HOT TO KILL

LINDA COLES

Blue Banana

All rights reserved. This book or any portion thereof may not be reproduced or used in any manner whatsoever without the express written permission of the publisher except for the use of brief quotations in a book review. This is a work of fiction. Names, characters, places, brands, media, and incidents are either the product of the author's imagination or are used fictitiously. Any resemblance to actual events or persons, living or dead, is entirely coincidental.

Copyright © 2017 Blue Banana

Chapter One

WEEK 1
One Friday in Summer

MADELINE WAS HOT, SWEATY AND VERY PISSED OFF.

"Oh, just get the hell out of my way, would you?" A moment passed and she yelled through the windscreen again at the driver in front of her. "Shift, for heaven's sake!"

She was annoyed, in a rush and gesticulating frantically for him to move the hell over, he wasn't budging. Drivers were getting more lazy and goddamn annoying. Did they not teach folks to drive properly anymore, have some manners, be courteous to other road users? If the driver in front had actually used their rear-view mirror, they'd have thought she was trying to get in to examine the inside of their boot she was driving so close.

When Madeline had first started taking lessons – what, thirty-odd years ago? – she'd been told not only to be courteous to others, but to get up to the speed of the traffic you were entering as quickly as possible so as not to ask others to stomp on their brakes as you merged into traffic at a snail's pace. And if you were going slower, then pull over to let others pass. It was common sense, something she assumed drivers of today left tucked away under their sodding beds of a morning. She hated outside lane hogs and, over the last few months or so, she'd noticed it even more. She'd also noticed her short temper getting shorter into the bargain, not to mention the tears at a moment's notice, and hot temper tantrums at all hours. What the hell was happening to her?

Eventually, the pea-brain in front finally remembered he had a rear-view mirror, and actually looked at it. He indicated to the left but then took another age actually getting over. Madeline hit the accelerator hard and flipped him the bird out to her left without actually looking his way, speeding down the bypass like an Intercity Express train heading full tilt into Croydon. Who needed eye contact when a middle finger would deliver the message just as nicely? She felt his stare as she sped by but still didn't look his way. She instinctively knew it was a 'him' – the stupid checked cloth cap on his head was a dead giveaway – and inwardly she was happy because she'd won: he'd shifted over and Madeline had got past. She broke into a smile, reached for her iPhone and asked Siri to play her ABBA playlist. 'Dancing Queen' blasted from all four speakers as she tapped the steering wheel in time to the beat. It was the small victories that pleased Madeline Simpson.

She was on her way to Sainsbury's, grocery shopping, something she'd used to enjoy, and still could do on rare days when she didn't feel so hot, sticky and angry. The summer heat wave was adding to her grumpy, distressed state. She never used to be this way all the time, but hitting the somewhat depressing age of forty-eight had changed all that, and a word she'd never heard of before became part of her vocabulary – peri-menopausal. That's what the doctor had told her the last time she'd gone to talk to her because she was feeling hot and sticky, sad and bloody grumpy all at the same time. The doctor had taken some blood to see where she was with actual menopause but had informed Madeline that everything was just normal – no sign of the full change as yet. So peri- or pre-menopause was what her symptoms all pointed to, though she'd never even heard of the first term. She didn't remember learning about it at school and certainly didn't remember her mum telling her about it. Nope, it had slapped her across her hot, sweaty face in a rush one day and it had been that way ever since. Some days she was good, and some days… Well, let's just say she was best left to her own devices and not spending time with anyone she cared about.

Today wasn't one of her good days. Just ask the guy in the stupid cloth cap, who likely had nothing but a blanket and collapsible chairs in his car boot, and possibly a flask for later while sitting in the park with his paper and silly small dog.

She flicked her indicator to turn right as she neared Sainsbury's and headed for the parking spaces that were furthest away from the front door. She always did that but wondered what it was with folks who needed to get as close to the entrance as humanly possible. It ended up being quicker to park a little way off and walk than sit waiting for a space by the disabled spots and the front door.

She grabbed her tatty old shoulder bag, checked for her shopping list, climbed out into the stifling heat, and headed for the trolley bay. As soon as she entered the foyer door, there was a traffic jam. Madeline rolled her eyes skyward and tried not to take the delay personally. What could possibly be holding everyone up getting through the automatic sliding door? She waited, reasonably patiently, trying her utmost to quell the internal rage that was building, but it was a struggle. Then she spotted the hold-up. Up ahead was 'Grandma' – not her grandma, but surely someone else's grandma – standing motionless with a trolley in front of her while she decided, painstakingly, whether she was going to turn left or turn right. Fruit or wine?

Oh, make a bloody decision, would you?

She was yelling inside, wanting to free the words from her chest in one big boisterous outburst, wanting to push forward and ram everyone in front of her in the heels with a turbo-charged shopping trolley from the 22nd century, complete with fully loaded automatic Tommy gun to blow them all out of the way forever, so she could shop in peace. She tried her hardest to plaster a fake smile on her face, forcing herself to leave it there, trying to pretend her wasted time wasn't a big deal. The old woman turned and their eyes met. There was little choice but to smile at her feebly, as if everything was just dandy

"Ohhh, ssorry," Grandma said in a frail and wobbly voice.

Madeline instantly felt bad for being such a cow with her thoughts, but it wasn't like the old woman could have read them anyway. She ultimately decided on turning right, so Madeleine instantly knew she herself was going to go left, even though she really need to go right. Towards the wine.

The old woman moved at the speed of a dying slug and Madeline prayed she'd not driven her car there, that her son was busy buying cigarettes at the kiosk and would be driving her back to her flat later. The old woman's reflexes would be nonexistent, and Madeline wouldn't want to be following her in her car.

Pushing her trolley to the left, headed for the fresh veg section first, she narrowly avoided another slow driver, this time a young mum with a little one in tow, pushing its own mini-trolley. At least that driver wouldn't be behind the wheel of a car anytime soon, and she smiled sweetly at it, destination carrots and spuds. She could be pleasant sometimes.

Thirty minutes later, with a full trolley and no more incidents to note, Madeline was back to feeling pleased with herself again. For a change, the whole experience hadn't been too bad, considering her previous foul mood and the heat – there'd been no major altercations in the aisles, no more flipping the bird to old men, and she was feeling calmer and more serene inside. She rolled up to the checkout and started to unload her groceries onto the conveyor belt. The woman in front of her was almost fully processed – which made her sound like a fish finger, she mused. The woman stood with her back to Madeline. She was wearing a cashmere sweater, a lovely pale pink colour, all soft and fluffy looking, that Madeline thought she had seen in M&S only last week. It came with a matching cardigan too, if you could afford both, but even for M&S she'd thought they were a bit pricey when she'd scanned the label. Why the woman was wearing such an item when it was probably in the low 90s outside she'd no idea. Madeline figured she lived in an arctic air-conditioned environment at home. Lucky cow.

Looking her up and down discreetly, Madeline wondered what she did for a living, if anything. A well-off husband, maybe? Pink Fluffy Woman was probably a bored but well-groomed housewife-cum-socialite if her long painted nails and perfectly streaked blond hair were anything to go by. Madeline touched her own brown and slightly greying lank head of hair and felt conscious that it wasn't looking its best. It hadn't been washed for a couple of days.

Pink Fluffy Woman was almost done. The cashier rang up the sub-total, Pink Fluffy Woman reached for her wallet – and then, with a little gasp and a self-conscious giggle, she committed the number one cardinal sin of shopping. She'd forgotten something, something she now needed to run back into the store and retrieve. She mumbled something about chocolates and her friend tomorrow, and then, with a click-click of her fine little heels, she was gone.

Madeline stood quietly for a moment then annoyance kicked right back in and hit her hard across the back like a slap. The cashier stood talking to her colleague on the next checkout, both with their backs to Madeline. Pink Fluffy Woman had been gone about thirty seconds, way too long for Madeline's liking, when suddenly Madeline spotted an opportunity to annoy her and get her own back for making her wait. A packet of iced buns was still on the conveyor belt, ready to be packed last on top, so Madeline slowly reached her hand out to them. A quick double-check around that nobody was watching, and then she pushed her index finger in through the wrapper and into the softness of the sweet iced doughy bread. It felt wonderful. If there'd been time, she'd have wriggled the finger around and made a larger hole but alas, not today.

Take that, Pink Fluffy Woman! See how you like having a hole in your iced bun while I've been standing here waiting for you to get bloody chocolates for the last 45 seconds.

"Retribution should be swift and hard and far outweigh the original crime," was her philosophy. She removed her finger slowly and slid the packet away gently so as not to arouse suspicion, like it was the most natural thing in the world to stick your finger into a soft bun, where it's not needed. She couldn't help the satisfied grin that was painted on her face, or the urge to lick her sweet finger, but when Pink Fluffy Woman came back, she made sure she was looking someplace less interesting.

"Sorry," Pink Fluffy Woman said brightly, showing her dazzlingly white teeth, drawing Madeline's attention back to her, the conveyor belt, and a box of Dairy Milk in her hands. Perhaps not that well-to-do after all, then, if she was only buying Dairy Milk. Could have at least gone for something a little higher-end –Thornton's, perhaps.

"No problem," Madeline gushed, which was obviously a lie. The chocolates were scanned and bagged and the buns placed on the top of the bag, the telltale hole just visible to the one who had created it. She watched Pink Fluffy Woman as she teetered on high pins and pushed her trolley delicately towards the exit and car park while her own groceries were scanned and packed. Perhaps she had been a tad mean, but that woman *had* made Madeline wait, after all. And that had annoyed her. Pink Fluffy Woman deserved it.

Madeline was soon back outside in the heat again, headed for her car, and was just in time to see the familiar pink sweater sliding into a fire-engine-red BMW. Its top was down, showing off cream leather lining that matched her hair perfectly.

Madeline clocked her private registration plate which read like a dog's name – and carried on loading her own car, thinking she could do with getting her tights off and slipping into something a bit cooler. And perhaps a gin. Without much tonic.

The thought spurred her on and she opened her driver's door and got inside, the heat punching her in the face as she started the engine. The air-conditioning rapidly kicked in and she allowed herself the luxury of resting her head back on the headrest and closing her eyes for a moment, relishing the cooling air blowing over her face, but more so the solitude and quietness the car gave, the outside world far away on the other side of the metal casing. She focused on breathing slowly and deeply, trying to calm harried nerve endings before pulling out of the space and starting the journey back home. The thought of cooking Gordon's evening meal was as about as scintillating as a long-ago-opened can of Coke. In her mind's eye, as she drove slowly out of the car park, she could see her prize for getting through the shopping ordeal in one piece, the whole day really – the distinctive blue Bombay Sapphire gin bottle that sat behind the kitchen cupboard door waiting for her to return. With cold tonic in a nearby shopping bag, it was going to be a long one.

Chapter Two

Wednesday morning

She'd been waiting for him for weeks. The landscaper had broken endless promises for longer than she cared to remember, but for some reason she'd kept on waiting, hoping that one day he would actually turn up when he'd said he would. But today, Madeline thought as she looked out the lounge window at a truck unloading a digger into the road out front, could be her lucky day. She stood transfixed, watching a short, overweight, grubby-looking bloke back the orange monstrosity onto the tarmac. With his arms covered in tattoos, his shirtsleeves rolled up to his bulging biceps, cigarette dangling from the corner of his mouth, wearing a high-viz waistcoat and undoubtedly stinking of yesterday's body odour, he didn't look to be someone you'd want to meet in a dark alley. His face was as red as a radish and probably as hot. Wondering what he was intending to do with the great orange thing, she thought she'd better go and ask him where he was going to put it. It certainly couldn't stay out front; the neighbours would have a hissy fit. Not that any of them were in during the day; they were all commuters into London, gone from dawn 'til dusk weekdays, which suited her just fine, but as the only part-time daytime resident of the quiet little cul-de-sac, it was down to Madeline to keep a relaxed eye on things when she was at home, and she sometimes did. She opened the front porch door and stuck her head out.

"Hello." Nothing, just the smoke from his cigarette and the blare of his cab radio playing something loud and nauseating, assaulting her eardrums. She tried again.

"I said, hello." Ditto. Useless. She made her way down the concrete front path and tried again as she neared the pavement, this time with a little more success. He turned at her enquiring but loud 'Hello' and smiled, his cigarette almost falling from his chapped-looking lips. He did actually have quite a friendly smile about him when she got up closer, not at all the thug look his body gave him – that was probably just for show, part of the heavy goods transport culture.

"Morning. Mrs. Simpson, I presume?"

Too bloody late now, Madeline thought. He's unloaded the damn great orange thing. What if she wasn't Mrs. Simpson?

"Yes, I am. You're not going to leave this great thing here, though, are you? That really wouldn't work for the neighbours. I'm sorry. Can you get it round the back?"

"Not a problem, my queen. Just show me where to drive it and I'll have it out of your way in no time." That big smile again, cigarette bobbing up and down precariously.

She wasn't quite what she had expected out of his mouth, but his calling her 'my queen' had thrown her a little. It was a bit familiar, actually, but she didn't let it show.

"Just round here and down the drive," she said, pointing a little behind and round. "Through the gate at the bottom, and if you could leave it in the far right corner, it's ready in the right place for when he comes to dig the pond hole out."

"Righto. Will do. Grand morning, isn't it?"

"Yes, I suppose it is. Thank you." And she left him to it. Such nice manners from such a grubby-looking tat-covered man. Would wonders never cease?

Back inside the lounge, she stood watching him through the window as he carefully steered the great orange thing with caterpillar rollers down the side of the house and out back, leaving dried clumps of mud the size of cow pats in its wake – another job to add to her bulging list. She moved back through the house to the bright kitchen at the rear where she could see out over to the garden and the fields beyond. The orange machine emerged into view as the man followed orders and drove the thing to the far right side of the garden. Maybe the pond digging would finally begin soon. She'd been waiting far longer than the landscaper had originally said, but now that his machinery had been delivered, perhaps things would move on quickly. She hoped.

Madeline waited until the man had walked back to his cab before going back outside to ask him what the plan was. Was someone finally going to come and dig the hole?

"Don't know, Queen. I just deliver 'em. I expect Des will be 'round soon to get started."

"That's just the problem. This should have been started weeks ago, and all I get are his broken promises."

"Ah, that's Des for you, but he's a master at his craft so hang in there," the man said amiably, and then climbed up into his cab and shut the door, cigarette still dangling, ash falling off the end of it. The door sign read "Sid's Transport," and she guessed he could have been Sid. He slowly pulled away from the curb and set off down the quiet road, waving a tanned muscly arm out of his window, heading back to wherever he'd come from. Madeline returned inside to put the kettle on. She was sure there was still some Battenberg in the cupboard with her name on it.

Chapter Three

THURSDAY

FOR TWO DAYS A WEEK, TUESDAYS AND THURSDAYS, MADELINE worked at Sally's, a café in the village, and for another couple of days, Mondays and Fridays, she worked in Croydon at an office equipment place. Wednesday was *Madeline's day*, the day to do whatever the mood dictated, her day all to herself, to do as she pleased. But today was Thursday, and that meant the café.

There was an old man that came into the café every day at lunchtime. He wasn't really that old, probably about fifty-five, but he just *acted* like an old man. Dressed like an old man, talked like an old man, and was as bloody grumpy as many an old man, which was a bit of a shame. She'd known, or rather seen him, for the last twelve months, which was how long she'd been working at Sally's, though the other girls talked about him coming in way before that. And he had always been so damn miserable. Madeline sometimes wondered why he was such a grumpy sod. Maybe he was shy, or maybe he was just wired that way because he was a distracted brain surgeon or a rocket scientist perhaps, something that demanded all of his focus so he had nothing left for the people around him, and didn't see the need to try and be civil. Regardless, there was no excuse for poor manners. A friendly welcome greeting or 'Hello' might even be nice, just once in a while. He gave nothing.

She'd never asked him his name. She didn't expect he'd give it without asking why she wanted it, and that would mean conversation, so she called him Grey Man. Even though she only worked there two days a week, she knew he went in every day and ordered a pot of tea and a tuna mayo sandwich. Every. Single. Day. He never deviated: no cheese alternative, no ham and mustard, no scone for a treat, nothing different, and he'd been doing that same routine forever. Maybe the rest of his life followed the same pattern: routine, routine and more routine.

He'd never really bothered Madeline, though. She just got him his usual and took it over to *his* place by the window where he sat each day and read his paper at exactly the same time. There was no real point in taking a window seat if you were just going to sit and stare at your newspaper or concern yourself with two down or eleven across each day, but each to their own; his routine must work for him. Madeline was reminded of her stepdaughter Ruth, who also did the crossword every day. She must get it from her father: crosswords frustrated the hell out of Madeline, but then it wouldn't matter whether she liked them or not because there was none of her DNA floating around inside Ruth's body to influence her from Madeline's side. No, Ruth was her stepdaughter.

Madeline pulled the door closed behind her and made her way down the side of the house to the garage and the car. The side door creaked loudly as she entered, reminding her to get it oiled. She pressed the button for the front roller door opener, and bright sunlight streamed into the dark space.

"Looks like another beautiful day, Dexter," she said to the big chubby cat sitting just outside the door, his deep ginger fur gleaming vividly in the morning sunshine. "Keep an eye on things while I'm gone, will you?" Dexter looked back at her as if he'd no intention of doing anything today but taking it easy, and certainly not keeping an eye open for rogues about the place. Most of his day would be spent on the sun lounger on the patio; then, when the sun got too hot he'd move to a shady concrete slab and coolness.

She got into her Audi and drove out of the garage, noting that Dexter still hadn't moved. She waved goodbye to him, like he was even once going to wave back, and set off into the village to Sally's and a day that would include the miserable Grey Man.

The morning flew by. Regulars called in for their mid-morning lattes and cappuccinos, the strong rich aroma of fresh coffee was always a welcome smell, and she watched the fresh cheese and rocket scones dwindling away to none, which was always the signal that the arrival of the lunchtime crowd wasn't far away. Some people used a watch to tell the time, but Madeline, for two days of the week, used cheese and rocket scones. They'd never been wrong yet.

At precisely 12.05 pm, Grey Man entered the little café and stood in the doorway. What was it about his miserable ways? If a child walked around looking like he did, Granny would've given him a dressing-down for dragging his chin on the floor and not picking his feet up. He was a grown-up version of that child, with no Granny handy to tell him otherwise. "My god," she thought, "he's got to be single. He never takes pride in himself." She surreptitiously looked him up and down from her spot at the counter and didn't worry that he might see her observing him because his face was permanently pointed to the floor. It must have been interesting. He never looked up, and when he ordered his lunch he wasn't any different. As he approached the counter where she stood, she could see great big beads of sweat on the top of his bald patch, making what little wispy hair he did have stick to the side of his head in a nasty, sticky, wet-looking way. He must have felt the moisture because he removed a large blue-chequered handkerchief from his pocket and gave his head a wipe, sending the wispy bits into tangled, damp disarray. Considering it was such a hot day outside, his dowdy grey suit, the same one he always wore and the reason she called him Grey Man, looked much too heavy for him, yet he hadn't thought to wear something lighter, or at least take his jacket off. A teeny-weeny part of her felt sorry for the man, at least until he opened his mouth.

"Tuna mayo roll and tea."

Here we go again. That was it. That was all he ever said. No please, no thank you, no nothing. And certainly no eye contact. She watched him studiously as he counted out the right money. Not many people used cash these days but he obviously preferred it. She scooped up the small pile of £1 coins and loose change and replied in an overly sweet voice, "I'll bring it right over," though he would never have seen the overly sweet smile that went with it.

He turned and went to his usual table, the sickly oniony smell of today's body odour lingering at the counter and clinging to the insides of Madeline's nostrils like thick cobwebs.

"You bloody miserable old git," muttered Madeline under her breath, heading out to the back kitchen to make up his roll and get his tea. "I should bloody spit in it," she mumbled out loud as she poured hot water onto a tea bag in a pot and mixed tuna and mayo for his roll, putting it together quickly and efficiently as always. Couldn't keep the man waiting.

She took his order over to his table, where he continued to completely ignore her and everyone else in in the café, and placed it down in front of him. His damp head was sticking out of the top of his newspaper. There was no 'Thank you,' though she'd have been more surprised if he'd said it than not. So she left him to it, noting his plastic shoes and his still-profusely-sweating balding head. A large wet bead turned into a small river and trickled down the back of his scalp to his collar, leaving a damp patch. *Gross.* It was enough to put other customers off their lunch.

Going back to her station at the counter, she busied herself with a cloth. A moment later she sensed someone approaching and looked up from what she was doing. Grey Man was back at the counter and that surprised her.

"Tea's stewed." Flat and monotone, no-frills delivery.

He was being clear about the problem, she'd have to give him that, but most people do elaborate with pleasantries around it, like maybe, "Sorry to bother you but my tea is a bit stewed. Can I get a fresh pot, please?" None of that for Grey Man, though. She looked at him and he looked at her. His dull grey eyes were the same colour as his dull grey suit, and the skin on his face was a lighter shade but just as dull and grey. The whole grey look he had going on matched the imaginary name she'd given him perfectly. Christian would have been proud of his grey-ness, though sadly for Madeline, they were worlds apart. She'd rather serve tea and a tuna roll to *that* Mr. Grey, given the chance... In fact, she'd happily serve anything to him full stop.

"I'll get you another pot," was all she said. If he only wanted to communicate in just a few words, two could play at that game. He slowly walked back to his table and half-eaten tuna mayo roll and sat back down, opening his paper and continuing on.

"What's up with him?" enquired Margaret, one of the other lunchtime staff. "He's looking his normal happy self."

"Sodding tea's stewed so I'm making him another pot," Madeline said wearily.

"Miserable old bugger." Margaret shook her head at him, not that he would have noticed, and carried on with what she'd been doing.

Madeline raised her chin slightly to her by way of agreement. She took his fresh pot over and placed it down on the table, smiling at him. Maybe she could teach him how to be pleasant? Nothing.

The words "Need a fresh cup" somehow left his mouth and ground in her ears.

For heaven's sake.

Wordlessly, she went back for a fresh cup, putting it down in front of him a little more heavily than she intended so that other customers looked round to see where the noise had come from. Grey Man still didn't make eye contact – no surprise there – so she left him to his fresh-brewed tea, the start of a plan forming in her mind. The old git deserved to be taught some manners. He didn't have to be so bloody rude, no matter what was going on in his tiny grey life. The plan developed quite rapidly. A knowing smile spread across her lips, and was duly noticed by Margaret.

"What you smiling at?" she asked lightly. "You look like you're up to no good."

She was bang on there.

THAT AFTERNOON AFTER WORK, MADELINE DROVE BACK HOME, parked the Audi back in the garage and went round to the back door to let herself in. As expected, Dexter was flat out on the concrete trying to keep cool in the shade. The heat from the afternoon sun was lessening a little, but wearing a thick fur coat couldn't be pleasant in high summer. He raised his head off the concrete just long enough to check who it was – no one to get excited about, no rogues about the place – and went back to his dream, his tail twitching ever so slightly, letting her know he wasn't pleased at being disturbed.

She dropped her bag on the breakfast bar and, before she forgot, which didn't take much, took a small tin of tuna out of the cupboard and opened it. She put the majority of it in a bowl for Dexter, should he decide to grace her with his presence later for his dinner, and put a couple of large spoonfuls in a small sandwich bag. She sealed it up and took it out to the shed. Opening the door, the heat from inside the shed nearly knocked her over. It was like an oven that had been on long and slow for a casserole, but she ventured in and put the little bag of tuna on a shelf.

"It won't take too long to do its thing in this heat. It must be ninety degrees in here," she said to herself, and closed the door again. The first part of the plan was already in motion. Shame she couldn't add the finishing touches until next week, but there was comfort in knowing it was in nature's hands, so as to speak. Patience and Madeline could be great friends when she wanted them to be.

Chapter Four

FRIDAY

ALTHOUGH SHE HATED HAVING TO GO TO SAINSBURY'S ON A FRIDAY afternoon, Madeline did look forward to Fridays because (a) it was nearly the weekend, and (b) more importantly, it meant girly lunchtime chatter with Rebecca. They'd been meeting up on a Friday for about three years, the time she had been commuting into Croydon to work at the office equipment place twice a week, and it suited them both really well because Rebecca worked nearby, at her husband Edward's office. She did a bit of bookwork, although knowing Rebecca, Madeline figured it was more filing her perfectly lovely nails rather than filing invoices, digital or otherwise.

Rebecca was her best friend. Rebecca and Edward had moved into the other side of the village a few years back and they'd seen each other at various events put on by the little theatre in the village or at the community centre and such like. Then they had bumped into each other at the street party that happened every year when the festival was on. It was always a bit of a riot, and they'd ended up sitting next to each other and just hit it off. Edward and Gordon had sort of hit it off, as only men do, but that hadn't stopped Rebecca and Madeline from becoming close friends. With her sons and Ruth having all left home, and Rebecca's children having done the same, they each had a bit of time to themselves. They both welcomed the female-only companionship, and when they realised they worked reasonably close to each other, the Friday lunch ritual at the Baskerville pub had started.

Madeline was ordering their usual at the bar, a gin and tonic for her, a glass of Sauvignon Blanc for Rebecca, when she felt her friend brush her shoulder and smelled her Chanel No. 5 – Rebecca always wore Chanel. Madeline turned to greet her.

"Hello, Rebecca," she said, and hugged her tight in a welcoming embrace.

"My god Madeline, what's with the bear hug?" Rebecca asked, laughing as she fought to pull away. "It's only been a week. Have you missed me that much?"

Oh, I'd love to tell you about my week... sticky buns and all.

"I've just been looking forward to seeing you, that's all. In need of a girly chat and lunch. I think my bloody hormones are out of whack again, and this heat is nearly killing me." It was the truth.

"Then you should just take the chemicals the doctor offers you and be done with it like the rest of us. None of that herbal nonsense. But I know you won't listen." Rebecca had been trying to get her on to HRT, but Madeline wasn't having any of it; she wasn't one for pill popping if something a bit more natural was available, although sometimes, just sometimes, she was tempted. Rebecca always meant well.

"Let's not go there. Let's have a drink instead," she said, anxious to get off the subject of HRT again. She picked up her gin and tonic and passed Rebecca her glass of wine, and they both headed over to their usual table in the corner, from where they could both see who came in and went. Madeline sat down with a heavy thump in the leather chair, then took a long drink from her glass. As she set it down she noticed just how much she'd just slurped down. So did Rebecca.

"Steady on, Maddy. You okay?" She and Gordon were the only ones who called her Maddy. Not even Ruth called her Maddy; that would be too affectionate.

"I'm good. Just needed a gin to kick back, which I've now got." She smiled. "Actually, I'm famished. Shall we order lunch now? Are you having your usual?"

"Yes, please. And let's share a bowl of fries too." Rebecca's idea of sharing meant she'd have four fries and Madeline would end up scoffing the rest, which was why she had an ample waistline and Rebecca didn't.

"Why not? I'll go and order it, then." She stood up to go and place their order at the bar. On her way over, she heard the distinctive ping behind her as a text landed on Rebecca's phone. She turned to see her friend reading it with a smile bending her perfectly filled red lips at the edges. She ordered and paid for the food and went back to join her.

"You look like the cat that got the cream." Rebecca had the decency to blush. Knowing Rebecca, Madeline had a fair idea what it was about. She bent forward and, almost in a whisper, said, "Come on, then. Who is he now?"

"That obvious, eh? Shit, I need to be more discreet."

The twinkle in her eyes made her a bit jealous. It'd been a while since Madeline's had twinkled quite like that.

"The gardener's son, Todd," Rebecca said. "Home from university and making his home at my place a couple of lunchtimes a week. Except he's not sleeping." Her eyes shone brightly, but at least she looked just a little embarrassed.

"Rebecca! I knew you had another," said Madeline excitedly, trying to keep her voice hushed. "You really are bloody naughty. That must be about five that I'm aware of since I've known you." But she wanted the gory details anyhow. "Go on, then, tell me more. Tell me all about it."

"Not much more to tell than he's twenty-one. He's –"

But Madeline didn't give her friend time to finish before she jumped in. "Twenty-one? Are you insane? You're nearly fifty!" Rebecca threw her head back and laughed, her expertly blended blond hair bouncing on her shoulders, her perfectly white teeth gleaming as she did so. She was a stunningly beautiful woman who always looked lovely without appearing to try too hard. She always wore just the right amount of make-up, and her hair was always perfectly coiffed. If she had to call her out for one thing, Madeline thought she dressed a bit too young. Cougar dressing, you'd call it.

And by all accounts, this cougar was happy playing with other cats' cubs.

"Go on, then," she said again. "How did it happen?" She wanted the details because she was intrigued as to how a nearly fifty-year-old woman could attract a much, much younger man. Although she already knew the answer – Rebecca's natural good looks and great body were all she needed. Madeline didn't have quite the same qualities; she was more quantity.

"He came with his dad working one day, and we just kept catching one another's eyes while he worked and I pottered in and out. Then one afternoon, he popped back on his own to drop something off and I took the opportunity. It wasn't hard – I knew he'd say yes. Not many young men out there would turn down the experienced older woman, and he wasn't one of them." Her mischievous smile suited her. She went on, "Garden shed was the first time. I never knew an old table could be so much fun! But now we've moved inside more. It's a little more comfortable." She took another sip of her wine then carried on, Madeline hanging on her every word, mesmerised by how the other half lived.

"Todd sort of looks like he might be into surfing, although I've never asked him. We don't talk too much." Rebecca winked and it was Madeline's turn to blush.

"Slightly longer sun-bleached hair," Rebecca continued, "and abs as tight as knots on a shoelace." She leaned in closer before saying, "And knows how to please me too, and not just for the standard twenty minutes that I've become accustomed to. We enjoy lively lunches." She winked again as she emphasised the word 'lively,' leaving Madeline in no doubt about what she meant. Madeline shook her head at her friend, feigning shocked disbelief, as their food arrived.

"Two cheese and ham toasties and a bowl of fries. Enjoy." said the waiter, and left.

"So, that's enough about me. What's been happening in your world since last week. Anything nice?" Rebecca shook salt onto the bowl of fries, then picked the longest one off the top and nibbled it like a rabbit eating a carrot.

That's why she's not the same size as I am. I don't nibble – I munch.

Picking up a fry and stuffing the whole thing in her mouth, Madeline poured tomato ketchup onto the edge of her plate to dunk the next one in. She shook her head in response.

"Really, I obviously need to get out more because nothing of note has happened. Unless you count getting road rage again last week on the way to Sainsbury's." Remembering Pink Fluffy Woman and the soft iced buns, she grinned.

"Now it's your turn to tell – what's that mischievous grin for?"

So, even though her tale wasn't nearly so exciting as Rebecca and Todd's antics, Madeline spilled the whole silly story, first of being wound up by a man in a cloth cap, and then the iced buns and the naughty finger.

"You did what?" Rebecca spluttered. "That's so wicked, Maddy. It's a wonder no one saw you. Do you know her?" She seemed a little surprised at the actions of her otherwise sane friend, and Madeline, as she spoke the words aloud, was a little surprised too.

"No. Never seen her before in my life, but I just felt so wound up, like I could have exploded, and after that slow bugger in the car that wouldn't move over... Then she made me wait while she went for a sodding box of Milk Tray. I mean, *Milk Tray* – had she no taste? I was gunning for a fight someplace. I just chose her iced buns." The vision of two iced buns duelling out in a forest surrounded by green fields sprang into her mind and she smiled despite herself. "Not quite as exciting as your week, but excitement nonetheless. Do you think bad of me?"

"Of course not, silly. I totally understand when the anger rages come. It's the hot flushes I can't bear, that sticky heat that bursts from nowhere, though I get less of them now with these tablets the doc's got me on. You should try them."

Here we go again.

"I call them temperature tantrums," Madeline said, "because they sort of stamp their feet as they fire up, and make me so damn hot and flustered. I'm bloody fed up with them – and before you mention chemicals again, no."

"Temperature tantrums, eh? That's a great name for them."

Rebecca threw her beautiful head back as she laughed, causing a couple of heads to turn and look.

Madeline bit into her toastie, melted cheese squeezing out the sides as she did so. "Oh, bliss. There's something about melted cheese, all the grease that makes it taste so good." She grabbed another fry, dunked it in ketchup and bit into it.

"Oh, and the digger has finally been delivered. Just need the landscaper now. Only been waiting sodding weeks, but it looks a bit more promising now, like the pond will finally get dug and I can sit and admire it for the rest of the summer. The digger's sat in the back garden ready to go, sort of taunting me that it's there but not actually doing anything as yet. I'm tempted to climb up and have a go myself."

"Now that I'd like to see. Do you think you could? Would you know what to do?"

"How the hell would I know? I can barely drive a food processor. Any more than two knobs or dials and that's me done." They both laughed. "No," she went on, "I expect I could if I really had to but I'll wait for him to do it."

"Can't Gordon have a go, then? Seems silly it just sitting there."

Madeline thought of Gordon. The closest he got to dirt was if there was a bit of mud on the path from her boots or the wheelbarrow. Or the hallowed ground at Crystal Palace. "I've a better idea: why don't you come over and have a go if you think it's going to be easy?"

Rebecca picked up another fry and nibbled it like the last one. Mutely she shook her head.

"No, I didn't think so," said Madeline resignedly. "Anyway, it's not terribly important. He'll come soon enough." Thinking, twitching both eyebrows up and down, she added, "Maybe he'll bring his son?" and they both burst out laughing again.

Chapter Five

Sunday

Ruth had entered their lives when she was fifteen years of age. Gordon and Madeline already had two sons and were shocked to find out they had a daughter too. Well, actually, that Gordon had a daughter and Madeline now had a stepdaughter from a one-night stand, a product of Gordon's early sexual adventures as a young man without many condoms. Ruth had grown up with her mum, but as she'd got older and more and more dissatisfied with her lot, living without much money, she'd set out to find Gordon, her natural father. It probably hadn't been too hard because both her mum and Gordon really hadn't moved far from each other after that single night of passion up a nightclub toilet wall in Croydon. They'd both been young and stupid, and Ruth had been the outcome. Of course, when she'd come knocking with the idea Gordon was her father, it had caused a great deal of upset, and they'd made sure of her claim and of the situation by having her and Gordon take a DNA test. It was a positive match. Gordon was indeed her dad.

Their twin boys, Andrew and Michael, were okay with it to start with. It was a bit of a novelty to suddenly have a fifteen-year-old stepsister hanging around the house, and it took a bit of settling in when she stayed over. Just practicalities like using the bathroom or her walking about in her underwear or the language she sometimes used in front of them all – she'd obviously been allowed a pretty free rein at her other home with her mum. Tanya had obviously been quite liberal. Madeline had never known her before, but not long after Ruth had come knocking, Tanya had shown up too. Just to chat, she said. Suddenly having a stepdaughter, finding out Ruth's real dad was Gordon, did indeed need a bit of a chat to straighten the kinks out. Tanya seemed all right, really. Her one-night stand with Gordon was just a blip in her life many moons ago, and on the surface she seemed like a good mother.

As time moved on and Gordon and Madeline had got to know their new daughter, Ruth had asked if she could spend more time with them. Tanya wanted to move out to France with her latest boyfriend and run a bar, and Ruth didn't want to go and leave all her mates. In the last couple of years of school, it seemed the sensible thing to do, and they'd said yes. How the hell they'd all got through those years without killing each other she'd never know. As soon as Ruth had moved in, things changed, like a switch flicking on and staying on – forever. The foul language, moody sulks, hidden alcohol and staying out after curfew were a constant battle, and everyone in the house felt it. Poor Gordon. He felt the worst, that it was his entire fault – and yes, a big chunk of it was his fault: he had created the little cow in the nightclub loo – but he hadn't had a hand in raising her or influencing her in any way. They'd all sympathised with each other, except Ruth, who was either blissfully unaware of the havoc she was wreaking or chose not to see it. Madeline had felt like getting drunk every night and resorting to violence.

I still feel like that now. Who am I kidding?

As the years rolled on, Ruth and Madeline's relationship had strengthened somewhat, but they were not particularly close. Ruth had always had an edge that Madeline really tried to soften and warm to, but she was sure the girl thought Madeline the dumbest woman in the world. She certainly took any opportunity to belittle her. Comments in passing like "Your roots are due. Why don't you get them done?" or "I saw a nice dress in town that would look really slimming on you" were common. One of her more recent digs was, "Why don't you get a nicer job than working in that café?" They were subtle, but Madeline got the messages; she got them all. Ruth thought that because she'd made a name for herself in her industry, all women should be as brave and strong as she was, be motivated to achieve something and be less dowdy. But Madeline wasn't like that. She was Madeline Simpson: not Ludwig Bemelmans' Madeline, or Madeline Kahn, but Madeline Simpson. And quite happy as she was, though wouldn't mind losing a chunk of weight off her middle. And her legs could do with toning, but whose don't? Despite everything, they'd grown a bit closer since Ruth had moved out at age nineteen, and while they still had work to do, they were making headway with each other.

It was Sunday, and Ruth was coming over for Sunday lunch. Madeline was cooking. Even though it was warm outside she had a joint of beef roasting in the oven and was in the process of making an apple pie. She'd been fancying some fresh apple pie for a week now. Those sweet imitation ones you could buy from the bakers, sort of Mr. Kipling–like, were just not the same; they didn't hit the right spot. Gran used to say, "They'll be alright with custard on," but that applied to anything sweet that was either burnt, stale or shop bought depending on what you'd done to it. Hot, thick custard was the fixer for anything that needed fixing. Much like the all-important cup of tea.

"Maybe Ruth will bring a boyfriend for lunch one of these days," she said to the kitchen window as she peeled apples. Now that Ruth was twenty-eight, Madeline thought they should have seen one or two men drift in and out of Ruth's life at some point, but no, nothing. "Or even a girlfriend?" In fact, she'd often wondered if Ruth was gay – not that it mattered but she just wanted to know. Her mind wandered a little, the apple and knife in each hand at a standstill. "And what is the politically correct word these days for a female that is gay? Is it lesbian, as in LGBT, or does gay encompass all of those that prefer their own sex to the opposite? So why have LGBT? Why not just GBT?" The window never answered.

She'd voiced her thoughts to Gordon, who thought she was just being silly and said, "Of course she's had boyfriends." But when Madeline asked him to name even one, he couldn't and had gone back to his newspaper to avoid any further conversation about it. Madeline suspected he suspected. A woman notices these things more so than a man and doesn't mind bringing them up, and on this occasion, she knew she was right. A part of her wanted to tell Ruth she suspected her sexual preference and they were cool with it, but she could only imagine the response back, something along the likes of "What the hell are you on about? I'm just busy, not gay!" or, "So what? I'm gay – you've only just worked it out?" No point in going there and upsetting the status quo.

From her vantage point peeling apples at the kitchen sink, she could see out into the large garden and the fields beyond. A couple of dog walkers were out for a stroll, with their charges running around chasing sticks or balls that were thrown their way. She had picked up another Bramley apple and started to peel it when she heard Ruth's voice through the now-open front door, chatting to Gordon about the journey over. Madeline turned to smile her 'hello' as Ruth came into the kitchen. They did the air kiss thing and Madeline turned back and carried on with the rest of the apples.

"Apple pie by any chance?" Ruth asked hopefully.

"Certainly is," she said triumphantly, turning back to her. She knew it was Ruth's favourite and a great way to keep her on side.

"Bloody marvellous. Not had that for ages. Custard or cream?" Madeline again knew her preference depending on the season.

"Cream of course, unless you'd prefer custard today? I can easily make some."

"Cream is perfect, thanks," she replied thoughtfully, and Madeline watched her as she opened the fridge, put a bottle of pink liquid in and took a clear bottle of liquid out.

"I brought a bottle of rosé because I wasn't sure what was for lunch and rosé goes with both sides in my book, so we can open that when it's chilled a bit more. Can I open this white in the meantime? I'm gagging for a drink."

She's chatty and pleasant today. Wonder what's on her mind.

Madeline watched as Ruth read the label with a look of confusion on her face. It dawned on her what Ruth was querying.

"I'm not sure what I picked up on Friday. I just grabbed one quickly, in a bit of a rush. Is it any good?"

Ruth carried on studying the label and replied with a simple, "Just not your normal Chardonnay, that's all. It's a dry Riesling. We'll soon see what it tastes like." She unscrewed the top off the bottle. Sticking her nose close to the neck, she sniffed loudly, though Madeline thought she wouldn't have smelled much from doing it like that. She opened the cupboard and took glasses out. There was the familiar *glug glug* sound as the pale, almost clear, liquid poured into them.

"Here you go, Madeline. Try that."

Madeline wiped her hands on her apron and turned to take the glass Ruth was holding out to her, then took a long sip. It was crisp and cold as it slid down the back of her throat, warming her insides as it went. She took another, smaller sip and tasted it properly.

"Now that is quite nice," she said, pleased. "What do you think, Ruth?"

"Not bad at all. Well picked, Madeline, well picked." Ruth left the kitchen with a glass for Gordon in one hand and hers in the other. Approval, mused Madeline.

Ruth was quite a striking woman, even from behind. At nearly six foot she had her father's height as well as his blonde-brown wavy hair, and the clearest hazel eyes you ever did see. There was no mistaking who she resembled, and she always looked lovely, looked after herself, went running daily. And she worked hard. She'd learned how to build websites with the help of a friend at college, and then more recently taught herself to create mobile apps, and had set up her own business. Judging by how many people she now employed, she was doing all right.

Madeline finished peeling and chopping the apples and put them in a pan with some brown sugar to cook slightly, then retrieved the pastry she'd made earlier that was resting in the fridge. Lunch was going to be a nice occasion; everyone was in a good mood. The sun was out, she had a glass of wine, the apple pie was on its way, Gordon was chatting with his daughter and the roast beef smelled divine in the oven. Taking another long swig of her wine, she stood for a moment letting the surge of alcohol soften the edges of her nerves. A couple of good deep breaths and another mouthful of wine, and she was feeling quite relaxed. She rolled the pastry out gently and carefully lined the baking dish with it, then sieved the apples into a colander and placed them in the dish, covering them with the remaining pastry, patting the edges together and crimping them expertly as Gran had shown her years ago. Last, she pricked a few holes in the top to let the steam out and painted it all with a little beaten egg. Standing back, she admired her handiwork and smiled at her accomplishment. It looked superb even raw, and she set it aside to go in the oven once the beef had been taken out. She went to join the others in the lounge with her wine.

MADELINE SHOULD HAVE KNOWN IT WOULDN'T LAST. THEY'D EATEN lunch, gorged on apple pie and cream and sat outside on the patio finishing off the bottle of rosé Ruth had brought with her. They'd all had quite enough to drink – maybe that had sparked the heated exchange that had happened. They'd only been playing Cluedo, for heaven's sake, and Gordon had been moaning about the fact that Mrs. White had been replaced by a new modern woman – Dr. Orchid, a sexy young biologist with a PhD in plant toxicology – and what was the world coming to? Why did they have to go and interfere with board game characters that had been around for what seemed like centuries almost? Ruth, on the other hand, thought it was a great move, very twenty-first-century. It depicted women a lot more positively than an old lady in a mob cap from way back when. Unfortunately, Gordon wasn't having any of it, but he took his turn anyway, so Madeline made a quiet exit and slunk away to find her book, leaving them to it.

Board games were not really her thing, but both Gordon and Ruth enjoyed them, as well as their fair share of puzzles. Both of them did the crosswords in the newspaper and Sudoku on their phones. With puzzles in mind, Ruth had actually started an online group, mainly for the locals about local stories and goings-on. It was quite a community now, and there were conversations about area vandalism or petty burglaries and the like. She called it The Daisy Chain, because when you made a daisy chain you made a necklace, a circle, and that was the end of it, all tied up – or, in the case of a puzzle, solved. Ruth spent ages on there, chatting about what was going on locally, and it had helped the police out in the past with leads and gossipy loose tongues. It covered the area around Croydon and South London, and Madeline was quite proud of her. Browsing it was a good way to spend some down time and she made a mental note to have a look later and see what had been going on in her digital absence.

Chapter Six

WEEK 2
  Monday

RUTH SAT IN THE WARM KITCHEN, THE MORNING SUN ALREADY promising another hot summer's day, just the kind she liked. She always knew she was solar powered; she hated the winter months with a vengeance and would have loved to live in sunnier climes all year round, but while she could work remotely, she needed to be close to those she loved and her business in London.

"One more cup of coffee and then I'll hit the shower," she said out loud to no one. Like clockwork every day, she rose at 5.30 am, put on her running gear and set off on her usual five-mile loop, come rain or shine. The loop took her to the nearby Beddington Park then back home to Richmond Road and her small but perfectly formed and positioned home. It was always so cheery, with the morning sunshine on the back, and in the afternoon on the front. She stood to put another capsule in the coffee machine and grabbed a clean mug for her second cup of the day, then turned back to the crossword puzzle she'd started just a few minutes ago. *Plop, plop, whoosh* sounded in the background, the promise of fresh coffee to come. This was the best part of the day. No one talking to her and disturbing her morning ritual, no one to please, and certainly no one to see her in her damp running sweats before her shower. And she loved her crosswords. She raced herself most mornings to complete each one quicker than she had the previous day, but she was not going to succeed today. She was stuck on seven down, 'Inclined to sag,' six letters. Nothing fitted, yet. The aroma of hot, fresh coffee filled the kitchen as the capsule emptied its rich contents into her cup. She walked over to the machine, added just the right amount of milk for her taste and took her steaming mug back to the table, sipping and moving on to the next clue, finding the answer almost immediately, and then the next. And the next. Now she was on a roll, and within ten more minutes she had managed to figure out seven down from the letters the rest of the answers had given her: it was 'droopy.' She sat back with a satisfied grin and heard the sound of familiar footsteps coming up the back path. Amanda. They didn't live together, just spent quite a bit of time at each other's houses, sometimes staying over but invariably going their separate ways at the end of their days. Ruth really loved her space, and both she and her partner worked odd shifts so they passed one another going in opposite directions like cars on a motorway. Sometimes they stopped and chatted. Sometimes they kissed. Rather than disturb each other's routine, they lived separately and made it work. The back door opened and Amanda walked in, the night's work etched in her face, the stress obvious to anyone, but particularly to Ruth.

"You look done in, Hun. Tough night?"

"Yeah, you could say that. But I wanted to say hi before you left, which is why I've come round. And get a hug. I need a hug." She stretched her arms out like a needy child.

Ruth looked at her tired face and stood to embrace her. "I'm still sweaty though. I've not had my shower yet. You sure you want one?"

"Hell yes, I'm sure. Come here." And the two of them stood in the warm kitchen embracing like the friends and lovers they were.

"Do you want a coffee or are you headed for bed?"

"No thanks, just needed that hug. I'm off home for a shower of my own, then bed for a few hours. I'm back on again at six pm unless anything happens in the meantime, and I bloody well hope it doesn't. So I'll see you tomorrow, perhaps? You in the office all day?"

"Yes, today and tomorrow, so if you get lonesome, we could grab a bite to eat somewhere, sometime?" It was a favourite saying of theirs; neither of them ever knew what that time and place might be until the last minute. They'd lived like that for months now and it suited. Others found it hard to cope with a lack of firm arrangements but that, Ruth decided, was their lookout. She and Amanda didn't have a conventional relationship, at least not in some people's eyes.

"Sounds good," Amanda replied, and gave Ruth a quick peck on the cheek. "I'd better get going. Thanks for the hug," she called over her shoulder as she headed back out the door. Ruth stood in the doorway smiling and waving at her retreating back, then went back inside and upstairs to a hot shower.

AN HOUR LATER RUTH WAS ON THE TRAIN HEADED INTO LONDON Victoria, then it would be a short tube ride round to Green Park and her office. She loved working in the city itself rather than in the suburbs; everything was just so handy. Her favourite weekday coffee shop with the lovely barista George was nearby, the drycleaners and a grocer's were only a couple of minutes' walk from the office, and some great restaurants fought for custom nearby. It certainly beat having to go into Croydon itself to do her errands – even though it was local, it was a bit of a detour.

Ruth also loved her job. Though she'd started out making and designing websites, over the last two or three years the team had been building more and more apps, some custom-made for individual business needs and some for commercial resale. Her favourite niche was intelligence, or spyware. Not the virus type of spyware, not things that did any damage, but more the safety feature sort of spyware —checking what your kids were up to, that sort of thing. Everything was available to be made for the right price, as long as it wasn't illegal. Some things they'd been asked to build had definitely crossed that line, but while the money was always enticing, she preferred her own bed to the striped sheets on a horsehair-filled prison mattress.

She stepped off the packed tube and rose up to the surface of the street, stopping for a moment to feel the sunshine kiss her skin before she crossed the road to the coffee shop.

"Morning, George," she called as she entered through the old polished front door.

"Morning, Ruth. Usual?"

"Yes, please, and a cinnamon roll too. They look divine. You make them?" she asked, already knowing the answer was definitely no, but she liked to tease the young guy. He knew she was gay, but that didn't stop him from flirting with her, like he'd made it his mission to somehow 'turn' her back to heterosexual again. She'd lost count of how many times he'd asked her out and she'd politely declined. Still, she enjoyed the fact she could still pull, even if he wasn't her type. Or sex.

She watched him put the cinnamon roll into a bag and finish making her coffee. He handed them both over with a smile, and she gave him her best flirty wink as she left, knowing it would make his day. And it did.

"So what you got going on today?" she asked Marcus, the head developer at McGregor and Co. as he stood next to her desk. "Pull up a chair."

Marcus dragged a nearby chair across the wooden floor. The legs screeched across it like a small jackhammer bobbing up and down. Ruth winced. Marcus didn't notice. He squeezed his rather large backside in and pushed his glasses back up his nose.

"Still trying to figure out a way to give the Burnwood account what they want and stay this side of the law, so we're on hold with that one until legal tells us we can go ahead with it. We're just working on finishing the job on hand at the moment. Any news on Liberty Investments? Have they decided whether to go ahead yet? We need to plan the workload in because it's going to be terribly involved. May even have to get some extra help in." He pushed his glasses up again.

"Should know by the end of the day for Liberty, and the same for Night Rider. Who'd have thought you'd call it Night Rider? Didn't we have a TV show called that some years ago?" Ruth asked.

"We did, though it was spelled differently. It was in the eighties, a bit before our time, though I believe there was something reborn a few years back. Not my thing really, talking cars. I guess it was quite futuristic back then, but not anymore. Everything talks to you now, even the damn fridge. Which reminds me, did you manage to get the correct accent that Spaghetti wanted for their voiceover?"

Ruth knew the client well. They had wanted a Liverpool 'chick's' voice, which had caused some headaches, but they had got there in the end. Spaghetti were sailing down the Mersey a very happy bunch. "Of course, and they're thrilled to bits with it. Took some doing, but at least we have the knowhow for when we need it again. Not everyone wants a soulless voiceover, and particularly when the roots of your business are set somewhere like Liverpool. Their dialect is almost a whole new language all on its own. They all talk like Cilla up there. It was Pete who actually managed to find the answer. That lad has worked out well."

"Yes, he has. Good of you to give him a chance with his background," Marcus said, though not maliciously; that wasn't him. Glasses.

Pete had started working with Ruth after a stint on the wrong side of the law. She'd given him a chance, and so far, he'd proven he was damn smart with the techy stuff. Young and keen, he'd quickly adapted to creating rather than breaking. He'd just needed something to fill his life with, something he enjoyed and was good at.

"Okay, I'll leave you in peace. Just keep me posted about Liberty when you hear, and I'll look at getting some extra tech students in to help with the hard graft."

"Righto. Speak later," she replied, and turned to her monitor, clicking another browser window open as he left her office. She picked up the familiar URL of The Daisy Chain and clicked the site open. There were a few new comments on the recent spate of car damage in shoppers' car parks nearby but nothing that needed her attention or moderation. Looked like Benjamin, another moderator, had been in ahead of her and done what needed doing. She closed the browser and went back to her email program, and work.

Chapter Seven

Tuesday

It was Tuesday, and that meant Madeline could put the second part of her plan into place – Operation Grey Man. The weekend had been as hot as a barbeque grill and the one time she'd been into the little garden shed for a plant pot, the stifling heat had nearly bowled her over. It had certainly been enough to bring sweat droplets to the surface of her ample cleavage. Now she was in the shed again, this time to retrieve the little plastic bag she'd stashed away last week. She slipped it into her handbag for later, closed the clasp and headed back out towards the garage, and Sally's. On the drive in she rehearsed in her mind what she was going to do and the best way to do it so no one got into trouble. That was, apart from one person – he was going to have a truckload of trouble.

The morning flew by, the scones' quantity dwindled downwards, and that meant one thing – lunchtime. At 12 pm, she knew she had just five minutes to wait.

"Tuna mayo roll and tea."

Madeline mentally rolled her eyes, though he'd have to look up at her to even have a chance of seeing her do it in reality. She was safe with her thoughts.

Hell, this guy really is something else.

She took the change he passed her and put the money in the till drawer, not even bothering to count it anymore. It was always exactly right, spot on, much like his dull routine. Dull with a capital D.

"Take a seat and I'll bring it over to you." As usual, nothing in return, just silence and that sickly-sweet onion body odour smell that seemed to cling to him all the time. And now it was clinging to Madeline. Again. Gross.

Slipping into the kitchen to prepare his pot of tea and make up his roll, she was ready for the next part of the plan. Luckily for Madeline, Grey Man was a creature of habit, so a few minutes ago she'd taken advantage of that knowledge and gone to her bag and slipped the little zip-locked food bag with tuna in it into her apron pocket so it was good and handy for when she needed it. The plan had been circulating around her head for most of yesterday and all of this morning. She'd made good and sure she'd covered enough details off so no one got into trouble, apart from a certain person, or more precisely, his stomach. This plan was going to work, and if she'd calculated the whole thing correctly, neither Sally's nor Madeline would be blamed.

A quick look around confirmed her colleagues were all busy with their own tasks, so she rapidly squeezed the bag's contents into a bowl, then added some fresh tinned tuna on top and mixed it up with a good dollop of mayonnaise. She zipped the empty plastic bag back up and put it back into her pocket to dispose of later at home. She had wondered if it would smell really strong, but it just smelled a bit extra fishy, a bit like the local fish market, and mixed with some fresh tuna he wouldn't notice anything different. He'd certainly feel it later, however.

She filled his roll with the tuna mix as usual, poured boiling water on the tea bag in the pot and took his order over to him. He didn't say a word, just as expected, so she went back to wiping the counter down and surreptitiously watched him eat. Then watched him drink. Then watched him leave. She smirked with that deep-down feeling of satisfaction you get when you know you're right about something and that you've won. She rationalised her actions in her mind: *People need to have manners, because if they don't they'll undoubtedly piss people off. And some people, people like me, won't stand for rudeness.*

Thursday would be the next time she was due to see his miserable face again, but she didn't suppose he'd be in for lunch the next day, and maybe not even the next. Instead he'd be having some quality toilet time. Alone.

"I hope he has some good quality soft toilet tissue hanging on his holder. He's going to need it," she mumbled.

"What was that?" asked Margaret as she passed the counter.

"Just remembering that I need to grab toilet roll on the way home. God knows how we get through so much of it," Madeline replied, and dried off the counter she'd been wiping down with a tea towel.

Chapter Eight

AMANDA WAS LOOKING FORWARD TO DINNER AND SOME GIRLY TIME with Ruth. Their schedules had not been in tune so much over the last week or so. Apart from that quick hug after Amanda's evening shift, they'd hardly spent any time together; she was getting withdrawal symptoms from lack of contact. In her kitchen, just a couple of miles away from Ruth's place, she stirred Bolognese sauce in the pan. Fresh spaghetti was ready to go into boiling water, and the garlic bread was ready to pop in the oven when Ruth arrived. She poured a top-up of Cab Sauv into her glass and took a healthy mouthful, holding it in her mouth for a fraction of a second longer than usual before letting it slip down her throat and relax her insides. Her stomach rumbled at the lack of food so she tore a piece off the end of the garlic bread that was waiting to go into the oven. The raw garlic was a little strong but she was hungry and swallowed it down, barely chewing it – no one would miss a single slice anyway.

Amanda checked her watch again. Ruth should be here any minute, all being well. She took her wine, the bottle and an extra glass outside onto the little back patio to wait for her. Knowing Ruth, she'd want a glass of wine to unwind with before dinner, and there was no rush. No, tonight she was determined there would be no rush, just relaxation. A car door slammed on the road out front and she heard the familiar clackety-clack of heels on the pavement, then a key in the front door. She smiled to herself but stayed put.

"I'm out the back," she yelled through from her spot outside. "I have wine for you."

"Oh boy, do I need that," Ruth groaned. She placed her bag on the floor by the sofa, kicked off her heels and padded barefoot through the kitchen and towards the back door. The coolness of the floor on her hot feet was bliss.

"Mmm – something smells delicious," she said, bending to give Amanda a peck on the side of her neck. "And I think it might be you. I can detect garlic. Have you been stealing raw garlic bread again?"

Amanda turned, caught her lightly back with a quick peck on the cheek and said, "Are none of my sins secret anymore? I made your favourite, but come and chill out a bit first. We can eat when you're ready."

"Your secrets are all mine anyway. I just don't know why you nick raw garlic bread, weirdo," Ruth said, and slipped into the chair beside her.

"Tough day at work?" Amanda knew Ruth had some big projects landed and about to land.

"Yes, but not so bad. You?"

"Not so bad either, actually, as it happens. Some of my smaller cases are getting tidied away and it's been a few days since we've had another groper issue, so perhaps he's buggered off someplace else. We can but hope, though not all the working girls tell us what they get involved with. They just tell each other, so we never really know how often and where an incident might have taken place. That said, the last incident wasn't with a working girl. Did you know about that one?"

"Yes, I'd seen something about that. Someone had posted it on The Daisy Chain. Maybe he's seen it, or seen the light and realised he's an arsehole. God only knows what he gets out of it." She took a mouthful of wine and set her glass back on the table. "Did you ever get any firm leads on him? The gossip online is just 'mid-fifties balding male,' but they're ten-a-penny. That's half of the Croydon male population. Rather a big pot of people to pick from."

"Not much more from the girls. He takes them by surprise and then he's out of there quick-smart. And because the girls don't work the streets the same anymore –it's all done via apps and online now as you know, so they just meet at the designated spot, like a park toilet if they're low-end girls – and he bursts in, does his thing, and then goes. And doesn't bother paying either. I guess he gets something from it, but like any of the weirdos out there, only he knows what that is. And the working girls aren't that bothered by him. They're more bothered about him wasting their time when they could be meeting someone a bit more 'productive,' shall we say."

Ruth nodded thoughtfully. "Well, let's just hope he stays away or, better still, stops doing it."

"Let's drink to that."

Ruth raised her glass and they clinked them together.

Amanda took a sip, then set her glass on the table and got to her feet. "I'll go and pop the garlic bread in. You pour some more wine. Enough shop talk for tonight. Let's enjoy some quality down time for a change. I'll be right back." Amanda patted Ruth's shoulder lightly as she moved past her towards the kitchen.

Chapter Nine

Wednesday morning

Gary smiled as the smell of his last fart drifted slowly around the interior of the van, seeping into his nostrils and making him gag at the same time. Even by his standards, it stank. That vindaloo he'd had last night with the boys after a few pints at the pub was repeating itself, this time from the other end, and it smelled rotten. He belched to add to the stinking odour and opened a window to let both smells out, the stench of last night's alcohol on his breath amplifying things tenfold. He wrinkled his bulbous red nose.

"Hell, that was a good'un!" He smiled in appreciation of his efforts.

Gary had left in rather a rush that morning, having overslept from his skinful the previous night and getting in late and then spending a good seven minutes on top of his sleeping wife. She was used to his demands; she just willed him silently to finish and couldn't care less anymore. He was almost comatose afterwards, quiet for a while before the snoring, and that's just the way she preferred him – asleep and half dead. One day, she figured, he'd actually go too far and kill himself with drink, or kill himself driving home drunk from the pub. She could only hope. Gary, of course, was oblivious to his wrongdoings: in his opinion all blokes acted the same – if they were real men, that was. And he'd been married a while and had spawned four kids from his fertile seed. Nobody could say he had a limp dick or no lead in *his* pencil. No, he was all man, and she was lucky to share his bed with him. He farted again.

But it was nearly lunchtime now and he'd missed breakfast because the bitch had gone to work and left him in bed, and there'd been no bread in the house to even make a couple of slices of toast. He'd have to have a word later, but right now he needed something to eat to stop his stomach rolling. He pulled off the road and onto the garage forecourt, parking in front of the car wash, thinking he might as well get the van cleaned while he ate his sandwich. He headed out into the stifling summer heat, walking towards the chill of the cashier's glass box inside. The air was refreshing as he entered through the door and went over to the cold cabinet to get what he wanted. He chose a sausage sandwich, a packet of ready salted crisps, a Mars bar and two cans of Coke. He was always thirsty these days and the heat wasn't helping, so he pulled the ring open on one of them and took a long drink, trying unsuccessfully to hide the belch that followed. The loud gurgling sound turned heads from those waiting to pay. The queue was longer than he'd have liked, but he joined the back of it anyway, opening his sandwich and taking a bite while he waited. The cold sausage tasted delicious.

It looked like there was a bit of a hold-up ahead: a middle-aged woman with a red face looking like she was going to melt, an old man behind her and then several people of various ethnic minorities, or was it majorities now? The UK had become a melting pot of everyone you could ever think of, and the Eastern Europeans had taken over, it seemed. And he resented them because they were cheap labour, and the influx of them teeming in from over the French border hacked him off. Now, the minority was blokes like him, the regular white Englishman, born and bred here with no unpronounceable names. The 'John Smiths' of this once great country were buried amongst the Polish, the Indians and the Syrians.

He took another large mouthful of sausage sandwich, crumbs along with a blob of tomato ketchup falling onto the front of his T-shirt, which stuck out with the size of his gut. He swigged back his Coke and belched again. The queue shifted slowly forward and by the time he'd reached the front, he'd almost finished his sandwich. A blob of tomato ketchup was still evident in the corner of his mouth, looking like someone's blood as he'd bit them, as if he'd left it as a reminder, something for later. A memento perhaps.

"Add a car wash, mate. That thing's dirtier than my neighbour's wife," he ordered, with a chuckle to Sanjay, today's cashier. Sanjay half smiled and pondered whether to say anything about the ketchup but wisely decided against it, processing Gary's payment quickly and moving on to the next in line. He'd seen men like Gary before and knew not to interfere or even try and be helpful.

Gary paid and made his way back out into the hot summer heat and his equally hot van, where he took his sweet time punching the code on the carwash keypad and getting in. He glanced at the car behind him. The woman sitting in her vehicle would just have to wait; he was in no rush now he'd got something in his stomach. He put the can to his lips again and, taking a couple of big slurps, checked his rear-view mirror and finally pulled forward, activating the soap from the wash program as he did so. He took the opportunity of the wash cycle to plough through his bag of crisps, start on the remaining can of Coke and open his Mars bar. By the end of the wash he was feeling much better. He must have needed the fuel, and the pain in his stomach wasn't quite so bad any more. It was a pity about his blood sugar levels.

He headed out on the Wickham road. Not twenty minutes into his journey, his phone rang; the caller ID showed his bookie's number. Suspecting Lionel wasn't ringing to tell him he'd won the jackpot, he didn't bother picking up. But Gary liked to gamble a bit, and not just with the dogs and horses. As an idea came to him, a smile spread across his red, unshaven, bloated face. He looked at the clock on the dashboard and figured, what the hell – he was already late anyway. He might as well be a bit later still and enjoy himself at the same time. He scrolled through his contacts to find the person he was looking for and clicked call. After four rings, a familiar voice purred, "Hello, Gary. What can I do for you?"

"A whole lot, Vivian, and that's why I'm ringing. When can you fit me in, sweetheart?"

"I'm free now," she purred again, though she never felt like she was purring with Gary. He was bordering on mean but he paid well. And the boils he had on his legs grossed her out, but when she closed her eyes... She said a silent prayer, glad she wasn't the one married to the prick.

"I'm on my way. Put that purple number on. It makes my cock as hard as a piece of wood, and I'm gonna show you a real good time."

The phone went dead in Vivian's ear and her stomach rolled just once, enough to remind her that she'd never liked him and this was definitely going to be the last time with Gary. No more.

Now he had something to look forward to, and he drove on with a smile on his face, thinking about what he was going to do to Vivian, and the cash in his pocket. But that was about to change: it was a pity he wouldn't actually get to spend the cash on Vivian, but he really shouldn't have pissed off Madeline Simpson.

Chapter Ten

It was Wednesday, and Madeline's full day off. No Sally's café and no Stanley's office equipment place to get to, and nothing else on at any particular time. The best part of any day off? Nothing in the schedule.

Madeline was sitting on the patio in one of the wicker chairs. She'd bought them so that she and Gordon could sit and enjoy some of the summer when Gordon got home from work, though he'd only joined her once since she'd bought them last month. Give him chance, she supposed. So there she sat, mug of coffee in one hand and a digestive in the other, perusing the garden and what she would do to it today. Apart from the bloody Great Orange Machine that still loomed in the far corner and which she couldn't do anything about, the flower beds were desperate for some attention, as were some of the hanging baskets. She made a mental note of what was needed from a trip to town. She had to go into B&Q; Gordon had dropped the Stanley knife down the grid, clumsy oaf, so they needed a new one to replace it, along with a new grid cover so he didn't drop it in again. She planned on treating herself to morning tea and a scone at the garden centre just out of town. She would get what she needed for the garden from there rather than the big-box store, even though the store would probably be cheaper.

She drank off the last of her coffee, took the mug back inside and put it in the dishwasher. Walking back through to the hallway, she could see the mail on the floor behind the door. It was as she shuffled through the three letters, disregarding two of them as junk mail, that she noticed a red one from the telephone company. She sighed heavily, looked at the demanding envelope that anyone looking, including the postman, could see was an overdue account, and tossed it onto the hall table. She wasn't going to get worked up over that blasted bill debacle on her one day off: it would have to wait.

"You can cut me off for all I care. Who needs a sodding landline these days anyway?" she mumbled, heading for the stairs and the bathroom to clean her coffee breath away before she left.

Five minutes later she was in the car, windows down and enjoying the breeze blowing through her hair as she headed down Stanstead Lane on her way to B&Q. It wasn't far into Purley, and she pulled into the car park easily. It was nice and quiet midweek, unlike the weekends when DIYers of all ages and abilities slowly made their way around the aisles looking for what they needed. She picked up a new Stanley knife plus a packet of extra blades for it and went off in search of a new grid cover.

Making her way to the checkouts, she headed towards the one with the shortest queue but was beaten to the post by an old man and his wife. Madeline seethed quietly: she knew for a fact the old bat had seen her out of the corner of her eye but had chosen to ignore her and pushed in anyway. Her mind starting rolling: Were they in a rush? What were they going to rush home for—a Rich Tea and a cuppa? They looked like they'd been retired for a good twenty years. She exhaled deeply, loudly, so they would know she was pissed. Even though Mr. and Mrs. Retired Couple probably couldn't hear the huffing and puffing just behind them, it made Madeline feel better.

The queue shuffled forward slightly as the person being served made their way off and someone else took their place. Madeline glanced over to the confectionery at the till point, scanning the Flakes and Turkish

Delights, trying hard to avoid temptation by telling herself they would probably be warm and slightly melted in the heat anyway, and she wouldn't enjoy them half as much as she thought she would. The queue shuffled forward again. The Retired Couple were next, and they loaded their few items... Ever. So. Slowly... onto the conveyor belt. Almost fit to burst, Madeline let out a "humff," and this time Mrs. Retired did hear and turned round to glare. It was quite a good glare as glares go, Madeline thought, and felt the woman's annoyance stick in her chest like a blunt dart.

I hope she could feel mine directed at her bloody push-in.

Not to be outdone, Madeline gave her best sarcastic smile back and the woman tutted like she was tutting to a child. That made her smile even more. Madeline – one point; Mrs. Retired Couple – nil points.

Finally they were through the checkout and heading outside. Madeline gave a low bird down by her thigh, more for her own enjoyment than for the old couple to see and be offended by. She emptied the three items from her basket quickly and efficiently for the cashier, who had her processed and back out the door quick sharp.

"Why couldn't other customers do that at the till instead of making it a bloody day's job?" she mused as she headed briskly out to the car park.

As she got closer to her car, she could see how dirty it was looking. It was all the dry dusty weather and the bit of rain they had had. It really needed a clean, and she decided to take it into the car wash before heading back home. She climbed in, turned the air-conditioner on full power and put the B&Q bag on the passenger seat next to her while she waited for the temperature to fall from what felt like a million degrees to something more human and less baking. You could have fried an egg on the dashboard. The noise of the fan on full reminded her of a hairdryer. As the temperature started to drop, she began to feel a little cooler, more refreshed. Pulling out of the car park, she headed out towards Purley Way, where she knew there was a petrol station with a car wash.

"May as well fill up while I'm here," she said to herself. "No point coming back at the weekend when it's busy." She topped the car up with petrol and headed inside to pay. Opening the glass door, the intense coolness of the shop hit her like a mouth-freshening extra-strong mint, making her nearly gasp out loud it felt so good and invigoratingly tingly on her skin. Could she just hang out here for the day without being done for loitering?

There were two people in front waiting to pay. She didn't mind standing there in the cold air—it was doing wonders for her hot and sticky self—but it seemed she'd found herself in yet another slow-moving queue. What the hell was taking so long up the front? The shop door must have opened at least half a dozen times as she stood waiting. Glancing behind her, she could see that quite a queue had formed. The man at the rear of the queue was a big sod, his flabby red arms sticking out of his sleeveless T-shirt, the name of a plumbing company embroidered on it. It was a logo she'd seen before, emblazoned on their vans. He wore a pair of dirty shorts and some old trainers on his feet without socks. His dirty blonde hair was stuck to his face in damp vertical lines like it had been tattooed in place. She turned back to wait patiently but grabbed a chocolate Flake from the display. It would be nice and cold from sitting in the coolness all day.

Finally it was her turn: she paid for the Flake, the petrol and car wash, and headed back out to the heat and her dirty car. Starting the engine, she drove around the back of the petrol station to the car wash entrance, and then halted abruptly. To her absolute horror, there was the plumber's vehicle, with no one inside, waiting to go into the car wash ahead of her. And she knew that Big Sod was at the back of the sodding queue inside.

"Is he trying to piss me off?" Her blood started to boil in her veins and a throb started in her head. She sat there in her car and cursed out loud, slamming the steering wheel with her fists and calling him every derogatory word under the sun she could think of, questioning his size, his heritage and then his birth status. The tirade that forced its way into her head and out through her mouth was worse than anything in the worst of the worst movies. It was appalling, even to her ears. But that didn't matter, nor did it stop her.

At last, like an engine sputtering, she ran out of steam. The torrent of foul names trickled to a halt—and then she remembered the brand-new Stanley knife, complete with nice new and super-sharp blade, sitting right on the seat next to her. A spiteful but clever idea thrust itself into her head and she knew just how to avenge this fat, inconsiderate and utterly grubby individual.

Acting quickly, telling herself he deserved it, she grabbed the knife, opened the blade, then took the Flake gently out of its wrapper, resting it back on top of the B&Q bag, naked, for later. Checking her rear-view mirror one last time, she slipped out of the car, bent quickly at the rear wheel of the vehicle in front of her Audi and stuck the knife blade into the tyre, making a short slash about an inch long and not quite all the way through the rubber. It didn't need to be big for what she was thinking would eventually happen. It only took a couple of seconds to do the deed, and then she straightened up and carried on towards the front of his vehicle to where the rubbish bin was situated and put the Flake wrapper in the bin. If anyone was watching, CCTV cameras perhaps, they would think she'd stopped to pick up the wrapper then placed it carefully in the bin nearby. Simple. Clever.

Madeline then got back into her car, wound all the windows down and waited for Big Sod to come out and get his dirty self and dirty van through the car wash before she and her Flake melted fully. She bit into her Flake with satisfaction; sprinkles of fine chocolate dropped into her lap and melted on contact. She wiped up what she could with sticky fingers and tried to suck them clean to avoid chocolate-covered clothes, but failed miserably. You just couldn't eat a Flake sitting down, but, typical, she had tried to anyway.

It must have been another couple of minutes before Big Sod approached his van and finally got in, and he didn't even acknowledge he'd kept her waiting. She turned her engine on in an effort to try and cool down, and after another five full minutes of his chosen van-cleaning program, she finally entered the car wash for her own turn, long overdue. She pressed the code into the keypad, drove to the designated spot inside and waited. At last, coloured foam hit the front window like party snow. Putting her head back on the headrest and turning it slightly, she noticed Big Sod's van turn left off the forecourt and wondered where he was headed and how long it would take before her plan came to fruition.

When her chosen and somewhat shorter program had finished, she drove out of the car wash and carried on, towards the garden centre and morning tea with just her own company. She switched the audio player on, and it immediately picked up the last playlist off her phone, a mixture of songs from the '80s and '90s. She turned the volume up and listened to Robbie Williams and a bunch of others rocking it. You're never too old to listen to rock and pop, she thought, no matter how frumpy you feel on occasion. It was a twenty-minute drive out to the garden centre but it didn't matter on a nice summer's day with great music playing. It was all part of the pleasure of gardening and time to one's self on a Wednesday.

About three miles away from her destination and a cup of tea, she saw the familiar flashing blue and red lights of either the police or an ambulance up ahead. In this case, it was both. The traffic in front was slowing to a crawl and Madeline joined the tail end of it, hoping that they wouldn't have to stop completely and spoil the trip out. Luck was on her side because whatever had happened up ahead was not actually on the road, but off to the side. As she got closer to the emergency lights, she turned the music down out of respect and could just about see what had happened. She peered over to her right; it looked like a van had overturned and landed squarely in the ditch, totally upside down on its roof. She wondered if the driver had perhaps misjudged the corner and taken it a bit too fast. There didn't seem to be any other vehicles involved, which was a blessing. Noticing the black tyre marks on the road, she deduced he'd left her side of the road rather than coming from the opposite direction. The van was covered in the detritus it had picked up as it had rolled, and the front end was crunched in like a discarded Coke can. This was a known black spot for accidents, so it wouldn't have surprised her if speed had been the issue.

The traffic in front pulled away as a policeman waved them through, and she trailed behind, looking at the wreck, wondering if anyone had been hurt. Then she spotted a familiar logo down the side of the van, covered in dirt where it had rolled but still recognisable to those who had seen it before.

The van belonged to Big Sod.

She drove past slowly, looking like a vulture at the upturned wreck. The ambulance crew were wheeling a large man on a stretcher to the waiting ambulance. Her intentions had not been to harm him. She certainly hadn't intended for him to flip his van—it was just supposed to be a slow puncture and an inconvenience in his day for making her wait to get the car washed and to teach him a lesson for being such an ignoramus. But rather than feeling appalled at what had happened, Madeline was smiling like a mad woman, satisfied and immensely pleased at what she had done.

As she turned up the volume on the audio system, Katrina and the Waves started singing, and she thumped the steering wheel in time to the beat. Even though she was driving along the Wickham road, inside she was walking on sunshine.

Chapter Eleven

Gordon was watching footy on the TV and Madeline was surfing on her iPad, pulling The Daisy Chain local page up to see what was going on. It was mid-conversation but obvious enough to follow what had been said. Particularly if you knew what you were reading about – Madeline assumed there wouldn't have been too many men admitted to hospital with an upset stomach.

@Jaybaby, I know because my mum's a nurse at the university hospital and she told me, though I agree she probably shouldn't have.

@Stargazer, What a terrible way to be ill. Food poisoning! I can't imagine the poor guy's pain or which end to deal with first.

@Jaybaby, You can be gross sometimes but I know what you mean. Yuck! It's bad enough just having the runs without the rest of it! #uncomfortableforsure

@stargazer, I wonder what he ate and where? #investigation?

@Jaybaby Who knows? But likely, I'd say. One case isn't much to go on but it sounds bad.

@Stargazer, If it's bad enough, I reckon they'd investigate it for sure. #haveto

@Jaybaby from @harold, Could have been anything gone off in this heat. Probably forgot and left his ham sandwiches in the car or something then ate them. I've done that before now.

@harold, That sounds dangerous, man. Shouldn't do that.

@Jaybaby, I learned the hard way too. Never again. Left a chicken once while I went to the grocers and post office.

@Harold, What happened to that? Didn't eat it, I hope? #deathwish

@Jaybaby, No, the smell put me off so I took it back to the butchers. He swapped it for me.

@Harold from @stargazer, Wow, you were lucky! #kindbutcher. But it seems the poor guy is okay, though he'll need time to recover, I expect. Not the best way to get time off work, eh?

@Stargazer, No, but at least the weather is good. Perhaps he's a gardener? There's always plenty to potter about doing on a warm day, and for that I do envy him.

@Harold, But not the rest, eh?

@Stargazer, Certainly not the rest! Over and out for now, my friends. My cocoa awaits me.

There was the conversation right in front of her eyes: a man, Grey Man, was in hospital with food poisoning and the local health board could well be investigating, although it appeared at this stage to be an isolated case. Well, they wouldn't find anything at Sally's. She'd been sure not to drag them into something they hadn't had a hand in doing. No, an investigation wouldn't lay any blame on them: plenty of people had eaten tuna that day, just not the variety that had been sitting in a sweltering-hot shed over the weekend.

Madeline closed the page on her iPad and went to make a cup of tea.

Chapter Twelve

THURSDAY

RUTH WAS AT HER KITCHEN TABLE, HER MORNING RUN COMPLETE and a steaming mug of coffee keeping her company as she scanned the newspaper.

"Same old same old," she concluded, then flicked to the crossword puzzle. Glancing at the kitchen clock, she made a note of the time. Could she beat yesterday's time? Her personal best was a slight 12 minutes. Could she do it in less?

"Let's do this!" She pumped the air in an effort to spur herself on, then checked the clock again, working out when she would need to finish to beat her PB. She quickly scanned the clues and immediately added the three she knew straight off. The skill in beating the clock was to get some traction with the ones you knew and work the rest out from that: no deep thinking and no hanging around. Much like *The Chase* on TV: if you don't know the answer, just pass or guess but don't dilly-dally around.

After a full 15 minutes, she relaxed a little. With two more clues to solve she'd resigned herself that her own PB would have to stay put for another day. She had just folded the paper up when a story at the bottom of the front page caught her eye. It was a picture of the mangled wreck of a van out on the Wickham road, where the van had somehow overturned and was sitting firmly on its roof. The headline read "Another black spot incident." She read, "A man was taken to hospital yesterday after his vehicle rolled, badly injuring the driver inside who has a suspected broken collarbone and facial lacerations, along with other cuts and bruises. While his injuries are not life-threatening, it is a reminder for everyone to buckle up and watch their speed on the notorious stretch of road. A tyre blow-out was thought to have caused the accident, but police said speed had likely contributed to the van rolling, and the man's injuries would likely have been less severe had he been wearing a seat belt."

She picked the paper up and added it to her recycling box under the kitchen sink, but the story of the accident stayed with her a few moments longer. Maybe it was the mention of the Wickham road. She knew Madeline regularly went to the garden centre and seemed to recall her mentioning going there on Wednesday, when the accident had occurred. She was glad Madeline hadn't been caught up in it.

At the breakfast bar in her own kitchen, Madeline was reading the report in the local paper too, front page no less, about a big sod who had got his comeuppance for pissing her off and making her wait at the car wash, though of course that's not exactly what was printed. Apparently, Big Sod had been out on the Wickham road and the police reckoned he had taken the bend too quickly and blown a tyre. The man was apparently quite badly injured, but his injuries could have been reduced had he been wearing his seatbelt. The police were reminding everyone to keep their speed to the conditions, particularly on known accident black spots, and of course to buckle up.

Madeline turned the page to read the other news and smiled to herself.

"Serves him right. Should have been wearing his seatbelt, silly sod."

Chapter Thirteen

Madeline had left the phone bill on the hallway table, not wanting to ruin her day off trying sort the damn thing out. She knew the bill was incorrect. She always paid the bills on time, usually long before they were due, and the phone bill was no different. But for some reason there had been a complete muck-up. The payment had been made – it had registered against her account – but from only god knew where, an extra charge of nearly £700 had attached itself, and it was nothing to do with her. Last month when she'd received the bill with the charges she'd tried tell that to the imbecile on the other end of the phone – when she was finally able to talk to someone about it, that was. But here the bill was again.

She checked her watch. There was just enough time to try and sort it out before she left for Sally's and another day of watching the cheese and rocket scones diminish. She ripped open the envelope and it was just as she'd expected: a red final demand for £700, or else they'd cut the line off. She dialled the account query number on the invoice and waited to be connected.

"Thank you for calling. Your call is important to us. We are currently experiencing heavy volumes of calls and your estimated wait time is..." The mechanical female voice hesitated while the other mechanical robot, another female but with a much deeper voice, filled in the blank. "Thirty. Five. Minutes." It then flicked back to the other female robot: "Please stay on the line, or try again later."

Since she didn't have that long to waste, she pressed 'end' and slammed the receiver back into the charging base, which didn't give nearly as much satisfaction as slamming the old style of phone down. There was no option but to have another go later from her mobile.

DEXTER WAS ON THE WARM PAVING STONES IN THE MORNING sunshine not far from the garage, and she wished him good day as she ventured inside to her car. He didn't bother lifting his head off the ground; too damn lazy for his own good.

"I wouldn't mind another day doing exactly what I wanted all day like you do, lucky thing."

No response, but none was expected really. Madeline drove out of the garage and turned out of Oakwood Rise, on her way to a another day and another dollar. Or pound, in her case.

"HE'LL BE IN SOON, YOUR FRIEND."

Margaret was trying to wind Madeline up. She nodded towards the big clock on the wall behind her head. It read 12 pm exactly.

"First, he's not my friend, and second, surely it's your turn to serve the old git? I had him last time."

"Ah, but he seems to like you."

"And how the hell do you work that out? He doesn't say anything more than 'Tuna mayo roll and tea,'" she said, deepening her voice to imitate him. "Hardly a conversationalist, hardly a sign of friendship."

"He's probably just lonely, or shy. Might be really nice if you got to know him. Give the guy a chance." Margaret smirked like she was fixing her up on a blind date.

Madeline rolled her eyes at her. "I don't think so. Not for me. If you feel sorry for him, you be his best buddy, but leave me out of it. He makes my skin crawl."

Margaret tut-tutted her mock disapproval and went back inside the kitchen area, no doubt to avoid the entrance of the infamous 12.05 pm customer.

As expected, however, Madeline didn't see him again that Thursday, nor the following week. In fact, she never saw him at the café again at all. No one missed him. The grumpy old sod was not someone any of them liked serving, and the general consensus was he'd moved away, or fallen out with his tuna mayo roll and tea combo. Good riddance to him.

AT 2 PM SHE FINALLY HAD TIME TO CALL THE PHONE COMPANY again. Pulling the phone bill out of her bag, she sat on the step of the café's back entrance and punched the number into her mobile. The sun was still blazing away, but the little overhead porch shaded her from its direct heat. The kitchen inside was a bit quieter now, most people having finished their lunches, so there was a lull before the few folks who wandered in for an afternoon cuppa. This time, the female robot informed her that the wait time was now less than five minutes, so she hung on, listening to the crappy piped music that was on a continuous loop. After one and a half times round of the same song, 'Natalie' came on the line and asked how she could help.

"Hello Natalie, Madeline Simpson here. Shall I give you my account number?" She set off being helpful, hoping this wasn't going to be a painful experience for either of them.

"Yes, thanks." There was the sound of typing as Madeline gave it to her. "How can I help you?"

"Well, as you can see, I have a strange charge against my account for seven hundred pounds, which is nothing to do with me, and it's now gone red so it's serious. I don't want to be cut off. Can you sort it for me?"

"You want me to pay it for you?"

"No, I don't want you to pay it. I want you to take it off my account. It's nothing to do with me."

"But it's allocated to your telephone number, so it must be to do with your account. It's for charges over the last month."

"But that's just it," said Madeline, struggling to keep her voice level.

"It's nothing to do with me. I've paid my bill, the usual amount give or take a few pounds. This is not mine." She took a deep breath and tried another tack. "Look, Natalie, I've always paid on time, but these charges are simply a mistake and shouldn't be on my account. Can you remove them, please, then perhaps someone can find out where they really belong?" She let out a long breath. Trying to be both clear and pleasant at the same time was burning her up inside and her pulse was beginning to race full throttle. And she didn't need the stress.

"I can't just do that, I'm afraid," said Natalie blandly. "I'm not authorised to do so. I'll have to put you through to my supervisor. Hold please." Then she was gone. An empty phone. For a moment.

The hideous piped music was back, and Madeline was left sitting there open-mouthed. Margaret called from out the front; it seemed she needed a hand. She stared at the phone in her hand, which was bleating an electronic version of "Yesterday" by the Beatles. Margaret called her again, her voice more urgent now. Madeline no choice but to hang up, exasperated.

"For heaven's sake," she cussed to the empty phone, Natalie in particular.

"Coming," Madeline shouted back. She stood and retied her apron, then went back towards the kitchen, putting a smile back on her face as she went, though throttling Natalie would have been much more satisfying.

Chapter Fourteen

SATURDAY

"Look Des, it's nothing personal, but no more. It's for your own good, buddy. You can't afford it."

Lionel, the bookie's shop manager, was not happy, but Des was even less so: he was desperate to put a bet on the 2.20 pm at Doncaster, a 'dead cert' according to his tip-off, and he certainly needed a win. For a change.

"Oh, go on, would you? You know I'm good for it, and the win will clear some of the debt I owe you, so a win-win all round. Go on, Lionel – what do you say?" Des hoped his smile would help win him over. It usually did. But this time he was mistaken.

"I say no, Des. You've already had fair warning. I told you last week, and the week before, and you just don't listen. It's for your own good, you know. You haven't got the cash to be splashing around, else you'd pay off your debt." Lionel lowered his voice and tried a different way to get through. "Look, you're going to end up in with a real bad crowd if you're not careful. I've already told you the big boss doesn't mess around with non-payment of tabs, if you know what I mean. 'Cos if you don't, I'll spell it out for you. It usually includes a baseball bat, just so you know, and be under no illusion: he'll not stop when you start squealing, and he won't stop hounding you until the debt is paid off in full. I've seen the way he works, mate. Believe me, you don't want to go there. Now clear off and go home – or better still, go and earn some money and pay your debt back."

He couldn't make it much clearer, but Des was desperate: the couple of hundred quid was burning a hole in his pocket and the tip-off was egging him on. He took the money out and waved it in Lionel's face as a tease.

Lionel let out an exasperated sigh. "I must be a soft touch, or stupid." Defeated, he said, "Give it here. To win, I suppose?"

Des nodded. "Yes, Troopers Gold, 33 to 1." He kiss-smacked his fingers like he was waiting for the juiciest steak to arrive and waited for his ticket. The winner's ticket. He could feel the excitement bubbling inside, the dead cert to win a way of getting out of his mess. Come 2.30 pm he'd be a richer man and he'd be able to pay some off his tab off, but the first thing he needed to pay off was his sister. He'd nicked her grocery money two days ago while she'd cooked dinner for him at her place – meat pie and chips with lashings of gravy, one of his many favourites. He felt bad about it, but who could resist a dead cert? And he knew she wouldn't miss the cash until next week when she went grocery shopping, so he had a few days to get it back to the tin in the kitchen drawer. She'd never even know. Hell, he might even buy her a bunch of flowers with his winnings. She deserved nice things.

Des took his ticket, thanked Lionel again, and headed off down the street to the pub for a pint and to watch the race. He figured he'd better not hang around the bookies much longer. After all, he'd had his warning.

At 2.30 pm, Des turned his attention to the TV in the bar and watched as the race got underway. Troopers Gold was leading the pack. "Go, go, go!" Des shouted at the TV. But his excitement turned to disbelief as Troopers Gold was overtaken on the final stretch and came second. On his 'to win' bet, which might as well have been last.

Des sat nursing his pint, looking much like someone close to him had recently died. In actual fact, it was probably going to be him when his sister caught up with him – never mind the bookie's boss. She'd rip a strip off him for sure. His day had well and truly turned to mincemeat, and he was up to his neck in trouble and debt. He tipped the remains of his beer down the back of his throat and slowly made his way outside like a depressed man on his way to a wake. What the hell was he going to do now?

Chapter Fifteen

Week 3
 Monday

Madeline and Gordon had had a lovely weekend: he'd gone to watch the match – Crystal Palace were at home – and she'd stayed at home, puttering around the garden. Even when the weather was hot and dry like it had been, weeds managed to find a way to invade the places you didn't want them, and it could take some considerable force to get them out. By early afternoon on Saturday, Madeline was soaked to the skin with sweat, her cotton shorts and T-shirt now too hot for the vigour and the heat of the day. She'd had to sit on the patio several times with a glass of cold lemon barley water with lots of ice cubes. Dexter had watched carefully out of one eye, half buried and looking out from under a low-hanging bush in the corner of his shady spot, not even contemplating entering the hot sun.

She'd bought a couple of steaks for dinner that night, to put on the barbecue, and there was a cold bottle of white wine in the fridge, along with a couple of beers for Gordon. She'd even bought raspberries, cream and meringue nests to make dessert. She'd hoped Gordon would join her for a while out on the patio later that evening, and he had, so it couldn't have been more perfect.

But on Monday morning it was time to go into Croydon and the office, so she finished getting dressed, put the pleasant weekend thoughts to the back of her mind and prepared herself mentally for the week ahead. And that meant having another go at sorting out that damn telephone bill again. It was still tucked away in her bag from Thursday; she hadn't had a spare minute to have another go that day, and by Friday she'd simply forgotten about it. The fog had rolled into her brain and it was all she could do to remember what was in front of her at work, never mind what was in her bag.

"Morning, Deidre. Have a nice weekend?" Madeline pulled up alongside her in the private car park, gravel crunching under the wheels, her passenger window open to call through.

Deidre smiled brightly. She always seemed to Madeline to be quite genuinely upbeat – unless something really got her back up, and then she was lethal. Much like Dexter in that respect: arched back, bared teeth and it was all on.

"Oh, wonderful thanks, Madeline, just wonderful. The grandkids came round and we filled the paddling pool and they had the best time with Granddad squirting water from the hosepipe too. Everything and everyone was drenched by lunchtime but the glorious sun soon dried things off. Then we put sausages on the barbecue and everyone stuffed themselves silly. You?"

"Same, thanks, though without the paddling pool and children. Just enjoyed the garden and the sunshine with Gordon after the match. Nice and relaxing, and quiet." She looked up at the deep blue sky. Even at just before 9 am it was a stunner; the heat was quite fierce already. "Shame to be stuck inside on a day like this, though I suppose it's a bit cooler in there," she said, nodding with her head towards the direction of the building they worked in. "Saturday nearly melted me like a popsicle."

They chatted and headed to the back door and the coolness that would envelope them both in the downstairs offices. Madeline opened the old wooden door that creaked like something in a horror movie. The whole building could do with a bit of modernisation, really; the dark downstairs offices sometimes smelled a bit damp. In winter the two women nearly half froze to death, but it was nice on a hot day.

"I'll make some tea, then there's one thing I need to get out of the way first off, and that's sort out my phone bill. They've added a seven-hundred-pound charge that's not mine, and I need to get to the bottom of it, because they keep sending me reminders and I'm not paying it."

"Heck. And it's a real pain dealing with companies like that," Deidre sympathised. "Same when I had an extra charge on my electric bill by mistake. Wouldn't listen. Drove me batty. In the end I got my son to deal with them. He had no trouble in getting it sorted – had them quivering in their boots. He can be quite cutting when he wants to be. A lawyer on your side can be quite handy sometimes." She smiled.

"I'll bear that in mind, then, if I don't have any joy."

Fifteen minutes later, Madeline was sitting at her desk, listening to crappy piped music once again, thrumming the fingers of her right hand on the wooden desk, making a hollow sound a bit like small galloping ponies on an old black and white movie. She'd been on hold for seven minutes already and wished she could have chosen some better music to listen to – the Death March sprang to mind. Finally, she heard a gap in the music and a real live person broke in, informed her his name was Julian and asked how could he help.

"Julian, I'm really hoping you can help me because those that have gone before you haven't managed it and, as a menopausal woman, I am almost at my breaking point." May as well go with the truth in a sort of threatening way. There was silence at his end. "Are you there, Julian?" she enquired.

"Yes, I'm still here. Just wondering how best to respond to you. I've some experience of what it's like to be a menopausal woman – my mother is one. So let's see how I can help your day get better, shall we? I'm sure you want the stress to go away."

Was he trying to be funny or was he empathising with her? She couldn't quite tell but his approach was certainly different.

"Why don't you tell me your name and what the problem is," he went on, "and I'll endeavour to solve it here and now." He sounded lovely, relaxing almost, genuine, and a little bit camp. Madeline bet his mother loved him deeply when she wasn't raging, sweating or crying. She took a deep breath and told him the whole silly story and didn't get worked up at all. Julian filled in occasionally with 'ums' and 'aha's' and when she'd reached the end, he simply said, "Not a problem. I'll put the credit through now for you."

"Julian, you are an angel. Thank you." She almost wept with relief. "You're a credit to your mother: she's damn lucky to have such a lovely son."

Credit where credit is due. I can be nice when it warrants it.

"It was my pleasure, Madeline. Now you have a nice day and enjoy the sunshine." He clicked off and ended the call.

Turning to Deidre, who was looking right at her, she smiled incredulously. She couldn't believe her luck – was stunned, in fact. "Well, that was nice and easy for a change. All sorted. And after all that hassle before, why couldn't the other imbeciles I'd spoken to earlier sort it out so simply?"

"Well, at least it's done and you don't need my David to get snarky with them."

"You're right there. Now I'd better get some work done before Stanley accuses me of slacking and I need a lawyer for a different reason." She turned her attention to a rather full inbox.

Chapter Sixteen

Week 3
Tuesday

"It's the best way, Madeline."

Dr. Bing was trying once again to get her to take a 'chemical' to help with the temperature tantrums and mood swings. She'd only gone to visit her for some cream for a skin irritation that wouldn't settle, probably something from the garden had bothered her, and the doctor had asked how she'd been since her last visit. Well, Madeline had been a bit worked up. And on top of that, she thought the doctor, though she meant well, was beginning to sound like Rebecca, wanting her to take something for her 'condition.' But Madeline wanted to do it naturally, not chemically, so if she was going to get some extra help, it would be more likely from a botanist than a chemist.

"I'm fine, really I am. I can cope with it all just as I am at the moment, though I would like some more cream, please."

Dr. Bing looked like she'd resigned herself to her patient being stubborn, and at the end of the day, it was her choice what she took.

She tapped the keys on her keyboard to create the prescription, and Madeline filled the empty air with light conversation.

"What a great summer we're having — lovely sunny days. And I must say, Gordon and I have been enjoying the evenings sat out on the patio with a glass of wine. Beats the TV any day." It was nearly true: she had been enjoying the patio, and the cooler evenings were pleasant, especially now, though Gordon still preferred the TV and the lounge.

Dr. Bing printed out the form and handed it to Madeline with a smile. "There you go. That should do the trick. And remember what I said about the other — just let me know if you change your mind or things get worse for you. Hundreds and thousands of women get support with tablets. No need to suffer on your own."

Madeline smiled, took the white slip and thanked the doctor, then left the small clinical office and headed over to the pharmacy to get the cream. Her phone clock said it was 9.30 am. She needed to get a move on because the car was parked in a sixty-minute space and time up was fast approaching. Luckily the pharmacy wasn't busy and it took only a moment for the pharmacist to stick a label on her cream. She was back out the door and heading for her car in no time.

But her morning was about to get a bit more stressful. In the distance she could see the uniform of the traffic warden, and he was looking at her car registration and tapping it into his small handheld machine. Flummoxed, Madeline checked her phone clock again and knew she still had another 10 minutes. Why was he giving her a ticket, she wondered? Only one way to find out.

"Morning."

Be nice, Madeline.

"Morning," he said back, keeping his head down and concentrating on his device.

"Can I ask why you're giving me a ticket? I still have at least ten more minutes left on the meter."

"That you do, Madam, but that's not why I'm issuing you with a ticket."

So am I supposed to guess why, then? Stay calm, stay calm.

"Then why the ticket?"

He still hadn't even looked up from his machine and that began to annoy her even more. Look what had happened to Grey Man. You can't talk to someone and not look at them. *Ask* him *what happens when you do that kind of thing.*

"Your wheels are over the white parking bay line, Madam, that's why. They have to be completely inside the box, otherwise you are in effect taking up two spaces."

Madeline took a step back to see what he was talking about. Yes, the front wheels were a little over the white road markings, but only by a couple of inches, four at the most.

"You've got to be kidding me. I'm getting a ticket for two inches over?"

Finally he lifted his head and looked at her as he ripped the ticket from his machine. "You are indeed. Two inches over is two inches over." He handed her the ticket and she just stood and looked at it.

"Whether you take it or not is of no concern to me. I've issued it now, so there is a record of it and I'd advise you to pay it sooner than later. It's cheaper that way."

Her best glare had no effect. She was sure he got verbal abuse all the time. She snatched it from his fingers.

"Sixty pounds?" she spluttered. But it was too late; he'd started to walk off and she was left standing at the curbside fuming with indignation. The warm sun, pleasant just a short time ago, was suddenly unbearable on her skin and beads of sweat started to roll down her cleavage, stopping only at her bra like a dam holding a trickle of a river back.

"Bloody nitpicking little shitbag!" she shouted after him.

The ticket found itself screwed up tightly into a ball and tossed over her shoulder. Madeline wondered if she'd be done for littering next.

"Little shit," she added more quietly to herself. She got into the baking oven of a car and turned it on, the air blasting her like a wind on a washing line in the desert. "Pity it's still too early for a gin and tonic," she muttered. "It'd go down nicely right about now."

She put the car in gear and headed to Sally's, wondering if Grey Man would be in today for his lunch. Probably not.

Chapter Seventeen

WEDNESDAY

WHEN WEDNESDAY MORNING CAME AND MADELINE ACTUALLY SAW the whites of Des's eyes smiling back at her as he stood by the digger in the back garden, she wasn't sure whether to thank him for finally turning up or kick him in the nuts for being so bloody tardy and causing her more and more annoyance every day. His rugged sunburnt face told anyone who met him that he worked outdoors for a living; his shorts and work boots were another clue. Still, he looked pleasant enough, though for what Madeline wasn't sure. Not a tall man, he looked like Joe Average. Save for the ruddy complexion. And at least he wasn't dangling a cigarette like Sid had.

"Better late than never, Mrs. S," he said to her. "Better late than never."

Like that would make up for everything. She felt her blood start to heat up in her veins, and it wasn't because she was having a temperature tantrum or because of the summer heat. "How dare he," she stropped inwardly. "One, be so bloody cheery and unconcerned, and two, call me Mrs. S. No one calls me that and gets off scot-free." A kick in the balls seemed like the best option, but she let the thought slip. She'd heard that to the untrained, it's actually quite difficult to get the kick absolutely right on target, so she'd probably end up kicking him squarely in the thigh, which would lose its desired effect and she'd just be embarrassed. And he'd be pretty damn mad. She chose to leave it alone for the sake of her escalating blood pressure.

"Yes, I guess so," was all Madeline managed, but in a sarcastic tone to let him know she was pissed at him.

"Any chance of a cuppa before I start? A nice strong one if you can, two sugars. Oh, and if there's a spare biscuit going, that'd be grand."

She couldn't believe she was hearing right, but found herself turning towards the kitchen and doing as he asked before she said something foul and unladylike. She muttered "Cheeky sod" under her breath and left it at that.

Kicking off her gardening shoes and leaving them at the kitchen door, she flicked the kettle switch, then went to grab the mail off the front mat while waiting for it to boil. Normally the mail was mostly junk mail, and today was no different. "What a waste of trees," she muttered. "If they banned junk mail, they wouldn't need bloody junk mail recycling bins, now, would they?" She sorted through it to double-check for any letters mixed in, and there was one – a phone bill. And it was in a red final demand envelope. Again.

"What the –?"

Clenching her teeth, she shoved the rest of the junk crap into the recycle bin in the kitchen cupboard under the sink, trying not to get worked up again. What with Mr. Bloody Cheeky outside and Julian another phone company failure, she wasn't sure who to get mad at first.

The biscuits were in the top cupboard so she grabbed the Rich Tea, vowing they'd have to do for him. He wasn't having her chocolate digestives, because she only had a few left until shopping again. She poured the boiling water onto the tea bags in the pot and waited for it to steep, all the while watching Des though the kitchen window. He stood surveying something or other in the distance, still not doing anything in the garden. Her nerves began to jangle again at his lack of concern for her damn pond.

"Will I ever get to sit by it and appreciate it this summer?" she asked out loud to the window. Madeline had always wanted a pond, a few fish swimming about, some pink water lilies perhaps, even a frog or two living nearby; something nice and tranquil, a place where she could sit and read on a fancy new lounger, perhaps with a checked sun umbrella to match. But it didn't look like that was going to happen anytime soon, not with useless Des standing with his thumbs up his bum.

She poured the tea, grabbed a couple of biscuits from the packet and took them outside to him. He blasted her with one of his no-doubt-practiced smiles.

"So you'll be finally starting the hole today?" She had to make a point.

"As soon as I've had me tea, I'm on to it. Won't take long to dig that hole, I expect, and you'll have fish swimming in it in no time." His cheeriness was both calming and annoying at the same time, if that was possible. She didn't need his damn cheer; she just wanted to see signs of activity before she lost her rag with him. She gave him her "better had" look, then turned briskly back to her own tea and chocolate biscuits waiting indoors.

Sitting at the breakfast bar, she grabbed the envelope with the telephone bill and hoped it was the credit notification she'd been expecting, but deep down she knew it wasn't. The envelope was red, after all. Madeline tore into it, only to find yet another bill, this one for just over £800.

"I don't sodding believe it!" she shouted into the empty kitchen. She felt a sudden surge of anger tighten in her chest. The thought of spending another forty-five minutes going round in circles on the phone listening to crappy piped music, trying to get now two bills sorted out before they eventually blacklisted her for non-payment or some such, was beginning to feel too much. The heat in her chest gripped like a strong hairy hand and she willed the feeling to pass, and quickly. It, however, had other thoughts, and wasn't going anywhere.

"Bollocks! Damn you!" she shouted again. She sat, seething, not really wanting to get wound up, but how could she not when faced with a dickhead outside still not digging up her garden and a dickhead at the phone company she'd soon have to try and deal with yet again.

Was the world out to get her this morning, she wondered, a conspiracy? Because it certainly seemed like it was. She tried again to steady her breathing as the doctor had told her to do when she started to get uptight. It wasn't taking much these days. Iiiiiiin... Ooooout.... Iiiiiiin.... Ooooout.

Breathe, Madeline, breathe.

She closed her eyes to help drain out the stress and heat invading her body, willing the deep breaths to work and her blood to stop hurling full speed through her veins, but she was struggling. After three whole minutes of trying, she gave up. The next best remedy Madeline had learned was scrubbing something, hard, so she filled a bucket with hot soapy water, retrieved the rubber gloves and Jif from under the sink and headed upstairs to clean the bathroom, again. Usually at the end of putting some energy into cleaning, she'd calmed down a little, but today was going to be different. After thirty minutes and a now-sparkling bathroom that Jif would be proud to feature in a daytime TV ad, she was still wound up, feeling the need to release even more pent-up pressure bubbling below the surface of her skull. Her head started to pound fiercely.

A knock at the back door got her attention, so she went back downstairs to see Des waving through the kitchen window for her to go to the door. She groaned inwardly but went to see what he wanted anyway.

As she opened the door, he said, "Need to talk to you Mrs. S. Come on out and have a look." He started walking off to the corner of the garden where his digger was idling, engine throbbing gently.

Madeline followed him, watching his lanky gait as he walked in front. For an outdoor landscaper type of guy, he had skinny, hairy legs and knobbly knees. As they neared the corner she could see he'd dug a hole about the size of a narrow grave, about the width of the digger's bucket and about four or five feet deep. The digger was parked up next to it, engine running, waiting patiently.

"The ground is too hard," Des said. "There's so much heavy clay, and without much rain, it's rock hard."

Why does that matter to me? she wondered. She still didn't trust herself to respond calmly, so she simply waited for him to continue.

"It's going to make the job a lot longer because of it, and that means the price will have to go up." He didn't dress it up: straight to the point. He didn't seem at all bothered.

You've got to be bloody kidding me!

So she was just supposed to say, "Okay, I've got loads of spare money," and he'd get on with it and that would be that? She wrenched her gaze away from the bottom of the hole, rolled them back to somewhere in the top of her forehead, then yanked them back to look level at him.

"Sorry?" she said frostily. Coolness had materialised from somewhere. "You quoted for the job, I accepted it and here you are here doing the job. We have a deal. You can't go back on it now." She hoped that made it plain enough. She really didn't need any more strife in her day; her nerves were already frazzled with the bloody phone bill fiasco and now she had a landscaper trying to up his price because the bloody soil was too hard and it was going to take longer. The coolness evaporated as quickly as it had appeared. Now she could almost feel steam percolating behind her eyes and ears, ready to explode from them, comic book-style, at any second.

"Well, I'm going to have to, I'm afraid," Des said blandly, "otherwise I'll be working for nothing. It's going to take me more than double the time to dig the hole, time I hadn't included in that quote." At least he looked honest about it, but his time wasn't her problem. "Come on, Mrs. S. See my dilemma and help me out here?"

She looked around the garden, at the hole, the digger, his tools lying around, his radio, his tea mug, actually her tea mug, and the pile of soil next to the Great Orange Machine. She was aware of him still rattling on but was someplace else, someplace outside of her normal self but looking in at the situation and not hearing a word of what he was saying. She stood there in the quiet of the garden overlooking the empty fields, only dimly aware of him jabbering on in his own defence and trying to get more money out of the job. A clarity hit – took over, really – and she knew just what she was going to do. Slipping on some nearby gloves, she picked up the spade he'd left lying nearby and turned towards him. His back was now to her as he pointed to a nearby area of the garden, still saying words she wasn't comprehending.

As calm as anything, Madeline lifted the spade and, harnessing all the excess energy bubbling inside of her, swung it with all her might at the side of his temple.

The metal connected to his skull with a sickening thump, and he went down like a paper airplane. The air was deathly quiet apart from the great orange thing gently throbbing in the corner. She stood for a second or two, still calm, and totally in control of what she'd had just done. She didn't feel any panic: no bad feeling, no 'what have I done?' Nothing. She let out a breath and looked around, mainly to see if anyone was there, although there was no reason they would be: it was her back garden and it wasn't overlooked by the neighbours in the slightest. There was no one. She calmly bent down and checked his neck for a pulse. It was still present. Madeline hadn't killed the man, merely knocked him unconscious. Was she disappointed? She wasn't quite sure.

Chapter Eighteen

Madeline stood there wondering how she was going to get out of this little situation. When Des woke up he was going to be pissed at her, to say the least. And she'd most certainly be in trouble. Grievous bodily harm carried a sentence if he pressed charges, and why wouldn't he? Being whacked around the head with a spade couldn't go unpunished. She looked at the hole, she looked at the great big orange machine with its engine still running, and she looked at the body of Des lying prone at her feet.

"Damn it! It's his own silly fault he's lying there," she told herself. "If he hadn't wanted more money and pissed me off on top of the damn phone bill, he'd still be stood upright."

Now there was a mess to clean up. She bent over him, grabbed his mobile phone out of his pocket and scrolled through the call log. Nothing since yesterday and no texts either, so she turned it off. Luckily it was an older-style phone, an old 'flip top' one, well before smartphones, so it only received calls and texts, nothing else. Madeline knew from watching enough episodes of *CSI* that they couldn't track it if it was turned off, and she'd just have to worry about pinging telephone towers later, although with no GPS or data capability, it probably couldn't be placed anyway. Luck was in her favour.

But who knew he was at her place? He probably ran his business off the back of a cigarette packet, and she hoped that meant no one knew, but it was an issue that needed resolving. What little she did know about him was that he lived alone, so he probably wouldn't be missed for a while if he didn't make it home at the end of the day. But someone would miss him after that. Probably.

She went back into his pocket to retrieve his van keys – another item to dispose of. She slipped the phone and keys into her own pocket and took stock for a moment. His cap lay nearby. What to do with the little problem of his prostrate body – let him live and risk his wrath, or finish him off? How the hell was she going to be able to explain away what she'd done when he woke up? That just couldn't be allowed to happen. She realised she had to finish him off. And now.

She glanced at the garage; the car inside had a decent-sized boot. She glanced over at the shed and the plastic bin bags and tools she knew were in there, and then glanced at the grave-sized hole that had started all this bloody mess. Finally, turning her attention once again to Des lying there on the hard ground, Madeline knew there wasn't long to decide, so she'd have to go for the quickest option, and one she could manage all on her own. That ruled out getting him into the boot of her car or putting him in bin bags in the shed and disposing of him later someplace. And cutting him up was not going to be easy or pleasant. The hole it had to be.

Madeline grabbed his arms, pulled them back over his head, and dragged him the short distance towards the trench, then rolled him over so he fell inside. With a thud, he landed at the bottom. She held her breath, stood very still and looked into the hole. Was he going to stir now? There was no obvious movement, and she allowed herself to breathe again. It seemed she was still safe, so she made her way over to the great orange machine, climbed into the driver's seat and looked at all the knobs and levers. How hard could it be to get the bucket to pick up soil and drop it in the hole a few times? She tested each lever in turn to see what it did and found it surprisingly easy to manoeuvre the whole thing. Co-ordination had never been a problem for her, and now it could be her saviour. She concentrated on the end where his head lay first, hoping he would suffocate quickly, and worked methodically down from there. It was only about thirty minutes or so before the whole thing was completely filled in. Satisfied, she drove the digger over the top of the offending spot a few times to flatten the soil down and generally neaten the previously dug area. Job done – for now.

Stepping out of the cab, she realised she needed to put the rest of her impromptu plan together: she had to clear the rest of the mess and evidence away. And quickly. First there was the small matter of his damn van sitting out the front of her house. She grabbed her own gardening gloves from the potting shed along with an old gardening shirt that was once Gordon's and could pass for one of Des's, went over and picked up the cap that had fallen off his head, checked her pocket again for his keys and phone and set off. Putting the cap on as she went, she kept her shoulders down and walked along the side of the house. She just hoped nobody in the quiet little cul-de-sac had decided to come home early. As it was only around lunchtime, that wasn't likely. Eyes low, she unlocked the van and slipped inside, where she let out the breath she hadn't realised she had been holding. She did a quick scan of the area. All was clear, so she put the key in the ignition and slowly pulled away. She wasn't really sure where to head, apart from keeping to the back roads and away from any known cameras.

How the bloody hell was an average Joe supposed to know where they all were exactly?

Madeline hadn't driven for long when an idea sprang to mind. What about if she left the van by the river at the reserve, threw the phone in the water and walked back home the back way through the fields? She would look just like any other dog walker, but without the dog, and not draw any attention to herself – just someone out for a walk on a nice day. Looking at the old shirt, she realised she'd be an unkempt someone, but she was running out of time: she had to make a decision, and fast. It had to be the reserve.

It's not as if I've lain in bed dreaming of this day, conjuring up the perfect landscaper murder plot. Really.

Less than 10 minutes later she pulled into the little car park area, hoping to be alone. It was deserted, so she said a little prayer of thanks. Parking up as close to the river and the little jetty as possible, she did one last check for nosey folks and then got out, leaving the van unlocked. With a bit of luck, some hoody-wearing youths would nick it later and set fire to it. She checked she'd not left anything of her own inside the van, threw the phone into the river then took the gloves and cap off. She deposited these inside her shirt to dispose of when she passed a rubbish bin on the way back. She'd left the keys in the ignition in the hope someone would think he'd just parked up and gone for a pee, or perhaps even had committed suicide. And of course it would make the van easier for an opportunist to nick. She needed Rent-a-Thug.

She paused for one last recon: Had she covered all the really important aspects that could lead this sorry mess back to her doorstop? She hoped so. Taking a deep breath, she set out down the road towards the shops and home. She left the gloves in one rubbish bin outside the chip shop, and dropped the cap in someone's wheelie bin that stood handy, ready for emptying, on the pavement. By the time the contents of both had been deposited on the landfill site somewhere later today, they would be impossible to find – at least, she hoped so, because her DNA was all over them.

Walking along, Madeline slipped off the old shirt covering her own and placed that in another wheelie bin, then took the grassy pathway that led up from the edge of town via the fields. One of the exit points was near her house, and a route she'd taken many times.

In her casual attire she blended in quite nicely. She made use of the time to think. Yes, she hadn't really wanted to kill him – that part had been an accident, of sorts – but she'd done it, so that left her with several problems. As she walked, she ran through what she'd done to cover her tracks so far and where she might have an issue to sort out, one that could attract unwanted police attention. The body was gone for sure, never to be smelled or seen for years to come, if ever, but she was left with all that loose dirt from digging that couldn't be explained – yet. The van was gone, but could possibly be linked back to being at her place if anyone had seen it parked up, so she filed that to the back of her mind to come back to as another loose end that needed tying up. His bloody great orange machine was still stood in the garden: how the hell could she explain that away? The phone wouldn't work again after a soaking, and any of Madeline's DNA should be lost on a landfill site by the end of the day, but she did need to clean his shovel off, then make it dirty again.

She brought the outstanding points together and let them rumble round inside her head, hoping a solution would show itself by the time she reached her gate. She'd heard that if you tell yourself to figure something out or try and remember something you've forgotten, and put a time to it – say you need the answer in two hours' time – then tell yourself to forget it until that given time, invariably your unconscious computer will come back to you with the answer. Worked nine times out of ten, roughly.

So that's what she did. Madeline gave herself until she got back to the garden to figure out the issue of all that loose dirt scattered across the lawn, the van, the shovel and the great orange machine, then put it out of her head until then.

AN HOUR LATER, SHE ARRIVED BACK HOT, SWEATY AND EXHAUSTED again at the house along with the solution to two of her problems. It was 2 pm, time to get a wriggle on, but her stomach howled in protest at the lack of food. The long walk back had made her feel like she was running on empty so she headed indoors to make a quick sandwich and survey the plan again while she ate. Would it really work? She grabbed ham, mustard and a couple of slices of bread and put a sandwich together quickly, then took it outside and sat on a canvas chair on the little patio in the shade for five stressful minutes.

The sandwich barely hit the sides of her mouth as she chewed and swallowed it down in a hurry, eager to get on with the next phase of 'operation cover-up.' A couple of minutes later, still with the last mouthful of ham sandwich going round like a cement mixer, she headed to the shed for a new set of gloves and made her way over to the great orange machine. She pretty much had the machine figured out, though that had only been for moving the original soil back into a hole that he'd dug. This next plan involved Madeline *actually digging* another hole, which was going to take much more intellect. And time. She climbed up into the cab as it sat at the scene of the crime and looked at the various knobs and levers again that she'd used for filling in the 'grave.'

You can't refer to it as a sodding grave, woman. It was a hole, okay?

The plan was simple. Dig another hole three or four metres away but still near enough to the original one, and pile the loose dirt from that one on top of the site of the original hole, the one where Des now lay dead – presumably – which would then mask the loose stuff lying around. Ingenious! It would also explain what Des had been doing here and why his van had been parked out front. If he was reported missing, and he would be eventually, his disappearance would likely be in the paper or on the local news. If someone had seen his van here they would then come forward. And Madeline would say yes, he had been here that day, though he was bloody unreliable and hadn't come back. He'd probably gone off to start another job, pissing another customer off by trying to overcharge them while he was at it. She could even add, "When you see him, tell him I've still a pond to be dug," though that sounded callous even to her own ears.

Her plan took care of both aspects – she hoped. The great orange machine would just have to sit and wait it out. It wasn't something she could easily remove herself: she couldn't exactly drive it into the river without drawing attention and looking like she was trying to dispose of it, now, could she? It had to stay put for now. Maybe someone would come and pick it up, that 'Queenie' bloke Sid perhaps. Right – she could ring old Sid to pick it up in a week or two.

It was much harder and slower digging the new hole. The ground was so damn hard – just like Des had complained. Madeline's hole digging was nowhere near as neat as Des's, but she got on with it the best she could. Within a couple of hours there was a tidy pile of soil on top of the original hole, the one containing a dead landscaper, so that part of the plan was complete. There really was no way to tell there was any other loose soil lying around, or a body underneath the ground: the new pile masked it all perfectly. And she had dug a semblance of a hole, though not as neat or as deep as his had been. She sat back in the cab to survey the work and was pleased with her efforts.

A glance at her wristwatch told her it was gone 4 pm, time to stop being 'Mad Madeline' and get back to being 'Mild Madeline' before

Gordon got home or someone else came knocking. She turned the engine off and left the machine right where it was, giving the steering wheel a quick wipe round with an oily rag that was in the cab. It was more from watching *CSI* than from need, because her skin hadn't touched it directly, but she wanted to be extra careful – she was a novice at killing a person, after all. As she headed indoors to get cleaned up, exhaustion from the last few hours enveloped her and she desperately wanted to crash, but that would have to wait.

It's bloody hard work killing someone, you know!

"Better start thinking about getting dinner on," she told herself as she entered the house and dropped her dirty gear in the laundry. Twenty minutes later she was showered and pouring her first gin and tonic of the day. It was slightly earlier than usual, but then this hadn't been the usual sort of day.

EARLY THE FOLLOWING MORNING, WHILE MADELINE STOOD IN THE kitchen in her nightdress waiting for the kettle to boil, she looked out of the window at the great orange machine in the distance, and the deadly secret that lay under the pile of earth beneath it. To her surprise she'd slept unusually soundly last night, one of the best night's sleeps she'd had in a good long time. She put it down to all her stresses being released in one go. She smiled to herself and then spoke it out loud to Dexter, who was busy weaving his way between her legs encouraging her to get his breakfast.

"I'm not advising going around killing landscapers or anyone else who pisses you off, but it was a good alternative to a chemical sleeping tablet."

Dexter purred loudly.

Chapter Nineteen

ROSE STOOD STARING AT DES'S DINNER IN THE FRIDGE. SHE'D MADE a lovely cottage pie with cheese on top, another one of his favourites. She couldn't believe he'd taken the money, her grocery money, though she shouldn't have been surprised; it wasn't the first time he'd done it. But usually her brother put it back, thinking he'd gotten away with it before she'd noticed. This time, though, he hadn't, and she hadn't seen him either, which was strange. No call, no nothing, and the cottage pie she'd saved for him was sitting in the fridge staring back at her like it was her fault. Since he hadn't returned any of her calls, she decided to drop in at his place before she went off to work and make sure he was okay.

Her toast popped up and she spread it with copious amounts of butter and lemon curd, causing a little puddle on the plate. Taking a big bite, she relished the lemony flavour. A little butter dribbled down her chin, which she wiped with the back of her hand and licked. Waste not, want not. Rose didn't have any vices to speak of, but real butter was her downfall and no amount of lecturing from friends could persuade her otherwise. If that was the worst she had, then so be it. Her philosophy had always been that it took a dairyman to make butter, and a chemist to make margarine, and if you ask which one flies prefer, they'd go for butter every time. She finished the two slices of toast with Des on her mind, then wiped the little plate clean with her index finger, not wanting to waste a drop of the delicious lemon and butter. The clock on the kitchen wall told her she had just five minutes before she had to leave.

UNSURPRISINGLY, THERE WAS NO ANSWER AT HIS PLACE, AND NO VAN in the driveway either. He should have been at work himself by now, so she let herself in with the spare key she kept on her keyring. They'd always kept a spare each, just in case it was ever needed. She called out as she opened the front door, though she already knew he wasn't in. Nothing in the kitchen had been touched and it looked the same as it always did, reasonably neat and tidy for a man in his forties who lived on his own. As she made her way upstairs to check in his bedroom, the house was as still and as quiet as a mortuary. It was obvious he wasn't in, and probably hadn't been since yesterday; she could just sense it. There were no smells, no last night's dinner, no burnt toast for breakfast, no deodorant lingering in the bathroom doorway. The bathroom towels hadn't been used this morning. No, she knew he definitely hadn't been home since yesterday. Now what should she do? She left the house and locked up after herself, deciding she'd keep trying him until lunchtime today. After that? Well, then she'd just have to call the police and report him missing.

Chapter Twenty

THURSDAY

"SO YOU'RE NOT SURE THAT HE'S ACTUALLY MISSING THEN?" DOUG Thompson, the sergeant at the front desk, looked sceptically at Rose.

"It's so unlike him to not be in contact. We speak most days and he was due to come round last night, but he never showed. I went round to his place this morning and it was obvious he'd not been home. And I'm getting worried."

"Could he be at a mate's house, a girlfriend's, maybe?"

"He doesn't have a girlfriend, well, not that I'm aware of, and I'm sure I'd know if he did have one. As for mates, none that he'd stay over at, and he'd still call me if he had. I've left loads of messages and nothing. Just goes straight to voicemail."

"Well, all I can do at this stage is fill in the relevant forms as a possible missing person, like we are doing now, but as he's of age, he has every right to go off on his own."

"Possible missing person? There's no possible about it – he's not here!" Rose fought down her frustration. "What about trying to find his vehicle? CCTV cameras must show it someplace. Wouldn't that be a place to start?"

"I'm afraid it's not as easy as that. We can't just put his registration plate details in and out pops his location. The general public wouldn't like us able to do such Big Brother things. Would be useful if we could, though," Officer Thompson explained gently. For the police, in reality, there was bugger all they could do unless there was evidence of a crime, and a grown man gone missing was not a huge priority, particularly when more serious crimes were taking place, like sexual attacks and burglaries.

Rose sighed heavily. What else could she do?

"Look, I'll pass this information on and see who has some time to look into it. You've given me as much as we need, but if you think of anything else, give us a call." He gave her a card with the branch details on it. "We've got your details, so we'll be in touch if we hear anything."

Rose had never felt so deflated. She knew Des wouldn't just wander off. No, something had happened to him, and she was afraid he was lying hurt somewhere, or worse. He'd obviously gotten himself into financial trouble with his gambling again; otherwise he wouldn't have taken her grocery money. Was it connected to that, she wondered? And should she say anything to the officer?

"Look, before you file that piece of paper, there may be something."

Officer Thompson looked at her sideways, a little annoyed she'd not said what it was a little earlier. "Oh? And what's that then?"

"He gambles. Quite a bit. And I noticed he'd taken my grocery money, about two hundred pounds' worth, and it's not the first time. Do you think his debt could have gotten him into trouble? Maybe his bookie's after him."

"Well, in my experience, if that's the case, that's even more reason for him to have run off, escape the heat, as it were. He's probably waiting it out until things have cooled off, but thanks for telling me. Who's his bookie?"

"It's Lionel, in the high street. Will you have a word?"

"I'll add it in to this report and an officer will follow it up, and it will also go onto the Police National Computer. Anything else you think could be relevant?" He peered over his half-moon glasses at her like a headmaster and she felt small.

"No. No, that's it. So I guess I'll just hope to hear from him, then?"

"He'll probably turn up in the next twenty-four hours. People who go missing generally come home when they either get hungry or realise they can't stay away forever. Come back and face the music. I hope he does." He smiled encouragingly at her and she managed a weak smile back. "We'll be in touch if we hear anything."

Rose turned and left the station, feeling despondent and useless. How the hell was she supposed to find him on her own? One thing was for sure: if he hadn't come home by tomorrow evening, she was going to put some pressure on the police to do something and investigate his disappearance a bit more seriously.

DOUG THOMPSON WATCHED ROSE LEAVE, SHOULDERS SAGGED, AND he knew how she must have been feeling. The truth was, there wasn't much they could do to help but he'd pass the missing person form on to someone to take a look at. The gambling angle could be something. How serious it might end up for him would depend on who he'd got mixed up with, but unfortunately the owner of the local bookies had a bit of a reputation for handling those who owed him money in some rather unorthodox ways. He hoped for Rose's sake he just walked in the door later that day. He walked back into the main squad room and passed the report to Amanda.

"What's this, Doug?"

"His sister just reported him missing and the gambling angle might be an issue. It's our 'friend' at the local bookie's. I figured if you've got time, you could take a look?"

"Thanks. Might be able to look at it later today." She dropped the report onto her desk and carried on with what she'd been doing.

Chapter Twenty-One

FRIDAY

AS ALWAYS, MADELINE LOOKED FORWARD TO LUNCH WITH REBECCA, and this week she was particularly looking forward to it, not because she was going to tell her about the dead man lying buried in her garden, but because she wanted to know how it was going with Todd. Of course, there wasn't anything going on in her own sex life that was noteworthy, but Rebecca's, particularly with this young man, was a bit out of the norm. It was more like a story out of *Woman's Weekly* than *Cosmopolitan*, considering their age group, but a juicy story nonetheless. She pulled up in the car park out the back of the Baskerville pub, named after the story by Sir Arthur Conan Doyle, who had lived nearby during the nineteenth century. She turned the engine off and sat and waited in her car rather than going straight in. Even though she'd slept well the previous night, she was feeling a bit rough around the edges after recent events. What she'd done was actually sinking in. She was hoping a girly chat with Rebecca about something fun would take her mind off the fact that there was a dead man buried in her garden and she was responsible for it.

Was that only two days ago? Yes, it really was only two days since he'd shown up at her door, they'd argued, and she'd seen red and whacked him with a spade. The only good thing to come out of the whole debacle was she could now operate a digger to some degree. Not that it was going to be a useful skill around Croydon on the whole. The great orange machine was still staring at her through the kitchen window each day, though now it wasn't mocking about the possibility of work being started: it was mocking in an 'I-know-what-you-did' kind of way. It was a good job diggers couldn't talk; she'd be in the shit for sure. Or cats. Dexter wasn't helping either, with his sideways glances as he passed her by, that 'don't come near me' look on his furry, knowing face. Or was she imagining it?

She wound the car window down to let some air in. The temperature at lunchtime wasn't as high as it had been, but it was still pretty hot, and the gentle breeze that blew in was welcome. She leaned her head on the headrest and closed her eyes for a moment. The breeze blowing over her face actually felt quite therapeutic and she breathed deeply, trying to help her frazzled nerves soften around the edges. There were consequences to what she'd done, and Madeline hoped that she never had to face them: being someone's bitch inside the 'big house' filled her with dread, but it was far too late to go back now. She thought she'd covered her tracks pretty well for an amateur, though caterpillar tracks were still evident across the garden. Who would think to look for a second hole with a landscaper buried in it next to one that he'd supposedly dug? Were they even looking for a murder victim, or was he just another missing person, another statistic that dropped off the earth every day of the week? The only reports she'd seen online were that he was missing, nothing more, and she hoped it stayed that way, though it was surely only a matter of time before the police turned up knocking. When they worked out he'd been at her place that morning, there would be questions, but as long as she told them what she knew as far as she could without actually telling them that she'd whacked him, there should be no suspicion. After all, she was just a regular middle-aged woman with no motive who had booked a landscaper who had since vanished.

The sound of another car pulling up beside her made her open her eyes. A smiling Rebecca looked back at her through the window, waving brightly. Madeline waved back, forcing a smile as she opened her car door and got out. Gravel crunched under her feet.

"Hello darling!" Rebecca said happily. "Why are you waiting out here? Aren't you hot in the car?"

"No, I've just got here and I was just taking a quiet moment to myself before you arrived. It's so peaceful here sometimes." She gathered her bag off the passenger seat and locked the car door, hooking her arm into Rebecca's as they walked over to the pub's back entrance.

"Well, if it's peace you want, shall I go?" Rebecca said, squeezing her arm to show it was in fun.

"No. Like hell. I want to hear the latest instalment of Todd and you, so no, absolutely not."

Madeline opened the door and they went inside. The pungent smell of beer lingered in the air. Since they were pretty much the first to arrive for Friday lunch, it must have been lingering from last night's bar.

"I'll get these," Rebecca said. "You go and sit down. You look done in."

Madeline did as she was told. She made her way to their usual spot, sat down and picked up the menu. She fancied something other than the usual cheese and ham toastie but nothing jumped out as she read. A moment later Rebecca handed her a gin and tonic and she took a sip, then another; the coolness was divine in her parched throat. She felt it immediately hit her empty stomach.

"What are you having then? Toastie?"

Same old, same old. Might as well, she thought. "Yes, but no fries for me unless you're going to eat more than two. I might have a slice of something afterwards if I'm still hungry."

I have every intention of having a slice of something afterwards.

"Good idea. You look like a piece of cake would fix things. I'll go and order, and then you can tell me what's on your mind." And off she went to place their order with the young barman who hadn't taken his eyes off Rebecca's backside since she'd walked in.

Madeline watched with interest as she flirted with him outrageously. She leaned close and gave him a meaningful wink as she finished placing their order, and the poor young man turned crimson as she turned and sauntered away, no doubt with a matching hot flush in his pants.

I wish my hot flushes happened just in my pants.

She sipped her gin and tonic and watched Rebecca sashay back to their table, all short cream leather skirt and long tanned legs. She would have matched the leather interior of her Mercedes perfectly, and Madeline thought back to Pink Fluffy Woman for a moment and the luxurious cream interior of her car. Had she ever found that finger hole in her packet of buns?

"So, tell me what's up Maddy. You're not your normal cheery self today."

"Oh, I'm okay. Just had a bit of a stressful week, that's all. I'm fine, really."

That's the understatement of the year, Madeline. You are now officially a murderer.

"But I'm dying to know more about you and you-know-who – Todd. So tell me more." She leaned in low as she said "Todd" and smiled encouragingly. Rebecca smiled, ready to tell all, and blushed ever such a little, just enough for Madeline to notice.

"He's lovely. And heavenly! I'm getting quite addicted to our twice-weekly sessions. I think I might get withdrawal symptoms when he goes back at the end of the summer." There was a teeny bit of longing in her eyes; she really meant it.

Madeline's danger radar started spinning. This wasn't supposed to happen: no falling in love, just fun.

"Oh dear, and you're off to Malaga soon, aren't you? How will you cope with just Edward for kicks?"

"I know," Rebecca said mournfully. "I wouldn't be so bad if he was staying at home like he did last year. I had a ball on my own back then. Perhaps I could fly Todd out with me…" Her voice trailed off.

Madeline had never seen her like this about one of her casual liaisons. Obviously this one was something more.

"Too bloody dangerous," she said. "Don't even go there, Rebecca. Where would you stash him – in the guest suite for a fortnight? I think Edward might just find him in there. And what's with this longing? It's not normally what you do. 'Just for fun,' you say. You sound like you've fallen."

"I know, and I *am* having fun, and so is he. But yes, I do feel a tad more for him than my other flings. He's so damn cute."

"And you should leave it at that – fun. You've too much to lose." She was being the voice of reason, sensible Madeline again.

"But life with Edward can be so drab on its own. He's always at work, and I'm damn sure he's screwing his PA on the side. That's why I have my little flings – I've got to get my kicks somewhere. *He* sure as hell is."

"Then why stay married to him if you think he's screwing around too? You're each as bad as the other."

Rebecca thought for a moment. "Simple. I love the lifestyle he gives me, pure and simple: his money, and my freedom to do what I want most days. It costs a mint to look like this," she said, waving her perfectly manicured hand around her head and shoulders.

Madeline's brow creased. She had never understood this side of Rebecca, and she didn't now. She herself didn't look like a trophy wife at business functions and was happy not to. If Gordon asked her to attend a company function, she squeezed herself into a body stocking girdle and put on the one black dress that she knew would make her look half decent. They didn't go out formally that much. Well, not much at all, actually.

"That's not a reason to stay married. What about love?"

"I still love him, just not like when we first married. We just exist together now, but we still have a laugh. We still *like* one another as people. The fireworks have just fizzled out now. No more *bang! bang!*"

The handsome young barman arrived just then with their food, and his ears turned bright red again at Rebecca's words. He placed the two plates of toasties on the table in front of them. Rebecca gave him another one of her flirty winks, making him red to the tips of his ears, and then they tucked in. The greasy melted cheese filled Madeline's empty stomach and, mixed with the gin, made her feel a little better about her own problem. She immediately felt herself brighten.

"You look a little tired, Maddy. Aren't you sleeping well again?"

I did fine on Wednesday night....

"Fits and starts. I go to bed and sleep really easily, but then I wake at about 3 am and then can't get back. It seems to happen for about a week out of every four, sort of part of my new cycle. Just means I'm knackered all week. And then the following week I sleep like a king, like I need to play catch-up. And when I wake up in the morning, I feel like I've been out partying hard all night, when all I've really done is read two pages of my book." As if on cue, she yawned loudly.

"That's no good. Have you tried a sleeping tablet on those nights?"

"You know my thoughts on chemical pills, Rebecca. So no, just a herbal sleep tea before bed. But I must confess, I have got some from the doctor. I've just not actually tried one yet."

"Well, I guess having them in your drawer is a start, Maddy. Just don't be afraid to try one. You might just get a good night's sleep for a change."

They both fell silent while they ate their toasties. Madeline was thankful for not getting a lecture on chemical help again.

"Can I run something past you?" Rebecca asked eventually.

"Of course. What is it?" Madeline enquired, taking another mouthful of toastie and chewing as she talked.

"Well, you know that landscaper guy that went missing?"

That caught her attention. What on earth was she going to say? She stopped chewing to answer. "Yes. What about him?"

"Well, I took Todd down to that reserve where they found his van, sort of on a date, and we parked up under the trees in Todd's car."

Oh shit. Where was this going?

"And?"

"And I remember seeing his van parked down there that day. Do you think I should go to the police and say? Only it could get embarrassing for me, if you understand. They'll want to know what I was doing there and who I was with, and I can't let that come out. What do you think I should do?" There was a tiny bit of concern in her voice.

"When was this – on the day he disappeared?"

Holy shit, I hope not. Had she seen me? I'd thought the coast was clear.

"Yes, it must have been about two o'clock, and it wasn't until we were ready to go that I even noticed it – not that I realised at the time whose it was or why it might be relevant to anything. I saw the report in the paper yesterday and put two and two together."

Madeline slowly let out the breath she didn't know she was holding. Rebecca couldn't have seen her at that time – she'd been back home working a digger. But shit, that was too close for comfort.

"I wouldn't worry about that. You didn't see anything, did you? Just his van, which you didn't realise at the time was significant. No one acting suspiciously?" She had to ask, just in case there was more Rebecca wasn't telling her.

"No, nothing. I was kind of busy at the time." She blushed. "Anyway, it's so quiet and peaceful down there in the daytime – not many people around. That's why I took him there."

Relief flooded Madeline's veins.

Yes, that's why I went there, too, though for a different reason.

"Then leave it be and think of yourself. Only embarrassment could come out of telling them what they already know about. It was just an empty van. There's nothing to be gained. And anyway, the bloke's probably just gone off and doesn't want to be found. He's a grown man, not a child, so he can do what he wants. Thousands of people do it every year, you know. You just never know what goes on behind the closed doors of people's lives."

'Behind closed doors,' indeed. Oh, the irony.

Chapter Twenty-Two

It was Friday and that also meant a trip to Sainsbury's for the weekly shop. Some folks called in every two or three days, for fresh veg and the like, but not Madeline. There was no way on earth she could cope with going in there more than was absolutely necessary. She dropped in to get fresh stuff from the local butcher and greengrocer in the town. Even though the prices were better in Sainsbury's, she liked the idea of supporting the little independent shops rather than the big chains all the time. It made her feel like she was doing her bit for the economy. It was the same with the recycling. She thought everyone should do what they could to make a little difference, however small it might seem at the time.

Driving down Purley Way on her way towards Sainsbury's and ultimately home, she ran through her head what to pick up for dinner. It was part of her Friday afternoon ritual: she bought something quick and easy and put it in the oven to heat up. Gordon was usually home at a reasonable hour on a Friday, saying the week in London was long enough as it was without eating into the start of the weekend, and they usually had a gin and tonic together while they waited for whatever to reheat, and discussed what they might do over the weekend. That was invariably nothing more than a trip to the garden centre for Madeline and off to see Crystal Palace play if they were at home for Gordon, but they kidded themselves with the idea of doing something different, exciting even; they never did.

It was bucketing down. The lovely hot spell of summer seemed a distant memory, although in reality it was only lunchtime when she'd been hot and sticky waiting for Rebecca. But as its reputation goes, the British summer consists of a few hot days, then back to sodding rain. And that's what the heavens were delivering right now – buckets of it. The only thing that really wanted rain was the garden, though it was a nice reprieve to feel a little cooler for a while.

She glanced into the back seat to make sure an umbrella was handy and headed into the car park. For a wet Friday late afternoon, it was absolutely mobbed and she slowly toured around near the front doors of the store to get a space as close as she could, not something she usually did. Normally she would rather walk a couple of extra metres and call it exercise. Today, though, she joined the mob in their quest for the space closest to the front door as the rain pelted down, not particularly wanting to get soaked to the skin. Cruising along, eyes searching through the frantic wash of the windscreen wipers, she spotted it. Up on her right, about ten cars up, the one and only empty space. She flicked her indicator on and prepared to swing in when out of nowhere a red BMW came suddenly around the corner from the opposite direction and swung straight in, right into the space, almost clipping her car. She saw red, literally.

"What the hell!" she exclaimed to the windscreen, and slammed the brakes on suddenly to avoid a collision. "That was my bloody space! Can't you see by my sodding indicator that I'm turning in, you shithead?" This was followed by a screaming "Argh!" and a hard thump on the steering wheel. The car behind sounded its horn because she had suddenly stopped and, with no sign of further movement, its driver was getting impatient. But Madeline was having a tantrum, and not of the temperature variety, but the good old-fashioned sodding angry variety. She pulled slowly forward to see who'd been so bloody rude as to take her space, but could see only the colour of the vehicle and the private registration plate. It looked familiar, and with a jolt, she remembered why: POOPSY, it read. It was Pink Fluffy Woman, back to torment her again.

"We'll see about this," she said through gritted teeth, though she wasn't sure how she was indeed going to 'see about this.' There was no chance of her getting out in the rain to have an argument or anything else at the moment. Growling, she released the brake, toured round a little further and resigned herself to a space three rows further back. Grabbing her bag and umbrella off the back seat, she set off at a slow jog in the rain towards the store. As she passed the red BMW she saw not Pink Fluffy Woman but rather quite a handsome-looking man emerging from the driver's side. Her partner, Madeline assumed, and from the bit that was visible as she went past, definitely worth a second look. He was just making his way to the store, pulling his hood up against the rain on one of those fancy lightweight jackets you can get from expensive gents' designer stores like Hugo Boss. Madeline was just guessing here, she didn't know those brands well enough to be sure, but she knew it wasn't from Walmart. And judging by the car, they probably did shop in nice places.

"It's good to see his fancy jacket getting just as wet anyway. Should have bought a fancy umbrella to go with it," she mused.

She entered the store, retrieved a trolley from just inside the door and waited, trying to look natural as he, too, entered the store. Obviously he'd no idea who she was or how she 'knew' either him or his Pink Fluffy Woman, so she didn't need to worry about being recognised. Taking the shopping list out of her pocket, she pretended to study it, waiting the few moments for him to enter and get a trolley himself. Once he was inside, she then began her weekly shop, one eye on minding her own business and one eye on minding his business. She was watching him for no other reason than he'd robbed her of a closer parking space in the torrential rain, and you just never knew how opportunities would present themselves. She travelled up and down the aisles, filling her trolley with various items: lasagne and garlic bread for dinner tonight, ingredients for a nice chicken tikka masala on Saturday, and a leg of lamb she'd do something with on Sunday, depending on the weather. She'd been meaning to make an apricot crumble for ages, so apricots went in too, along with various staples. If it was too hot on Sunday, crumble would become a fool instead.

One thing she'd noticed over the last three or four years was her cravings: they now tended to be for the more old-fashioned and heavier styles of foods from when she was a child. Rice pudding, apple pie, any kind of meat pie, sausage rolls and kids' party food in general, anything that was the home of large amounts of calories rather than simply a sugar fix or a bag of crisps. She'd even bought a large sausage roll last time she'd filled the tank with petrol, stuffed it into her mouth in record time and then hidden the bag in the rubbish bin before pulling off the forecourt. She didn't even want to take the incriminating evidence home, not that anyone would have seen it.

And look at me now: I've got a whole lot more important incriminating evidence in my garden than a naughty sausage roll wrapper, for heaven's sake.

And Madeline's food cravings were not so good for the waistline either, something else she was finding harder and harder to control. Elasticated waistbands were starting to look appealing.

A quick check of the shopping list, then a check of where her latest 'surveillance victim' was: he was just turning down the aisle where she was standing, the wine and spirits one. Picking up a bottle of Bombay Sapphire and putting it in her trolley, she moved along slowly, her back towards him, to choose some white wine for the weekend. Nearby she could hear a man's voice mid-telephone call. He sounded like he was wound up about something; his voice grew louder and louder as he got closer. But her back was to him, so she couldn't see anything, though she was tempted to turn and look. Perhaps she should have.

"Ah!" Madeline shouted, and stumbled forward. She turned to see who had hit her. It was Pink Fluffy Woman's partner. "Watch where you're going!" she fumed, and bent down to check the rear of her ankle. There was a trickle of bright red blood rolling slowly down it. It started to throb almost instantly.

"Oh, I'm so sorry. I was so busy on the phone I didn't see you. Are you hurt?" *The stupid sod ran his trolley into my heel, which is now obviously bleeding, and he asks me if I'm hurt? Of course I'm sodding hurt, and pissed off! Stupid man.*

"Yes, I am, thanks to you! Pay a little more attention, would you?

Look what you've done to my heel!" She was tempted to hit him around the head with the leg of lamb that was in her trolley, but it was a bit too public for that. And look what had happened last time she hit someone around the head. She harrumphed and, turning her back, shoved her trolley down the aisle away from him.

"Once again, I'm sorry," he called after her, but she ignored him. Huffing and limping, she managed to grab a bottle of white wine as she passed by. She had no idea what she'd just picked out; life would just have to be an adventure this weekend. Since Ruth had approved of her last 'grab,' she wasn't unduly worried, but still. Without looking back at Mr. Pink Fluffy, she hobbled to the checkouts in one almighty huff.

She wanted nothing more than a quick exit right now, and briefly considered the self-serve checkouts. No, with so much stuff it'd be far too much work on her part, not to mention annoying and stressful, with the stupid automated woman inevitably advising there was "an unexpected item in the bagging area," even though there never was, and then having to wait for someone to reset the robot, only to then try and get an oversized cauliflower or package of toilet roll into a plastic bag and be told to "please place your item into the bagging area." She'd been known to yell, "I'm bloody trying! Shut the hell up, will you?" which always got a supervisor over quicker than quick.

She imagined the Tannoy announcement: "Menopausal woman at self-serve checkout needs assistance urgently. Please respond before she obliterates the machine." No, Madeline was in no mood to deal with that stupid automated voice today, so, with a heavy sigh, she headed for a human checkout operator. She tried to guess how long it would take the cashier to ask if she had a Nectar Card, another game she played in an effort to make the whole experience a bit more pleasant. They beat her at getting the card out every single time.

My god, I need to get out of here.

Madeline joined the shortest queue, and thankfully the operator was an efficient one. She was soon by the door putting her umbrella up. She glanced down at her red heel which, though bloody, had started to dry, but was still throbbing to a beat of its own. She pushed her trolley out into the rain, driving it with one hand, the umbrella covering her against the elements in the other. She squeezed down the shortest route to her waiting vehicle. The rain sloshed into her shoes, soaking her feet but at least rinsing the blood off her ankle.

Then she saw The Car. Not her car, but the red BMW. Madeline the Mad raised her ugly head with an idea.

"Well, since I now have a red heel with a piece taken out of it, let's see how *you* like something red with a piece taken out of it." She did a quick reconnaissance of the car park. All clear. She pushed her trolley forward at an angle, scratching straight down the passenger side of the red BMW. She could hear the screeching sound as the trolley made contact and gouged the paintwork as it went. She was careful not to hit the innocent other vehicle on the other side.

"It can be hard pushing a full trolley with one hand," she told herself. "Accidents can happen." From the scraping sound as she'd gone down the passenger side, she knew there'd be damage, but she didn't have time to hang around and look – or be seen doing so.

Her mission accomplished, Madeline carried on walking so as not to draw attention to herself and pulled up at her own car three rows further on. She quickly loaded her bags of shopping into the boot then returned the trolley to the trolley park. She grabbed a couple of straggler trolleys sitting close by that other people had dumped in the rain and shoved them in after her own. That neatly buried the offending one, stowed away within the pack. Anyone looking at CCTV footage would just think she was a good sort for tidying the trolley bay up in the pouring rain. By the time she'd got back in the driver's side of her own car, she was soaked. Whoever Pink Fluffy Woman had lent her car to wouldn't even notice the damage when he got back in the driver's side, so they would probably never know when or where it had been done when they did eventually find it. Madeline, on the other hand, knew exactly where and when. She started her engine and slowly drove out of the car park and back towards home, the thought of a large G&T, lasagne and garlic bread on her mind, and the fact that once again she'd won. It made up for the throb in her heel.

Chapter Twenty-Three

Week 4
Monday

Every time she looked out of the kitchen window, Madeline was reminded of the day last week when she'd turned into 'Madeline the Mad' and done something a bit crazy. A lot crazy, actually. Though since that day, she had found herself in a number of situations where she quite possibly could have done it all again, given the amount of aggression and anger that bubbled to the surface with surprising ease, taunting and goading her to do something else dumb. But the damn Great Orange Thing stared back at her, silently reminding her of her sins buried beneath it in the corner of the garden.

Gordon had come home that night as usual. She'd poured him a glass of wine and they'd made small talk about the day while she'd cooked spaghetti Bolognese for dinner. He'd asked about the landscaper and she'd stuck to her story, telling the truth to a certain extent: he'd turned up, started digging the hole, and then vanished. Never heard from him or saw him after that morning. Strictly, she hadn't lied;

he had been in the hole after that, so no, he hadn't been 'seen' or 'heard from' again. It would pass a lie detector. Hopefully.

She'd promised Gordon she'd call him the following day and see when he was coming back, and had even left a message, though one thing she hadn't gleaned from *CSI* was whether the police could actually retrieve texts and voicemail messages from a phone that was turned off, and without the actual phone. She suspected they couldn't, as yet. If they could, there'd be people screaming privacy issues all over the place, thinking that the FBI or CIA or MI5/MI6 or some such would be listening in to their non-important and no doubt extremely dull everyday conversations. And they weren't. So she felt sure she was safe there. But just in case, in the name of honesty, she called him once again and left a message, knowing full well it would never get played. Des would never hear it. And Gordon hadn't said much more about it – how could he? There was nothing else to do: he knew she'd called him and not heard back, so that was that, in his eyes.

Madeline did, however, guess correctly that the police would want to question the last person to see him alive. And that was her.

Chapter Twenty-Four

Tuesday

"Afternoon," Madeline said politely to the two plainclothes police officers at the door. Their identification cards were displayed ready for her as she opened it. "Oh," she said in surprise as it registered who they were. "What can I do for you both?" She wiped her hands on her leafy printed apron; flour was dusted down the front from rolling pastry in the kitchen.

"I'm Detective Jack Rutherford, and this is Detective Amanda Lacey. Are you Mrs. Simpson?"

She nodded at him. This looked serious and she knew why – and she hoped she wasn't about to show it.

"We are investigating the disappearance of Des Walker, a local landscaper. We believe he may have been working here recently. May we come in and ask you a few questions?"

She nodded again, unsure of what else to do or say at this point. She opened the door wide and let them both inside.

Relax, Madeline. It's just routine and you've been expecting them.

"Can I offer you both some tea?" she asked, smiling at them both in turn as they walked down the short hallway towards the lounge.

"No, thank you. We won't keep you long."

"Please, go through to the lounge," she said holding her arm out to the left by way of direction for them. Entering, they both hovered, waiting to be seated. "Please, take a seat," she offered, and everyone sat. Madeline perched on the arm of the sofa. She took the opportunity to size them both up. Jack was stockily built and had the most hideous moustache she'd ever seen, but was smartly dressed in a navy suit that, while it had been well kept, was obviously quite old because it was double-breasted. She'd not long since cleared Gordon's old suits out of the wardrobe and taken them to the charity shop, so she knew it was all single-breasted nowadays; the charity shop volunteer had enlightened her with that titbit.

"Now, how can I help you both?" she asked, and then resumed her summing up of them. He looked a bit older, fifty-five maybe, with hair that was more salt than pepper, and had a bit of a brusque way about him, like he was really trying hard to be nice, but it was something he might be struggling with. Conversation and friends might be tough for him outside of work, she noted. The deep creases around his eyes told her he'd spent a good deal of time laughing, and that settled her inside somehow. Maybe he laughed in his own company.

"We are just doing some routine enquiries at this stage about Mr. Walker. You may have seen the story of his disappearance in the local paper?"

"Oh Lord. Yes. It's terrible." Madeline looked away, wondering what they would want to ask next.

"So he did come here, then?" Detective Lacey asked.

Tell the truth, Madeline, as best you can without putting your foot in it.

"Yes, he did. Stayed a couple of hours and then disappeared, and I've not seen him since. I did try and leave a message on his mobile, but nothing. He never called me back, or came back for that matter. Do you think he's okay?"

Dexter chose that moment to make his entrance and padded into the lounge, making a beeline for Detective Rutherford, rubbing himself around his legs like he was an old pal.

"Come away, Dexter." Too late: Dexter's hairs were already stuck to the bottoms of both of Jack's trouser legs. He tried in vain to brush them away, looking slightly irritated, but he needed something stronger than his fingers to dislodge them.

"Well, we're treating him as a missing person at the moment," Detective Lacey went on. "His sister reported it to us after he didn't show up at her place as arranged and she couldn't get hold of him, and no one has seen or heard from him since."

Detective Amanda Lacey looked a bit butch to Madeline, with tidy short-cropped hair and functional but neat clothes. Highly polished Doc Martens and a light smatter of make-up completed the look. A uniquely striking woman, though she supposed a detective had to dress for all eventualities, chasing gunmen and burglars and the like. No point doing it in heels and tight skirts like Ruth wore or detectives seemed to do on TV. Madeline bet she was single.

"Oh dear. I'm not sure how much I can help you both. I still have his digger machine sat in the back garden waiting for him. Do you think someone will come and pick it up for him? Maybe the chap who dropped it off?"

"Someone dropped it off, did they? Any idea who, Mrs. Simpson?" Rutherford was asking the questions again and Lacey was taking the notes.

"I don't know his name. Kept calling me 'Queen.' The cab signage said 'Sid's transport.' Quite a pleasant sort really, considering he was tattooed from head to foot. He looked quite intimidating when I first met him – I didn't really want to go to the door, but he was really quite pleasant. Drove a big truck with the digger on the back. Dropped it off, oh, a good couple of weeks back. That's about all I can tell you. Sorry." Madeline was trying hard to just stick to the facts, not elaborating and keeping from getting in a muddle or saying too much like she was covering something up. Telling the truth was always much easier than trying to remember than a concocted story, and she was managing to so far. As long as no one asked her if she'd hit Des Walker over the head with a spade and buried him in the garden and covered him over, she'd be okay. And she wasn't actually expecting anyone to ask that.

"So did he tell you where he was going when he left here that day?"

"I'm afraid he didn't. He didn't even tell me he was leaving. Just here one minute and gone the next."

Isn't that the truth.

Madeline could feel the questioning drawing to a close already. There really wasn't much else they could ask. They were just questioning her because they had to at least ask the person who potentially was the last to see him, and were trying to determine whether he'd left to run an errand or see another customer. The female detective, Lacey, smiled at her and offered her thanks, said they were done for now, and asked her to call if she heard anything from him, or indeed remembered anything else to do with him, anything at all, no matter how small it might seem. Maybe he'd said he was going somewhere in passing; it could be valuable in locating him.

She handed Madeline her card, which she looked at and slid into her apron pocket, saying she would call if she remembered anything. She smiled as she showed them both out of the front door, and watched them walk down the path and get into their car. When she finally closed the door and was safe in the privacy of the hallway, alone, she let out a long breath. While she'd been expecting them, she hadn't been expecting them quite so soon, and had actually found the whole experience quite unnerving. She'd never had the police in her home before, never mind two detectives asking questions about a missing man, a man she'd personally disposed of. Not an experience to repeat. Even an innocent person must feel a little bit guilty even when they've not done anything, she thought, a bit like when you see a police car behind you when you're driving – you feel the same 'oh shit' moment in your stomach even though you've done nothing wrong. But of course, in this case she really *was* guilty.

Madeline headed for the kitchen and the cupboard up top with the distinctive blue bottle of Bombay Sapphire. She didn't bother with a glass, just swigged a couple of mouthfuls straight from the bottle to steady herself; never mind the time. She slumped down into the comfy chair in the corner of the kitchen feeling like someone had deflated her, sucked all the air out, and left her slung in the corner like a blow-up doll with no bung in the hole. But had she passed the test?

Chapter Twenty-Five

"What do you reckon there, then?" Amanda asked Jack when they'd got back in the car. "She's the last person to see him alive; no one's seen him since that morning. But he has a reputation for always being late for his jobs and we know he gambles." They both fastened their seatbelts but she made no attempt to start the engine.

"That's true, but we don't know whether he's gone off voluntarily or if something else has happened to him, and there's certainly no evidence that she had anything to do with his disappearance. His van was found down by the reserve, keys still in the ignition – remember? He could have just gone for a walk and decided to have a bit of a mid-life crisis and bugger off someplace else, stage his own disappearance – particularly with the amount of debt he had. And stealing off your own sister is a bit low."

He had a point about Des maybe not being dead, just having taken a hike – and a long one at that.

"And she certainly doesn't look strong enough to murder a big man like Des and do away with his body," Jack went on. "Not without help, anyway. And her husband was at the office all day. I don't think she's involved. Why would she be? What's her motive?"

"I don't know. I just have this gut feeling it's more than that, you know what I mean? More than just gone off on his own: more like gone off permanently. Like down the river."

"He'd more than likely have surfaced by now," said Jack. "And anyway, she'd never have been able to get him into the river. No way. And amateurs who dump bodies in the river don't usually do too good a job of weighing them down. Depending on all sorts of anomalies like the current and the weather, it's actually quite hard to keep the secret: they surface. No, he'd have surfaced by now if he was in there. And like I said, what's the motive?"

He sounded so confident. Amanda knew he'd seen some stuff in his twenty-odd years in the force, and she respected that. But he could still be wrong.

Amanda started the engine, pulled out from the curb, turned left out of Oakwood Rise and headed back down Stanstead Road towards town. As she drove, she said, "Then let's look at the facts that we know of again." She used her fingers on the steering wheel to note the points. "Number one. He turned up as planned to use the digger that was dropped off beforehand, dug a hole, then got in his van sometime later that morning and drove to the reserve.

"Number two. Nobody saw him arrive at the Simpson place, or leave, because they were all at work and it's a nice quiet cul-de-sac.

"Number three. No one saw him drive to the reserve, but CCTV caught him just before he turned into the car park at eleven fifty-three am. The pictures are grainy, but his sister recognised his cap so we have to assume it was him. At this point, there is nothing to suggest it wasn't.

"Number four. No one saw him leave the van and go for a walk. His mobile isn't turned on, and his bank accounts haven't been touched since two days before when he drew out his last fifty pounds from the ATM in the high street. We've checked the cameras there, and it's definitely him withdrawing the money. Amounts of around two hundred pounds were not unusual for him, but his account was nearly empty. We know he liked the horses and bet on them regularly.

"And number five, his bookie said he was a decent bloke, though up to his eyes in debt – so much so he had been instructed not to take his bets any more until his tab had been paid off. He owed several thousand. He also said he's not the type to just run off, but then also wondered why anyone would want him dead, if that's what had happened. There's no point in killing a man who owes you, or you'll never get it back. I think he thought we'd be looking at him, or his boss, MacAlister, again. So, apart from maybe mistaken identity as a reason to dispose of him, it's a real mystery what's happened to him." Her thumb and four fingers stood elevated on the steering wheel like a low wave to an oncoming vehicle.

Jack was still silent, thinking it through.

The rain started to fall and immediately went into torrential downfall mode as it often does after a hot sticky day. Amanda turned the windscreen wipers on, brightening the star-shaped red lights that were coming from the tail-lights of the cars in front. She cursed at the deluge.

"I thought this was meant to be summer," she moaned, then waited for Jack to say something. Jack was his usual contemplative self at times like this, and there was no point in pushing. Her experience of working with him over the last ten years had taught her that silence was usually a good thing; he was a man of few words. He never felt the need to fill a gap with conversation, and when he did speak, it was in bullet points, which to the uninitiated often seemed weird and rude. Many people who came into contact with him instantly disliked him, which was fine by him. He didn't feel the desire or need for friends, and his unsociable ways were simply accepted as his normal way by those who knew him well. The others? He didn't really care about them.

He also preferred surnames to first names, feeling they were the stronger part of a person's character. Rutherford and Lacey sounded too much like a department store chain or an American cop duo for Amanda's liking, though, and some of the other officers thought it was a great source of amusement, particularly when they went to the pub after a shift and had had one or two. She preferred to stick to first names.

"Let's see what the media appeal surfaces once we've weeded out the nutters, weirdos and clairvoyants," he said now, "and take it from there. Something's bound to show up if there's anything to show. It usually does." Then he went back to being silent.

The rain kicked up another notch, pelting the windscreen hard, and it was the only sound audible as they drove back to the station. Amanda was glad of the relative silence, and used the opportunity to think things over again in her own mind. Deep down, she knew an adult had every right to 'lose' themselves and not tell anyone where they were going or why. Thousands did it every year. And Des might just be one of them. Unless there was evidence to the contrary, eventually they would have to give up looking. A combination of not enough man-hours and other more pressing crimes would eventually reroute their attention. It wasn't right, but those were the facts. She felt sorry for his sister, who was obviously extremely worried.

"Fancy a burger before we get back?"

"Why not?" Jack said, and she pulled off the A23 and into McDonald's.

Chapter Twenty-Six

Wednesday

Every once in a while, Madeline liked to go into London and do a bit of shopping, usually window shopping. She'd treat herself to lunch in the Harrods food hall, eating at one of the upmarket food bars downstairs, then go to the big M&S at Marble Arch to see all the gorgeous clothes and furnishings they wouldn't be getting in Croydon. Afterwards, she would often grab something for dinner from the food department downstairs to reheat later. Her day was all very civilised and a treat, an experience she enjoyed probably once a month. It was also a time when she could indulge in her favourite bookstore, Waterstones on Piccadilly, which claimed to be the largest bookstore in Europe – with 200,000 books on several miles of bookshelves, it probably was. It was a cross between modern and traditional and had a lovely feel about it. It had lots of nooks and crannies to get lost in, and if you were still in town later in the evening, it stayed open until 10 pm. Sometimes she went up to the fifth floor and sat at the bar there for a while, in a world of her own, just watching and thinking. Then, when it was time to leave, she'd buy the two or three best books she'd chosen then head back out to the riot of the streets of London.

They say that New York never sleeps. Well, it's much the same in London: there are people shuttling around like rats on their way to someplace important at all hours of the day or night. Someone also said that 'books are theatre for the mind,' which to Madeline's way of thinking was a good explanation of why you should never watch a movie made from a book you'd read. The characters would never be the same. You just know in your mind what the characters you are reading look like, and when you see them on the big screen they're never what you imagined in your head. A thriller series that Madeline particularly enjoyed involved a detective called Will. He was tall and blonde with fair skin in the story, but for some reason known only to Madeline, he was a Denzel Washington lookalike in her head. How anyone could get a dark-skinned, dark-haired man from a tall slim blonde one was a mystery in itself, but that was the theatre in her head.

Perhaps it should be closed down, she thought with a wry smile.

She'd just entered the train station car park and was looking for a spot. Because she lived on the commuter belt, there was no way in hell there would be any free spaces close to the station end. People started filling them from about 5.30 am. By 8 am, everyone going in to the city for work that day was already parked up and well on their way. The next time slot was for people like Madeline, the day trippers heading in at about 9.30 am on the cheaper train fare and staying until around 4 pm, with commuters idling back until around 7 pm, hoping someone at home had cooked them dinner and looking forward to a chilled glass of wine to ease their stress.

She drove down to the far end of the car park and found a space, backing in for an easy getaway on her return. She stuffed the current book she was reading for book club into her bag to read on the way before tomorrow night's meeting and locked the car. It was another beautiful fine day, and the heavy rain the previous night had helped clear the sultry, sticky air, though the temperature would soon be cranking up again. The sky was a lovely shade of blue, reminding her of the cornflowers in the field behind the house. The sun warmed her face as she started the walk back up the car park towards the station, taking care where she put her feet on the rutted, potholed surface. There were puddles everywhere and she did her best to avoid them. The silly deep puddle scene from *The Vicar of Dibley* popped into her head and made her smile. She and Gordon had both howled at the scene, in which Dawn French stepped in a puddle and went in all the way up to her neck. Later, wiping their eyes, they had reminisced that TV at Christmas was not as good as it used to be when Noel Edmonds had a Christmas show.

The glare from the sun was already intense. She grabbed her sunglasses out of her bag and carried on walking with a lighter feeling in her shoulders as she looked forward to her treat in town. In the distance, heading towards her, she could see a car coming down the same route she'd taken just a minute or two ago, except he was driving a lot faster. As he neared, she could see it was a man at the wheel, aviators gleaming as they caught the sun, his mouth moving animatedly as he spoke into a mobile phone that was jammed to one ear. He didn't look all that old – she put him in his thirties from what she could see – and as he neared she noticed he was reasonably good-looking. It was obvious from his speed he was in a bit of a rush.

Watching him as he got closer, she didn't notice the large puddle that was in his direct driving line, and neither did he: he sped through it, and a wave of filthy, dirty water splashed up her bare legs and sandals in great big dirty grey globs. She stood stock still as he drove on, oblivious, looking down at the mess he'd created. Dirty water was dripping down her legs in rivulets, grey dirt resting in small clusters on her soaked toes.

"What a bloody mess." Madeline glanced back his way and could see only his tail-lights as he pulled into a parking space just a couple down from where she had parked.

"Asshole," she cursed. She yanked the wet wipes out of her bag and began wiping her legs and feet down in a huff. "How bloody inconsiderate." She briefly considered chasing him down and doing something to his car, or him, in revenge, but the more pressing need to catch her train steered her in the right direction.

She set off again and threw the grimy wipes in the rubbish bin by the station entrance. She put her credit card into the ticket machine and bought a day pass, then made her way over to the platform and waited, trying to ignore the feeling of gravel between her toes. To her astonishment, moments later the rude driver sprinted through the doorway and headed for the same platform, all 'skinny suit' and attitude and obviously an Oyster Card carrier. Madeline glared his way, but it was wasted on him.

She felt the familiar rumble as the train tracks vibrated with the arrival of an incoming train, its two bright lights shining as it slowed into the station. The front-most carriage glided to a standstill right in front of her. As the automatic doors pinged open, she entered and turned right, making her way to the centre of the carriage in search of a seat. There wasn't much space on board even at this hour. She spied one just ahead, but unfortunately Skinny Suit had seen it too and was approaching it from the other direction, aviators still in place, his mobile phone once again glued to his ear. He got there first and sat down with a sigh of satisfaction. Madeline stopped in her tracks, tutting with irritation: she wasn't sure if he'd even seen her or not but that wasn't really the point: he'd now pissed her off twice in the space of ten minutes, and that made him a prime target for revenge of some sort. Resignedly, Madeline stood, along with the other new embarkees, and held on to one of the vertical poles to steady herself. The doors bleeped as they began to slide closed again, and the train edged out of the station. In the confines of the airless steel tube, she knew, it was only going to get hotter as they neared Victoria Station, picking up more passengers on an already warm morning. The journey wasn't going to be pleasant.

Like I need it to get any hotter?

Madeline could feel the familiar heat starting around her shoulders and chest, and working its way up her neck. She knew she'd soon be quite red in the face – it doesn't take the brains of the Archbishop to see when a woman of a certain age is suffering.

A trickle of sweat rolled down her cleavage, and she felt the start of another drop on her temple, which she wiped away with the back of her hand before anyone noticed. Her overheated body screamed for cool ventilation, but there was none to be had. It was at times like this she was glad of the invention of the smartphone, because everyone had their heads down and nobody was paying any attention to her temperature tantrum. She could do nothing but wait for it to pass and dab her wet face and neck with a tissue to keep herself dry. She desperately wished menopause would bloody hurry up and buzz off somewhere else, because there didn't seem anything to gain from it. At least when you went through puberty and had periods, you knew you were on the right track to womanhood and a baby maybe, but all there was to look forward to with menopause was things drying up or, in her current state, getting wetter. And slowly wizening up like a prune. She was so very definitely over it before it had really even begun.

"Perhaps I need some chemical intervention after all," she mumbled under her hot breath, feeling like a dog that had been running hard and was wet from a dip in the sea, though she hoped she didn't smell like it. Another stop at another station only made the journey worse. Another large group of day trippers squeezed their way on, so everyone had to shuffle up even tighter into the middle of the carriage and stand even closer together. She remembered the book in her bag she was supposed to be finishing, ready for book club tomorrow night, but there was no conceivable way she could stand and read it now unless she held it an inch from her face. Since she didn't want to be in bother with James, the host, again, she decided to give it a go and retrieve it from her bag, not wanting to give him the satisfaction of having something to say again about people's dedication to the group, or lack of it, mainly her own. He thought she was a bit of a flunk at the best of times.

"How can we discuss a book as a group if no one's read it?" he'd say, like an old hospital ward matron, though they all knew he did have a point.

She rummaged with her one free hand into the bottom of her bag to locate the book and reading glasses at the same time, which proved too difficult in the cramped space. Her bag swung a little to the left, catching Skinny Suit on the shoulder. He looked up and glared from behind his aviators, the thin line of his mouth doing what his eyes couldn't portray. Mouthing a 'Sorry' at him, she again tried to get her book and glasses. Her bag touched his shoulder again, but this time she ignored him: one thin lip glare from him was enough to shame her. If he'd just let her have the seat that she had been aiming for in the first place, she wouldn't be standing trying to get her book and glasses so haphazardly and bumping into him. When she'd finally got her glasses out and firmly parked on her damp, slippy nose, she opened her book to begin reading and let a slow sigh escape from her lips as she began.

Relax, relax, relax.

After about ten minutes she was engrossed in the latest Lucy Bridges romance, reading about the lovers' breakdown and everything that had sent the main character spiralling to the dilemma he now found himself in. "Who knew what being married to a sex addict could do to you emotionally?" she wondered, and felt sorry for the guy, but it was only fiction, so she read on. When she raised her head out of her book again, they weren't far from Victoria Station and they would all soon be off the sweatbox they were confined in.

It was about then that Madeline felt a gurgle in her gut, just strong enough for her to feel and hopefully for no one to hear. Clenching her butt cheeks to be on the safe side, not wanting to embarrass herself and break wind in such a confined space, she willed the gas to pass quietly. A moment later she felt another gurgle begin to form, the bubble popping internally but not escaping fully, but putting her on notice she needed to get out and let it out in a safe space. The train couldn't get to Victoria fast enough for Madeline, and with one more gurgle she felt the air leave, thankfully quietly. But her backside was positioned just level with Skinny Suit's face.

She had to stand there pretending nothing was amiss as the train finally arrived at the station and came to a standstill. The doors opened with a whoosh, driving the air back up into her face. She knew from the whiff as it rose to her nose it wasn't pleasant. Last night's Rogan Josh had caught up with her, and Skinny Suit, though she couldn't risk a glance at him for confirmation, must have known she was responsible for the fog he was now sitting in. She fought back a smile: tough. He'd soaked her legs with dirty water back in the car park and stolen her seat so this had turned out to be the perfect a way to get back at him, even though it hadn't been planned that way. She'd won, again. She gave herself a silent high-five as she cleared the carriage and the cooler air blowing along the platform engulfed her hot sticky body. First stop, the toilet.

Chapter Twenty-Seven

At nearly 2 pm Madeline had had enough for one day. The heat in the city centre was too intense, her feet were throbbing even in flat sandals, and she was sick of the smell of other people's body odour mixed with random cooking smells from food chains and street vendors. She'd stayed a bit cooler in the air-conditioning of M&S, and treated herself to a couple of high-cut summer dresses that covered a multitude of sins except her bat wings; she felt sure she had something to put over them buried away in the back of a cupboard at home somewhere. She took the elevator down to the basement food floor to pick something up for dinner, wondering as she went what Gordon might like. She grabbed a basket from the stack at the bottom of the escalator and headed over to the cold fridges in search of ideas.

"What haven't we had in a while, then?" she muttered, slowly scanning the vast fridge spaces filled with just about every conceivable type of food the world had to offer. Gordon wasn't too good with Asian-style food. He enjoyed his Italian and his Indian, but as for Thai or Vietnamese he wasn't struck, so she moved along to find something more to his taste. Nothing seemed to inspire, so she switched fridge rows and tried another aisle. Then she saw it – the upside-down prawn and Marie Rose sauce salad with grated cheese, grated carrot and small pasta shells in it.

"When did we last have that? Perfect." She grabbed a large one, then added a pack of fresh strawberries and a small pot of cream to her basket. "Good find, Madeline."

She took the few items to the checkout and once again chose a human to do the processing. This particular human made polite conversation about not having had the salad herself for ages, though she'd tried Jamie Oliver's version in one of his cookbooks and it hadn't turned out bad. Madeline wondered why, when she worked in the damn food hall, this woman would be bothered boiling pasta shells and grating carrot instead of just buying a ready-made one herself with her staff discount? It made no sense, but she kept her mouth shut; there was no need to be mean.

As she rode back up to street level on the elevator with her purchases, the intense heat of a stifling hot London afternoon hit her as she opened the door and entered the throng of people once again. The walk back down to Oxford Street tube station with throbbing feet was marginally better than one moment longer on the tube so she decided to jump on the Victoria line there. She was on her way back home, where a gin and tonic waited with her name on it, to be quaffed while sitting on the patio before Gordon got back. She hoped the journey would be less eventful than the journey in earlier that morning.

When she got down onto the platform, she was glad to see there was a vacant seat just along a bit. She sat down with a thud and retrieved her phone from her bag, pulling up the Daisy Chain page. There didn't seem to be much of interest as she surfed through – and then a short post caught her eye: there'd been another attack by the groper, and it wasn't on a prostitute.

Holy hell.

She rested her head back on the cool tiled wall for a moment, eyes shut. This guy really needed catching – and soon. If he was now bothering ordinary women, that meant he was getting less choosey. All women needed to be aware.

It wasn't long before she heard the familiar rumble of the approaching train, so she gathered her things and stood up. The lights of the train reflected back from the shiny white public-toilet-like tiles that decorated the inside of most tube stations in the city. She stepped forward, ready to grab any available seat the minute the doors opened. The familiar "mind the gap" sounded mechanically, warning all passengers to be aware of the sometimes quite large gap between the platform and the actual train.

"Ruth should talk to London Transport about getting a nicer tone for their automated recording. Perhaps someone a little less severe and a bit more British," she mused. The doors pinged open and to her delight there were several seats free, so she chose one at the end near the door that connected the two carriages together. This would allow the draft from the open window to blow across her as the train sped through the tunnel. No matter that it wasn't the cleanest; it was certainly the coolest on offer.

Grateful for the seat and a relatively un-crowded tube train so far, she relaxed her shoulders while waiting for the doors to close and the train to pull out. Suddenly she sat upright again: through the window she saw a familiar figure, briskly walking from one end of the platform where the public toilets were and heading for the street exit upstairs. He was quite clearly on a mission, and not one back to the South London area like she was. He may have just needed the loo, but something made her look at him more closely: what was Grey Man doing down there, and why was he in such a hurry?

Chapter Twenty-Eight

THURSDAY

It was a balmy summer evening, and book club time. And she'd not fully read the damn book. Again. And that would mean a *tsk tsk* from James. And that would mean she was going to be pissed at him because he'd be pissed at her, though actually, if he stopped behaving like an old matron and being so pissy and condescending, he would see that it was all just petty. book club was supposed to be enjoyable, but sometimes, just sometimes, it was a giant pain in the arse, though she always enjoyed the company of the others. They were quite an eclectic little group of seven, including Madeline, and they'd been meeting up regularly for about four years, though a few members had come and gone. Madeline had been the last to join, two years ago.

James, the book club's self-proclaimed leader, was actually called James Peterson and thought of himself as the real-life James Patterson. He quite closely resembled him in a lot of ways: his age, his build and his glasses, and the fact that he liked to write, though their James had never published a thing. He just sounded like he had. An engineer by trade, he ran a successful local business, though he should have long since retired. They met at his rather swanky place every fortnight to discuss the current two books on the go and share a bottle of wine, usually with some cheese and crackers. He was still a little stuck in the '70s with the cheese and wine thing, and Madeline always half-expected a cheese and pineapple hedgehog with cocktail cherries for decoration to appear one day. The other members ranged from a student called Josh to a couple of teachers named Pam and Derek, a really quite wonderful artist called Annabel, and Lorna, a housewife. Then there was Madeline. So it was quite a varied group, and they all got along nicely, except when a book hadn't been read. Like tonight.

"If you haven't read it, then how can you have an opinion on it? How can we discuss it properly? You can't just agree with what the others think. They are not your views." James was on his soapbox, and poor Pam was getting quizzed this time. Madeline chipped in to help her out, knowing from experience what it was like to be the chosen one.

"I agree with Pam, James. The story was actually quite steamy and it was a little uncomfortable to read it in places, so I skipped over some of the pages too. If I'd been reading that sitting on the train I would have blushed hot for sure. It's bad enough having hot flushes sneaking up on you without adding any more in. I think we got the gist of what was going on without having to actually read every word."

Pam, clearly embarrassed at being singled out, looked at Madeline now like she was her saviour.

"I've pretty much finished it," said Josh, the youngest of the group at 22, and a real bookworm, "and I thought it was a good read. And because it's written from both his and her points of view, it was good to get both their takes on the hot bits." He smiled coyly before adding, "Made good learning for me actually." Now it was his turn to blush a little.

Lorna caught his eye and grinned at him. "Then that's a great way to use the book, Josh – a good storyline and an education." They both tittered like silly teens. Lorna herself was probably only about 29 years old, with a lovely young family she cared for at home while her affluent hubby went into the city every day. She got as bored as all hell on her own without adult conversation to stimulate her mind and looked forward to book club for just that.

"Let's get back on track, please," intoned James in his deep baritone voice. "We've still got the other book to look at yet." He looked at his wristwatch, which was something quite old and classic-looking, with a worn, leather crocodile-like strap. Madeline wondered if it was perhaps his father's or grandfather's even. Not many men even wore a watch these days; everything was all on smartphones. The small clock on the mantelpiece said 8 pm.

Thinking she'd take some of the seriousness out of the room, she offered to refill wine glasses. "Top-up, anyone?" She stood hovering, the remains of the bottle of white poised to pour into the glasses of whoever wanted it. Pam nodded, so she stepped over to her and refilled her glass, smiling in appreciation. She looked around the group and, as no one else wanted any, poured the rest into her own glass.

"Can we please get on?" James sounded anguished.

Oh, shut the hell up, James. Stop being such a bloody matron.

Madeline could have withered under his glare, but chose to ignore him and sat back down. He could be such an old man sometimes.

"Let's move on to the Hawkins book, shall we?" Derek hadn't said a word all evening, but he clearly thought it was about time to contribute and cleverly changed the subject to the other book they'd agreed to review, the massive bestseller *Girl on a Train* by Paula Hawkins. There was a collective exhale as they moved on from hot, steamy sex scenes to thriller. Madeline had quite liked the steamy scenes herself, just not when out in a public place – and Gordon seemed to have enjoyed them too.

"Oh, what a great book," Lorna chirped. "So much going on, so intriguing! It reminded me of some of Hitchcock's work. I could almost hear the birds screeching in the background as I read it. Couldn't put it down."

James glared at her for her outburst of unsolicited opinions, and she abruptly quieted down and shrank back into her chair.

"Let's look at the story as a whole first," he said officiously, "then we will talk about the various aspects and key characters and their involvement, and how the author could have done a better job."

How the author could do a better job? Does he know how many millions of copies it's sold? Eleven million, last count. Really, pea-brain.

Madeline again inwardly sighed. She'd read quite a bit of the book but hadn't quite finished reading it all, so she was now going to find out the ending before she really wanted to. Thankfully, Derek had read it all and was happy to oblige James with his opinion about the various aspects he wanted to talk about.

Deciding to keep quiet and let him revel in having done his homework, she picked up her glass of wine and took a long mouthful, probably a bit too long, and reached for another cracker, placing a cube of cheese on top. It really was a bit too tall for her mouth and she struggled to get it all in without the cracker breaking. Crumbs fell down her front, balancing on her T-shirted chest like little golden pieces of Crunchie Bar. James was looking at her, but again she wasn't going to wither. So she smiled brightly in his direction, which was unfortunate because she hadn't quite finished chewing all of the cheese and cracker. He wrinkled his nose and looked away again.

She swallowed her food, then sat back and listened to Derek and his account of Rachael the Drunk, and left the rest of them to discuss the book in its entirety, nodding here and there to show them she was present and taking notice. The group used to be so much fun. Why was it so damn serious now? Book clubs weren't supposed to be this serious, were they? By 9 pm and the end of the get-together, not only had Madeline drunk too much wine, spilled crackers down herself and been told off for not reading the raunchy bits of the first book, she also knew who the *Girl on the Train* murderer was.

Not much bloody point in finishing that one, then, is there?

Everyone was on the move now, gathering their belongings and taking their glasses into the kitchen. Madeline joined them, still thinking gloomily that the session had been just too stressful, rather than pleasant like it was supposed to be. And it was all down to one person. If this little group was going to carry on and become fun again, something had to change. *Someone* had to change, actually, and it wasn't going to be her.

Everyone filtered outside to vehicles parked out front on the leafy upmarket street. The night was still close, humid and sticky even at that hour, which meant another warm one in bed tonight and probably little sleep. Lorna shouted good night.

"Are you not driving, Lorna?" Madeline said, pausing with her keys in her hand.

"No, I walked over for the exercise. It's not far back. And it's a nice night."

"You can't seriously be thinking of walking home on your own, can you? You do know there's a nutter knocking about?" Madeline wasn't trying to scare her, but didn't know if she'd heard about the groper.

"I'll be fine, thanks. It's really not that far."

"Nonsense. Get in." She indicated the passenger side. "I'll drop you round. Better to be safe than sorry."

Lorna stood tentatively for a moment, then smiled and started to walk towards Madeline and her car.

"Okay. Thanks. It must be awful having someone jump out at you and do something like that. I couldn't imagine it." She opened the passenger door and climbed in. So she *had* heard about the groper.

"No, bloody scary, I expect. And I read on The Daisy Chain he's not just targeting prostitutes anymore, so there's no point in giving him the opportunity. Easy enough for me to take you home." She pulled out from in front of James's house and took a left on her way to Lorna's place. It was only a short drive, and as they turned right into her lane, a familiar figure caught Madeline's attention. Out for a stroll in the fading evening light was a grey-looking man who, at that moment, turned left down a leafy alleyway and out towards the park. There was no mistaking who it was. Grey Man – again.

Chapter Twenty-Nine

AMANDA LOCKED HER CAR AND STROLLED INTO THE STATION BACK entrance. Jack was waiting for her. He looked a little agitated; he was fiddling with his moustache as he did when something was up, and he was deep in thought. Some people had other tells; his was fiddling with his moustache. She wondered what her own was, and hoped it wasn't as obvious.

"Spill. What's up?" she asked him as she took the steps two at a time. Functional clothing and footwear allowed her to do so.

"Well, if you'd slow down a little so I can keep up, I might be able to tell you." He was a bit out of breath, which was a bit of a worry considering the small amount of catching up she was making him do. He needed to get more exercise and stop eating such crappy food. She stopped for a moment to let him catch up.

"Another attack on a woman," he said between gasps. "Toilets yesterday, and get this, again she wasn't a working girl. By her description, it sounded like the same guy who's been grabbing the prostitutes, but this woman is different. She went to use the loo, and he followed her in and groped her when she was washing her hands. Grabbed her tits and stuck a hand between her legs. She screamed and he legged it; that was it. CCTV doesn't show much apart from a blurred bloke with a balding head leaving the toilets at that time. Lucky for him he gets lost in the crowd, and a couple of the cameras are out."

"I wonder why he's changed tack and again not targeted a prostitute – that is, if it is the same guy. Could be a copycat? Maybe someone trying to cop a feel for himself and fly on the coattails of another offender?" Amanda didn't know the answer and was just throwing the notion out there.

"Well, it could be, but either way – a copycat or a perpetrator who's changing tack – it's bad news. We kind of thought this was just a naughty John who wanted to hook up without handing over the cash and got his kicks from a free touch-up, but now this – a second one who isn't a prostitute?" He waved his arms in the air to suggest a much bigger problem. "This will have the greater public worried now, never a good thing."

"Have you interviewed her yet, the latest victim?"

"No, I was waiting for you, but she's here at the station so we can both talk to her. Or you may be better on your own, being female and all. She might prefer that."

"Okay. What's her name?"

"Gina Harris, aged fifty. Lives in Croydon. She's in room two when you're ready. Here's the notes I have so far from the duty sergeant who took her in." He handed them over to her.

"I'll let you know how I get on, then. Anything else to report?"

"Not yet, but the day, as they say, is still young."

"Night."

"What?"

"Night. They say the night is still young." She left him standing there thinking, twiddling his moustache again between his fingers.

"Hello, I'm Detective Amanda Lacey. You must be Gina Harris."

"Yes. Hello."

Amanda could see the woman still looked quite shocked, and she'd obviously been nervously picking at her previously well-manicured fingernails because they were now all chipped, and the skin around them all red.

"I'm here to take your statement, your account of what happened, and any details you can possibly remember about the incident. Anything at all, even the smallest detail, might help, so tell me as much as you can. All right?" Amanda placed a hand on the woman's arm briefly, as a gesture of comfort, and proceeded to take down her statement, stopping her every so often to clarify the facts as she went.

After fifteen minutes there wasn't really anything left to tell. It had all happened so fast and unexpectedly. Gina had added in that she now felt disgusting after a stranger had touched her in that way, and she was still clearly quite upset. With the interview part complete, Amanda asked her if she'd like counselling support organised. She said she'd think about it, then Amanda offered to drop her back home.

"That won't be necessary, thanks. My husband is on his way over to collect me. I wasn't really sure I was going to report it, you see – I felt so embarrassed. So when I decided, I just jumped in a taxi. But I don't want others to have the same experience. That's the main reason I'm reporting it. For others, you understand." She trailed off as she got to the end of her sentence.

"Let me give you a number to call in case you decide to go ahead with counselling," said Amanda gently. "Sometimes talking really helps you get over something like this." She took one of the cards she carried out of her jacket pocket, wrote her own direct number on the other side, and handed it to Mrs. Harris.

"Here's my direct number. If you want to chat to me or if you remember anything at all, just either text me or call me, okay?"

"Thanks. I will. Do you think you'll catch him? Is there enough to go on?" She looked frailer now than when they'd first started talking.

"It sounds like the same person who attacked the others, I'm afraid. But hopefully your evidence brings him a little closer to being caught and we can find him before he offends again." Amanda smiled at Mrs. Harris in a comforting way, hoping that she would at least *feel* she was helping put him away.

"Let me show you back out to the waiting room. Maybe your husband is here for you now."

They both stood and Amanda followed her out, guiding her with gentle directions back out to the front. As soon as she was in the waiting area, her husband came forward and wrapped his arms around her in comfort and support. Amanda stood until they had left through the main entrance doors, watching as he helped her to his waiting car – a fire-engine-red BMW convertible.

Chapter Thirty

SUNDAY

RUTH WENT ROUND TO MADELINE AND GORDON'S FOR SUNDAY lunch, which, in the heat of summer, was certainly not a roast lamb dinner as planned. As it was too hot for indoor cooking, Gordon manned the barbecue outside and cooked sausages and burgers. They ate M&S potato salad with them and had trifle for desert. It was actually quite enjoyable, one of Ruth's better visits – after a glass or two of wine inside her, she was actually quite easy to talk to. Madeline and Ruth were getting on better and better as time went by. And that was nice.

"What's with that orange digger, Madeline?" The Great Orange Machine still stood out like a sore thumb.

"Well, the guy came, then went, and we haven't seen him since. I rang but he's not returned my call, so who knows what the story is." Madeline smiled like a regular nice part-time housewife rather than a murdering maniac.

"He's the guy who went missing, isn't he? Saw it in the paper," Ruth said drowsily from her sun lounger in the shade.

"Yes, the police called round here asking questions. Seems I was the last person to see him that day – not that I could be much help."

"What sorts of things did they ask you?"

"Just routine stuff, you know, like what time did he arrive, what time did he leave, did he say anything about where he was going. Like I say, I couldn't tell them much. I don't know much."

Not quite the truth, though, eh, Madeline?

"You didn't tell me the police had been round asking questions. Where was I?" Gordon sounded a bit indignant, like he'd have enjoyed being present. He too was lying on a sun lounger with his eyes closed, soaking up the afternoon sun, the remains of his third glass of wine just evident in the bottom of the glass he was holding. He'd be asleep in less than an hour.

"You were on your way home from work, I expect. It was late one afternoon earlier this week, and like I said, nothing much to tell them."

"Well, that digger needs bloody shifting soon. And that hole he's dug won't float many fish either."

Madeline smiled at that one.

You mean the hole that I dug, surely?

She could hardly correct him.

"Not sure what else I can do in the meantime. It took him long enough to get here and start the job in the first place, so I expect he's gone off to start someone else's job and stop them from grumbling too. I bet he's got half-happy customers all over the place."

"That'll be right," said Gordon drowsily.

Madeline glanced across at Ruth, who had closed her eyes too and was lying back on her lounger, wine glass lightly dangling from her hand. Madeline got up and took the wine glasses from both of them before they dropped on to the patio and smashed, and placed them on the mosaic garden table. Sitting back down, she glanced over to the Great Orange Machine just as Dexter made his presence known, rubbing his hot ginger fur around her ankles and flopping heavily on to the concrete.

She smiled at Dexter. She smiled at the whole silly situation – here they were talking about a man who wasn't much more than a few feet away, and a few feet deep, under a pile of earth that she, Madeline

Simpson, bulldozer driver extraordinaire, had dug. Was there no end to her newfound talents? Ruth was spark out. Like father, like daughter. Two peas in a pod they were.

Sitting back, Madeline sipped her own glass of wine and let her mind wander in the peace and quiet of a Sunday afternoon. The gentle hum of a distant lawn mower was the only audible sound. Dexter softly purred his appreciation of the tranquillity.

Chapter Thirty-One

WEEK 5

"The results from the van examination came back, and there is one thing you might find interesting." Amanda was talking to the back of Jack's head; he was busy filling his mouth with a ham salad sub. He turned her way to find out what it was, mayonnaise clinging to his moustache, and spoke with his mouth full, spraying little pieces of lettuce onto his lap.

"Damn. Sorry about that, Lacey. And what's that, then?"

Amanda grimaced a little, watching him wipe the bits of food away.

"Cat hair. In fact, ginger cat hair. Found on the driver's seat, and some on the floor."

"And? What's relevant with that?"

"Madeline Simpson has a ginger cat. So I'm asking myself, what would her cat's hair be doing in the van of a missing man?" Amanda looked a bit too smug for Jack.

"Well, I'd say that as he was working there, albeit for a short period, the cat hair probably transferred onto him somehow, then into his van. Remember the state of my trousers after our visit? Damn hair all over them from the little sod. But I'm detecting you think it's more than that?" Jack took another bite of his sandwich and mayonnaise gathered again, this time hanging tight at the corners of his mouth.

"I just think it's a bit of a coincidence is all. She's the last person to see him alive and her cat's hair turns up in his van. And yes, it could have simply been transferred. The rest of the van was reasonably clean, for a landscaper's vehicle, anyway. There were some other hairs we presume are from his sister that are still to be confirmed, but they look like hers. There's also a mixture of soils, as you'd expect from various jobs, plus litter and general debris. No real evidence, except the cat hairs." She watched as he finished chewing his current mouthful, thankfully, before he spoke again.

"Not much else to say, then, really."

"So that's it, then?"

"Well, we still don't know whether he's dead. We've nothing to go on and there are no suspicious circumstances – just the cat hair, and that has a simple explanation for it. There are no signs of a struggle, no blood, no footprints, no injury that we know of, no robbery, no text messages, nothing. No evidence at all that points to anyone or anything. He's vanished. I say it's done with, unless something says otherwise. We've got too much else going on to worry about a bloke who's done a runner on his life and disappeared."

Amanda knew he was probably right, but she couldn't help the feeling that something wasn't as it seemed. Something bothered her. Though what, exactly? People went missing all the time and had the right to stay missing if they chose, leaving their families and friends behind to worry, and this guy did have a gambling problem. Maybe he'd done the same? There was one thing for sure, however: she wasn't going to file the paperwork away in her head as completed. In her eyes, it was definitely still pending, and she'd work on it in her own time if need be. But she'd get to the bottom of it.

Chapter Thirty-Two

Friday

Rebecca wiped another tear off her beautifully made-up face. There wasn't a drop of dirty black mascara staining her cheeks, nor were her eyes red and puffy like when anyone else got upset. No, even in the throes of misery she was gorgeous. All Madeline could do was say the relevant 'ah's' and agree with her while rubbing Rebecca's arm gently as she let it all out. It was a good job the pub was quiet this lunchtime.

"I feel such a fool," she said, half-wailing. "I really liked Todd, and I thought he liked me, but now I've gone and ruined everything."

"It had to come to an end sooner or later. I guess you just brought that day forward a little, unintentionally." Madeline's comments probably weren't being much help under the circumstances, but she made them with the best intentions nonetheless.

"Why did I get so greedy?"

There was no answer to that that wouldn't upset her even further, so Madeline kept her mouth shut and thought about what had happened to her friend. Edward had never really been enough – no news there – but to have Edward, Todd *and* the young barman on top, pardon the pun... How many men did her gorgeous friend really need? A little part of Madeline was a teeny bit jealous of Rebecca's antics, and all she could do was console her until the tears passed.

"Look on the bright side. At least Edward didn't find out, and it was only Todd who found you in the pool house. It could have been a whole lot worse. You've still got your lifestyle intact, just not your heart."

Rebecca sniffed in response.

Rebecca had been waiting at the pub when Madeline arrived, sitting slumped in their usual corner, the remains of her first wine sitting in the bottom of a glass, pale pink lipstick stuck to the rim in a patterned crescent. It was obvious she was upset, and Madeline had immediately sat down and put her arm around her while she'd poured out the whole story of getting found out – by Todd, not Edward. It seemed the barman, known as Gabriel, or Gabe for short, had been doing a little more than flirting at their last lunch date and had slipped Rebecca his phone number. She hadn't been able to resist, naturally, and had arranged to meet up with him at his place for a drink one afternoon. Well, it was obvious what was going to go on there, wasn't it? On the second date, back at her place, she'd forgotten completely that Todd was scheduled to work in her garden, and she'd been busy with Gabe in the pool house, which hadn't gone down too well with Todd. A bit of a fight had ensued. Gabe had got a bloody nose for his trouble and Rebecca had got dumped for hers.

And I thought my life was full of events. Maybe I should change tack and find myself a young man for the garden rather than the dead man I have lying around. Could be more fun and less troublesome overall.

"Shall I get us some food and a drink?" Madeline said. "Have you eaten today?"

"No, I haven't. Couldn't face it this morning. I've not been into work either. I told Edward I wasn't feeling well and not going in."

"Well, you can't drink wine on an empty stomach. You'll kill yourself driving around like that. I'll go and order, and bring you a soft drink. Wine will make you feel even more maudlin." She left to order their usual toasties. There was no sign of Gabe at the bar today and she wondered why not. Perhaps he'd got a black eye as well as a bloody nose and had decided to stay away out of embarrassment. A pretty brunette was filling in for him. Perhaps she worked in the evenings. Madeline had never seen her before.

"I'll bring your toasties over when they're ready," the brunette said, and smiled nicely. Maybe she had seen Rebecca crying.

When Madeline arrived back at their table, Rebecca's tears had stopped but she still looked like her world had caved in. Was she really that besotted with Todd, knowing he was going back to university at the end of the summer anyway? She took her lemon, lime and bitters and sipped at it, curling her nose up at the taste of no alcohol.

"The sugar will do you more good today than the fuzz from wine, so drink it and tell me about the rest of your week," Madeline said briskly. "What else has happened?"

"No, you tell me about your week. Let's change the subject from my life – yours will be infinitely better than mine this week. I'm guessing you haven't stuck your fingers where they've not been wanted?" She raised a weak smile at her own joke.

Madeline just grinned at her, wishing she could tell her what she'd really been up to. She thought there was no harm in telling of farting in Skinny Suit's face on the train, if only to get her friend to smile and think of something other than Todd, so she took a sip of her drink and launched into the tale. When she got to the part about the rumble in her gut and letting a smelly one out into his aviator-framed face, Rebecca nearly fell off her chair laughing. She'd told the story well, emphasising the main bits like it was a scene in the best movie ever, and Rebecca reared her pretty head back with laughter, curbed only by the arrival of two plates of toasties.

"I'll have a glass of what she's having," said the pretty barmaid as she handed out knives and forks to both. "That lemon, lime and bitters must be more potent than I thought." And with a beaming smile, she left them to it.

Rebecca was finally looking more like her old and seriously gorgeous self. "I'm famished. Let's eat," she declared. And they did. At least Madeline's antics could be used in a positive way occasionally.

Chapter Thirty-Three

"I'm going to go back and dig a bit more at Madeline Simpson's. Something doesn't add up."

Jack rolled his eyes at Amanda and fiddled with his moustache, deep in thought. "There's nothing *to* dig up, is there? I thought we'd been over all this – deduced he's buggered off, escaped his gambling debts and his sister and has gone off because he can't face the music? Is that not the end of it?" His voiced was slightly raised and that was never a good thing. To be fair, the case did look pretty much closed. Just not to Amanda Lacey.

"I'll go in my own time, see what I can find. Maybe woman to woman, and with a bit of time passing, she'll get sloppy and say something, drop me a tad to work with."

"You're sniffing up the wrong tree with that one. No motive and no evidence. Up to you, though, but count me out. I've bigger fish to fry and so, incidentally, have you. You waste time on this, you'll screw it up with Sir up there," he said, pointing to their superior's office door with a podgy finger.

She knew he was right. "I'll stay below the radar, and go and see her later on my way home. He'll never know. And it's barking up the wrong tree, not sniffing." Amanda knew she was skating on thin ice, but sometimes, she knew, you had to keep picking at the bone, and this bone needed picking.

IT WAS AFTER 5 PM WHEN SHE REACHED MADELINE'S HOUSE. The warm afternoon sun was still quite strong when she knocked on the door. A moment later Madeline Simpson stood before her.

"Oh, hello again," Madeline greeted her brightly. "Would you like to come in?"

Amanda was watching her face and movements carefully, looking for any telltale signs that she was perhaps a little flustered, guilty, anything that she could see and use, but there was nothing. Either Madeline Simpson was actually innocent, or she was a damn good actress.

"Thank you, yes. I just have a couple of questions I'm hoping you can clear up for me." She followed Madeline back down the hallway to the lounge. Madeline certainly wasn't going to take her to the kitchen. The Great Orange Thing and the scene of the crime were quite visible from the window, a constant reminder of the wild events of that day.

"Would you like a cold drink perhaps?" she offered with a smile.

"No, thanks. If I could just ask you about your cat?"

"That's a strange question. What about him?"

"Well, an odd thing was found in the missing landscaper's van." Amanda watched Madeline like a hawk as she spoke, but still nothing registered. "We found cat hair, ginger cat hair actually, and I'm wondering how he had ginger cat hair in the driver's seat of his van. He doesn't own a cat, you see, but you do."

"Well, I expect he picked it up off Dexter, then. The stuff is everywhere, on every chair inside and outside, plus Dexter will have climbed all over that digger while it sat here waiting for him to turn up."

Amanda knew she was indeed right, but needed to ask, to see her reaction.

Madeline changed tack for her. "So he's still not shown up yet, then? Do you think he's just buggered off someplace?"

"We're pursuing different lines of enquiry at the moment. Why do you ask?

"Oh, only because it's a local story. There's been a bit about it in the papers. I did hear on the grapevine he liked the horses. I bet he's in hock up to his eyeballs and run off to hide out from the people who are looking for him. That MacAlister, the one that owns the bookie's, he's not got the friendliest reputation around here, but I'm sure you already know that. It would explain why he wanted to put his price up on me at the last minute, though, but I wasn't having it. A deal is a deal in my book."

Madeline was aware she was rambling a little, but she also needed to make sure she did her best to deflect suspicion away from herself and point the finger somewhere else. She wanted their line of enquiry to be a long way away from her front door. "That's what I reckon, anyway: too much debt and gone off. His gambling seems to be common knowledge now." She watched Amanda right back. There wasn't a clue on the officer's face that she'd given herself away, and Madeline felt pretty sure she'd done a decent job with her little charade.

Amanda knew she had nothing else to ask or go on, so she made her way slowly back to the front door with a simple, "That's all, then. Thank you for your time."

Madeline had one final question for her, though. "Is it okay to get that digger shifted now? Only it's killing the grass and I need to get the pond dug if I'm ever going to enjoy one this summer."

"I don't see why not. We don't need it now. You'll ring the guy who delivered it?"

"Yes, I'm sure Des will be wanting it back when he decides to turn up and do some work." It sounded callous even to her own ears, but Madeline knew she had to be convincing. She was grateful for her amateur dramatics classes all those years ago as a young woman. You just never knew when experience might come in handy. Detective Lacey's slip of "We don't need it now" was not lost on her: maybe the investigation was finally over.

With the front door open, she followed Amanda out with her eyes as she walked to the pavement and unlocked her car door. Standing on the step in the late sunshine, Madeline watched as Amanda started the engine and drove away. She let her shoulders back down to their normal height, took one deep breath in and out and headed to the blue bottle in the kitchen cupboard, hoping there was plenty of ice left in the dispenser.

Chapter Thirty-Four

WEEK 6
Thursday

JAMES LIVED ALONE. HE'D BEEN ALONE SINCE HIS WIFE HAD PASSED almost twenty years ago, when he was in his forties. The lack of companionship had troubled him at first but as he'd grown older he'd come to the conclusion that he was actually quite at ease with his own company. His time was his own. No more did he need to think about being someplace at a given time, worry about someone waiting for him with his dinner on the table, or consider someone else when choosing a restaurant or going on holiday. Plus, there was the fact he was already married to his job. His late wife had worked there with him until she had fallen pregnant with their son, who had sadly then been stillborn, and she'd suffered greatly with the loss. And so had he, but not to the same extent: she'd never really got over it and had never returned to work. She had chosen instead to paint her sadness away, spending her days in a back room of the house painting whatever she saw in her head. Those paintings never saw the light of day, were never hung on the many walls of the big house and never made it as Christmas presents for others, but they had served their purpose in keeping her mind as sane as it could be under the circumstances. He'd wanted to help her at home rather than send her off somewhere, packaged up with a suitcase, and soon to be forgotten, and he had hoped she'd appreciated his choice. It was a relief, therefore, when she'd finally passed some years later of cancer that had never been diagnosed or treated. He'd locked that room where she used to exist, and not even the housekeeper, Mrs. Stewart, had ever been into it. So he'd rattled around the big silent house on his own for as long as he could remember, book club and a couple of other visitors aside, but that was it.

He had learned over the years that he could still get the odd bit of pleasure that a man needed without going through the long-windedness of finding another partner, and once a month took to the services of one lady in particular, though there had been a few more visits from someone else much earlier on. Now his monthly visit was enough for his needs and they had a regular set-up – the first Friday of the month. Her name was Vivian. And the first Friday of the month was tomorrow night.

Chapter Thirty-Five

SHE'D FAILED. FAILED ONCE AGAIN TO GET A FULL BOOK READ SINCE the last book club, but this time Madeline wasn't so bothered – because she had a plan for cantankerous old James. He'd made her and poor Pam a little uncomfortable last time with the raunchy romance scenes, so it was payback time, although Pam didn't know it yet. Madeline was sure she wouldn't mind: this was just going to be a bit of fun, no harm done. It would be something to snigger about later in the evening, knowing what would be happening upstairs in James's bedroom after they'd all gone home.

The thought made her smile even now as she pulled out the drawer of Gordon's bedside cabinet. Inside was a little box containing powerful blue diamonds, and not the kind that jewellers use. They were more the kind that those looking for some longer-lasting fun in the bedroom department would use, and yes, she and Gordon used them occasionally too, just for the fun of it.

Undoing the small box, she took one out and slipped it into her trouser pocket for the first part of the plan. Since James had made them both feel uncomfortable, this little initiative was going to do something along the same lines to him.

Making her way back downstairs, she took two teaspoons out of the kitchen drawer, placed the blue diamond between the two and pressed down, turning the little blue tablet into potent dust. She then tipped the contents onto a small piece of plastic kitchen film, pulled in the four corners and twisted the edges together to seal the powder in, then slipped the little parcel into her pocket. The plan was pretty much all set as long as no one joined her in the kitchen when it came time to get wine and nibbles. Hiding the blue powder in cheese and crackers wasn't going to work, so she had bought a tub of M&S smoked mackerel pâté and some rye crackers and planned on using those to deliver the message. She just hoped James liked smoked mackerel pâté or else it wasn't going to work at all.

The clock on the kitchen wall said it was time to make a move, so she headed outside to her car with the pâté and crackers balancing just inside the top of her handbag. A few minutes later she was pulling up outside James's huge house again. It had been two whole weeks since she had last been there. Where the hell does time go when you're having fun?

"Evening," Annabel shouted, and waved brightly as she locked her car just along the road a bit from Madeline. "Another balmy one, but better than that rain we had yesterday."

"Hello, Annabel. Nice to see you. And yes, the rain was welcome in the garden, but who doesn't prefer the sunshine?" She retrieved her bag off the passenger seat and the two women headed to the front gate and up the neat front path. Turning to Annabel, Madeline said, "I thought I would bring some crackers and pâté for a change to cheese. Do you think James would mind? Cheese is a bit too much for me in the evening. Gives me a headache."

"Oh, I think that's a great idea." Annabel was always so over-the-top cheery, and you couldn't help but love her for it – she brightened everybody's day. "I don't think he'll mind at all. In fact, maybe we could suggest we take it in turns to bring something to nibble on to the meetings. James has always supplied the food and wine since we first started. Shall I suggest it?"

"Yes, do that." Madeline smiled back just as brightly at her. "On another note, though, have you read the book this week?" She hoped she had so that at least one person could talk about it in the absence of her own knowledge. All she'd managed last week was the *Woman's Weekly* and the opening couple of chapters of what they were supposed to be reading, which hadn't grabbed her at all.

"Yes, I've read it. Not quite what I thought it was going to be, but it was okay. I can see why she wrote it under another name." She was talking about JK Rowling and her pseudonym, Robert Galbraith. The book they were reading was the first one in 'his' new series, *The Cuckoo's Calling*. It was a murder mystery, but there were too many words Madeline just didn't know the meaning of and she had given up early on. She knew she should try harder.

"No good?" she asked curiously. They were nearly up to the front door.

"Ah, it's okay. A little slow, I thought. I guess sales weren't that strong under the male name, so that's why we all know it's her now. May as well use your name if it can make you some money," she said, giggling.

The front door was open on such a warm night and they both sauntered in. James greeted them with a deep "Hello" and both women replied with big smiles.

"I've taken the liberty of bringing some pâté and crackers, James," Madeline said in her most charming voice. "I hope you don't mind. It seems the burden of nibbles is always on you, the host. Is that okay?" She gave him her best killer smile and headed out the back to his massive kitchen that rarely saw action.

He followed her in, looking a little surprised at her smile. Maybe it was a tad overdone, but it must have worked because when he'd recovered, he stammered a little as he replied to her retreating back, "Yes, yes, of course. How kind."

I can be kind when I feel like it – or when I have a motive.

She dropped her bag on the floor by the breakfast bar stools, slipped the pâté into the fridge for later and left the crackers on the side.

"I'll come back out and get them for supper a bit later," she said as casually as she could.

Other "hellos" could be heard down the hallway as the others arrived and greeted one another, so Madeline took the tray of glasses and the bottle of wine and went to join in the greetings and be sociable in the lounge.

It wasn't long before they were all discussing the recent weather and other snippets of news, particularly the fact that the groper was still at large, and now targeting other women, not just prostitutes. Josh was most interested in it; he read far too many murder mystery novels and fancied himself a bit of a Miss Marple. Perhaps he was getting writing ideas of his own. "It said on The Daisy Chain earlier in the week that there has now been more than that one attack on a member of the public," Josh said. "He's not just targeting hookers anymore. It's a bit of a worry really."

The others did a collective head nod and Derek chimed in with, "And I believe the last one was only down the road on the edge of the park, though it wasn't serious, thank god. She got away quickly and because she was out for a jog and he'd surprised her, she managed to hightail it before he could do much. Ran straight home and called the police."

"He can't be that smart if he was trying to get hold of someone jogging, now, can he, really?" James clearly wasn't impressed at Derek's common sense and went on, "I mean, we all read enough books. Well, some of us do." He aimed a meaningful glance at Madeline. "At any rate, most of us know how these things work, and to aim at a running target seems pretty thick to me."

He was right, but the comment about *some* folk reading books landed in Madeline's stomach with a thud. Slipping her hand into her pocket, she was comforted by the little plastic-wrapped package that was still there.

Just you bloody wait.

James decided it was time to officially start the club meeting and called for attention. The chatter stopped immediately.

"Excellent. So, *The Cuckoo's Calling*. Who would like to start with their overview first? How about you, Madeline?"

Awkward sod – like she wouldn't realise he'd done that on purpose.

"Oh, you move on to the next person and come back to me. I'll just go and put some pâté on a few crackers. Back in a moment." She smiled at everyone as she stood and made her way back through to the kitchen. As Lorna was giving her thoughts on the book in her absence, she knew she hadn't got too much time: she had to act quickly. She opened the fridge to retrieve the pâté, took a knife from the drawer to spread it with and prepared a dozen or so crackers for everyone. Madeline then tipped the contents of the little package of blue powder into the remaining pâté, slipped the plastic film back into her pocket, and stirred the pâté and powder mix, creating a potent paste. She stuck her finger in to test it wasn't obviously crunchy, but the particles were nice and small. No one would ever know there had been anything added.

Yessssssssssss.

Loading up more crackers, she set them down on one specific corner of the plate all together. James would surely eat the ones that were closest to him; she'd just make sure it was them. She wondered for a moment what would happen if Pam or Annabel had one by mistake, but this was no time for pondering. She put the remainder of the pâté back into her bag on the floor, picked up the plate of crackers and went back to the front room where she rearranged the coffee table slightly, making sure the 'naughty' crackers were facing the person they were meant for.

Derek made an "ooh" sound and leaned in to get a couple, with the others following suit. James, not wanting to be left out, joined in and took two, which he ate immediately. So far so good: he'd taken the ones specifically for him. Madeline joined in with a couple of crackers for herself, washed them down with a mouthful of wine, then set about thinking what she was going to say about a book she'd only read about fifty pages of. When it came round to her turn, she managed herself quite well considering, taking points from the others' reviews and basically putting them into her own words, though she suspected James knew what she was doing.

When she was done she sat back, chancing a glance at the cracker plate. She noticed James had gradually taken all that had been meant for him, plus a couple of others. The plate was empty, so it was obviously a popular choice for book club snacks. And the deed was now fully in motion: there was no turning back.

It wasn't long before the first signs appeared, but they were probably only visible to someone in the know – Madeline.

"Derek, would you mind taking over for a minute or two? I think I need a glass of water. Back in a moment." Everyone watched as James got to his feet and left the room.

"He doesn't look too flash," said Josh. "He's looking a little hot. Do you think he's okay?"

"Well, it is still quite warm. He's probably overheating a bit, that's all. A glass of water will do him good," said Annabel, cheery as always.

A moment later, James returned and sat back in his chair. He did indeed look rather warm.

Josh wouldn't let it go. "Are you okay, James? Do you feel unwell? Only you look a little on the warm side."

"Actually, I really don't feel my best at all. Must be this damn heat. I do rather feel quite hot. Perhaps if nobody minds, we could draw to a close early tonight? I might just sit out the back and get some air." It was obvious he was suffering with something, and Madeline had a fairly good idea of what, exactly.

"Of course we don't mind," she exclaimed happily. "If you're feeling under the weather, an early night is the best idea. We'll wash up the glasses and leave you be."

"No," James said, a little too fiercely. "I mean, no. Don't worry about the glasses. Mrs. Stewart will do them in the morning when she comes in. But I'll take you up on the early night idea. Sorry, everyone."

Everyone stood and grabbed their things, making their way back to the front door. Madeline nipped back to the kitchen to retrieve her handbag and the pâté tub containing the evidence. She and Annabel were the last to leave, and they both wished James a peaceful night as she pulled the front door closed behind them. Little did Madeline know that for James, it really would be a very peaceful night.

JAMES SAT IN HIS ARMCHAIR FEELING A LITTLE HOT UNDER THE collar. It wasn't just the cloying heat of the summer evening, even though it must have been about eighty degrees outside. Something felt wrong. And then there was the feeling he was getting in his pants. He was more than a bit puzzled by the slight erection he'd sprouted. They certainly hadn't been talking about a book with sexual elements – not this time, anyway. It had made him feel intensely uncomfortable in a room full of people, and he'd needed to get rid of them, to make them leave so he could do something about it and relieve the tension.

An idea came to mind. Loosening his collar, he went upstairs, cell phone in hand, where he took his clothes off and got in under the sheets. He prepared a text.

Vivian, are you free now, can you come over? JP.

He hit send and waited. A moment later, her reply landed back on his phone with a ping.

Give me forty-five. Can't wait until tomorrow eh? Naughty boy. VV.

He'd never known her surname, but she always signed her texts off with VV. He replied with, *I want you now, tonight,* clicked send and reached for a magazine from under his bed to wait for her to knock.

Forty-five minutes later, Vivian stood knocking, but James didn't answer the door, or her repeated texts that evening. Though it was strange, there was nothing else she could do. Eventually she gave up and left.

Chapter Thirty-Six

Madeline climbed into her car outside James's house. The temperature inside was still hot enough to roast a chicken, and sweat immediately started to glisten on her top lip.

"Poor old James. He seemed a bit warm himself just before he asked us to leave," she mused. She knew exactly what was going on in his body right about then. His thinning blood would be starting to heat him up inside, focusing in on one spot. "I'm pretty sure he only had the one glass of wine. Shouldn't do him any harm." She chuckled out loud at what she'd set him up for – a night of extreme, urgent discomfort unless he relieved himself. But even then it might take more than once or even twice. Yes, James was going to be a busy man for the next while. She grinned.

She drove off towards home feeling pleased. "That should teach him a lesson for making me and Pam feel uncomfortable with that last book."

The journey home was short, and she parked the car in the garage as normal, grabbing her bag containing the night's evidence off the seat beside her.

"I'm home," she called out, sing-song-like, to Gordon as she opened the front door.

"You're earlier than normal. Everything go okay?" he said, coming into the hall to greet her with a peck on the cheek.

"Yes. James was feeling a bit under the weather, so we finished early. Fancy a cuppa?" She made her way to the kitchen, Gordon following like a puppy. Flicking the kettle on, she opened the fridge to put the remainder of the pâté in and was just about to put the crackers in the cupboard when a hand stopped hers.

"Oh – crackers! And was that smoked mackerel pâté I just saw?"

Oh dear.

"Yes, the last bit. There's not much left, really." But it was too late. He reached for the crackers and retrieved the pâté, taking both to the kitchen bar, grabbing a knife from the cutlery drawer on his way past. Madeline watched, helpless, as he scooped a dollop out and smeared it over half a dozen or so crackers that were now lined up ready to be eaten. Knowing they were contaminated, she could only watch. And wait.

Chapter Thirty-Seven

"YES, JACK? WHAT'S UP?" AMANDA WAS STILL CHEWING HER TOAST. A marmalade 'stick' clung to her chin like a glistening golden matchstick. She wiped the sliver of peel with her fingers and popped it into her mouth with the rest of the toast as she spoke.

"I'm guessing you're still eating breakfast by the sound of the chomping coming from your mouth. Some of us have been at work a while already, you know."

"Stop your whining, Jack, and tell me what's up." She added a mouthful of coffee into her food processor of a mouth. Jack grimaced as he guessed rightly what she was doing.

"We have a stiff. A Mr. James Peterson," he said, a chortle in his voice. She could hear him consulting his notebook. "Seems he got a little excited last night and now he's stone cold dead. I'm at his place now. When you've a minute, why don't you come over?"

Amanda took his insults in stride, bouncing her head from side to side and making a face as he spoke.

"Address?" She wrote it down and took another swig of coffee. "I'm on my way. See you in ten." A minute later she was jogging down her front path and getting into her car for the short journey to James Peterson's place. Jack had sounded calm enough about it, so she figured it was something quite straightforward. Had it been a mass murder or a gruesome stabbing he'd have said something in warning, if only to protect her stomach.

She pulled up outside the big house where flashing blue and reds were parked and went inside. Jack was in the kitchen with an elderly woman. He turned and excused himself from her when he saw Amanda enter.

"That's Mrs. Stewart, the housekeeper," he said. "She came in this morning and found the body, so she's obviously in shock. Body's upstairs in the bedroom." He started to move down the hall and up the stairs, and Amanda followed his lead.

At the top of the stairs she could see the bedroom to the left, where a couple of uniforms and a photographer worked the scene inside. When she entered the room, she saw what Jack had meant about 'having a stiff,' which in hindsight seemed crass and disrespectful, even for Jack.

The dead man was on top of his bed, completely naked, surrounded by magazines and used tissues. As she got closer, the subject matter of the magazines became clearer – ancient copies of *Playboy* and *Hustler*.

"I see what you meant earlier now. My goodness, these date back more than ten years. Without any puns, Jack, is there any suggestion of foul play?" Amanda was deadly serious.

"Not at this point, but it's still a working scene and the doc hasn't been in yet. En route. But it looks pretty straightforward from what I can make out. From the size of him it's my guess the guy had a dicky ticker, and got a bit overactive. I bet you a tenner he died of a heart attack." He really could be crass sometimes.

Amanda carried on scanning the room, taking it all in. The bachelor-style décor told her Peterson was probably single. Adding to that theory was the housekeeper downstairs, plus what he had so obviously been doing before he died. Alone. How sad, she thought.

"Still don't know the exact time of death until the doctor gets here, but he's stone cold so it's been a while. Mrs. Stewart came in at 8 am as usual but didn't come up here until around nine am, after she'd done whatever housekeepers do downstairs. Apparently, Mr. Peterson is usually up and out for his walk early, so she just assumed he was outside somewhere. Then she came up here and saw the curtains still closed. When she saw him, she just called us on the phone in the hallway."

Footsteps were coming up the stairs and Amanda turned to see Doctor Mitchell, bag in hand.

"Morning, all." A bright-spirited person, though Amanda wondered how that could be when you were dealing with dead people for your entire working day.

"Morning, Mitchell. Come on in," Jack said, pointing the way to the bedroom. "Looks pretty straightforward to me, but then I'm not the doc."

"That you are not, but thanks for the round-up. I could have done something else with all my years of medical training instead of wasting my time." Mitchell was in a good mood, though she never failed to put Jack in his place if he guessed the outcome without evidence or overstepped his mark. She winked at Amanda, who returned the knowing look.

Faith Mitchell took in the room and the body of James Peterson. At this point only James knew what had gone on, but he was no longer in a position to say.

"I see what you mean, Jack, but it's not our job to assume anything, I look for the facts and work with them." She bent down to undo her bag and retrieved her thermometer. Amanda and Jack stood patiently and waited for the body temperature info, the ambient room temperature info and the estimated time of death that followed.

"Based on rigor, the temperature of his body and the ambient temperature in here over recent hours," said Mitchell, "I'd estimate the time of death to have been around ten pm last night. I'll have to do an autopsy and tox screen back at the lab and let you know what I find, but he's a big man and, judging by the medication on the bedside cabinet, he had a heart condition. Angina probably, but I'll know more later. Who found him?"

"Housekeeper, downstairs. Mrs. Stewart. She's been working for him for some years and is obviously in a state of shock, poor woman. Can't tell us anything except he's just how he was when she found him."

"Okay. Well I'll get on with my examination and fill you in when I have some results."

Amanda nodded in response and started back down the stairs, Jack on her heels. She said over her shoulder, "I'll go and check on Mrs. Stewart and have a chat. You hanging around or going back to the station?"

"Back to the station. Can't see I can do much here until Mitchell has finished. Let me know if anything comes up and I'll see you later."

"Okay. See you back there. I shouldn't be long, unless anything surfaces, of course." She watched as Jack headed off. It seemed straightforward, but then again, you never could tell.

She turned into the kitchen, where Mrs. Stewart was sitting at the kitchen table with a female officer, a china cup and saucer in front of her. She looked to be around seventy, though she had remarkably good skin and only a few wrinkles on her face. It was her neck and hands that gave it away.

"Hello. You must be Mrs. Stewart. I'm Detective Amanda Lacey. I believe you found Mr. Peterson?"

Mrs. Stewart dabbed her nose with the screwed-up hankie that was in her hand and said, "Yes, I'm afraid I did," then sniffed loudly.

"Are you able to answer a few questions for me?"

"Yes, though I'm not sure how much help I can be. I just came in as usual at around eight am and tidied round down here, then made my way up to make his bed." She started to cry again at the thought of what she'd found, fat tears slipping down her face and dripping on to the table top.

Amanda felt sorry for her; it couldn't have been easy.

"Mrs. Stewart, do you have someone I could perhaps ring to be with you? It's an upsetting time, I know. It might help."

"Not really. My daughter is away in France at the moment, and James – I mean Mr. Peterson – was probably the one closest to me after her. We go back a long time, you see."

"Did you see anything unusual, or anyone unusual, out of the ordinary perhaps, when you got here? Anything out of place, maybe? Any sign of an intruder, an unusual window open, perhaps? Anything at all?"

Amanda could see the question moving around in the old woman's head. She came up blank.

"No, nothing. Just Mr. Peterson, in his bedroom." Her eyes met Amanda's. Their red rims looked sore already.

"What were you doing downstairs before you went up to his room?"

"Just some washing up. He runs the book club every fortnight and it was here last night, so there were a few wine glasses to clear away."

"How many glasses, do you remember? How many came to the book club?" Amanda was taking notes down onto her pad.

"Oh, let's see now. I think there were six wine glasses in all and a couple of water glasses. And a plate. They usually have cheese and crackers. James is – was," she corrected herself, "always extremely generous and always supplied a nice bottle of wine and something to eat." She smiled weakly at the thought.

Amanda joined her. "Do you know who attended? And what time does it start and finish?"

"I can write their names down for you but I don't know where they live or anything. They are local, of course. They would be gone usually by nine pm, James wasn't a night owl and liked his bed. Early to rise, though. Didn't believe in wasting the day." She dabbed her nose again. It was a deep pink colour now. Amanda handed her a pen and note pad for the names. Mrs. Stewart hesitated a moment.

"Why don't I write them down?" said Amanda, trying to help her. "Who is the first one?" She smiled encouragingly at Mrs. Stewart and waited.

"Oh dear. Let me see. Joshua, then there's the teacher – Derek, I think. An artist lady, Ann something, and a couple of others. Oh dear, I can't think of their names." She looked even more distressed than she had at the beginning. "Oh! Is it important, do you think? I'm all confused and mixed up."

"Not to worry for the moment. I can probably start with what you have given me. In the meantime, why don't I get an officer to drive you home. Do you have a friendly neighbour nearby? We can talk again a bit later."

"Yes. Thank you. You're very kind. Yes." The old woman was

clearly flustered, and Amanda was a little concerned for her. The female officer who had made her a cup of tea moved forward at Amanda's nod.

"Let's get you home for the moment," she said soothingly, "and I'll come and talk to you again later when you are feeling a bit better." Mrs. Stewart stood on wobbly legs and the officer helped her out of the kitchen and down to her patrol car. It was a slow journey.

Amanda stood at the door and watched them both leave. She'd catch up with the officer again shortly and arrange to see Mrs. Stewart later, but for now she needed to find out about Joshua, Derek and the others – whoever they were. If Derek was a teacher, the schools were the obvious place to start looking for him.

Chapter Thirty-Eight

FRIDAY

"So you're saying you never actually met him last night?" Jack had volunteered to talk to Vivian. They went back a long way; she had been one of his first ever arrests when they were both young and stupid, and he'd been known to be stupid *with* her on occasion. Right then they were sitting in her small lounge, in a house Jack had visited many times over the years, sometimes for pleasure. The text messages found on James's phone together with local knowledge had brought them back together this time.

"No," she sniffed into her tissue, dabbing her bright red nose in the process. "We weren't due to meet until tonight, but I got a text from him saying he wanted to see me last night so I got ready and went straight over. Probably about forty-five minutes from getting his text."

"And what happened then?"

"Well, I knocked, but there was no answer. I don't have a key – refused to have one though he'd offered it to me. Didn't want the responsibility. In case I lost it, you know?"

"Go on."

"So I sent him a text saying I was outside waiting, which you've probably seen by now, but he never answered. I gave up in the end, came back home. Figured he'd fallen asleep or changed his mind, but it wasn't his way to let people down. And now he's dead. I can't believe it. It's too much to take in."

"Do you know why he changed the day to see you? Did he mention anything earlier on?" He twiddled his moustache thoughtfully.

"No, and it was out of character. He liked the routine, seeing me on a certain day. We'd done the same thing for more than ten years, always the first Friday of the month, and he always looked forward to it." She sniffed again. James had been a gentleman, unlike others she could mention. He took care of her, and sometimes they even ate together, shared some supper, and had a laugh. It was more like a friendship than a business transaction; they were two people who had sex with each other occasionally, and she knew she'd miss him.

"Thanks anyway, Vivian. We have to ask because you were texting each other last night, so we have to follow up. We'll have the tox reports back soon, see if that shows anything, and of course the autopsy will tell us more. You want me to get you some tea or something? Maybe something stronger?" He slipped his arm around her shoulders in comfort.

"I'm fine, Jack, but thanks. I'll just sit here and try and make some sense of it. I knew he had a heart condition, and we were always careful, but a man needs a release, let off some steam. You know what I mean?" She wasn't embarrassed in the slightest. Her profession was just like any other job to her; she could have been talking about car maintenance or a lettuce in a greengrocers. It made no difference to her. "He figured we all have to go sometime, and what better way to go than mid-orgasm, if that was to be." She smiled weakly, then started to cry gently into her tissue again. Tears ran down her cheeks in slate-grey rivulets.

Jack felt sorry for her. She shouldn't still be turning tricks at her age, but while there was custom and she was willing, he guessed she'd carry on.

"You go, Jack. I'll be fine, and if you need anything else, sing out. But do me a favour?"

"Of course. What's that?"

"Just let me know what you find out. I'm sure it will just be his heart, but I'd like to know. We were quite close."

"Will do. I'll let myself out. Goodbye, Vivian."

And he was gone, still twiddling his moustache as he walked back to his car. He knew Vivian, and he knew there was nothing there. If James had died on the job, or in this case, before the job, there really wasn't much left to investigate, unless the tests showed anything. He doubted that would be the case, but you never know. He ran through the scene from the bedroom earlier and tried to recall everything about it. To someone looking at it, it was most certainly an older man having some fun with girly magazines, his paid escort on her way. It was sad, he thought, that he'd never got to see her.

Chapter Thirty-Nine

MADELINE'S PHONE CHIRPED WITH THE ARRIVAL OF A TEXT.

"I'm driving so you'll just have to wait, whoever you are," she said to the phone buried in the bottom of her handbag. It was Friday and that meant two things: lunch with Rebecca, and the weekly trip to Sainsbury's again later. She was only five minutes out from the pub; she hoped it wasn't Rebecca cancelling their girly lunch date for some reason. She needed filling in on the latest instalment of Gabe or whoever it was since Todd had dumped her. How the hell Rebecca had never been caught over the years was a mystery in itself. She always managed to keep her liaisons secret somehow, unless Edward did suspect but couldn't give a rat's arse because of his own antics. Her indicator clicked as she turned into the pub car park. With relief, she saw that Rebecca's car was already parked over in the corner, its gleaming nose trying to take advantage of the dappled shade of a tree. Slipping into the space next to hers and remembering the text, she quickly rummaged in her bag to find the phone. It was a group text sent from Derek, which was strange in itself. She read it out loud:

Sad news. James died early this morning. Heart maybe. Keep you posted of funeral news. Derek.

"Holy sodding moly. He's dead!" Madeline was stunned, absolutely stunned. Then realisation started to dawn. "Did I do that? If I did, that wasn't meant to happen. I just wanted him to be uncomfortable for the night, not wake up sodding dead." She thumped the steering wheel in frustration but missed it entirely and hit the horn instead. Its loud blare made her jump.

"Oh, for feck's sake!"

And of course now she was frazzled again. The heat in the car was starting to build up with the engine turned off and the windows closed, and a familiar bead of sweat ran down the back of her neck. She opened the door for air but didn't move for a moment. What she'd done and how she'd done it played through her mind like an old 8 mm film movie reel, complete with flashing numbers counting down. She wondered whether she'd been clever enough, or if an avalanche of shit was now going to fall her way. And add that to a missing landscaper... The pile could indeed be deep.

Her throat was dry and her head was spinning, so she picked her bag up off the seat and slowly walked to the pub entrance, lost in uneasy thought. It was another baking hot day, which wasn't helping her sort through the flurry in her head. She went inside and asked for a glass of water.

"Are you okay, love?" the young barman asked as he handed her a tall glass, which she gulped down quickly.

Rebecca waved to her. "Maddy? Maddy! Come and sit down." Madeline set the empty glass on the bar and walked over to her friend. Her legs felt like tree stumps. Rebecca peered at her, her forehead creasing in concern. "You're as white as a sheet. You look like you've seen a ghost." She perched Madeline on a bar stool, for which her wobbly legs were grateful. Somehow she found the words to speak.

"It's James, from book club. He's dead. Just got a text." She turned to face Rebecca, ashen-faced. "He's dead. I can't believe it."

"Let's get you something stronger to drink and some food inside you, then you can tell me all about it." Madeline stayed put as Rebecca ordered food and drinks, then stood and let Rebecca help her over to their usual table. She felt strangely light-headed, as if all the air had gone from around her. Now there were two people dead because of her, one sort of planned, and one definitely not. And then there was

Big Sod, who she assumed was still alive in hospital though she didn't know for sure. So that could be three.

Shit, Madeline. What's happening? Have you truly turned into 'Madeline the Mad'?

She picked up her gin and tonic and drank the whole thing down in one, the cold liquid soothing her parched throat and making her nerves sing at the same time.

"Steady on, Maddy. You've got to drive back to work yet."

"I'm not going back this afternoon now. I'll text them in a minute. Shit. I can't believe it." She was, of course, more worried that the police would come looking for her again than in shock at the fact that James had died – that was her main, actually her only concern. If they put her name together with the disappearance of the landscaper, it was going to look like one hell of a coincidence, and she wasn't sure how she'd talk her way out of that one. An image of striped prison sheets thudded into her mind. And a horrible sense of being a bitch. One thing was for sure: she needed to keep her head down and not get involved in any conversation with the police, or the other book club members. Not yet, anyway. If she stayed low, kept out of their way, they'd have no choice but to interview her last. And it might all be over by then.

"I'm feeling a little better now. Perhaps the G&T has done me good." She forced a smile Rebecca's way, and Rebecca smiled weakly back at her, not entirely convinced.

"I've ordered you a toastie as usual," she said. "Should be here soon. That will make you feel better. I bet you've not eaten since breakfast, have you?"

She'd had a doughnut with her morning coffee but didn't admit to it. Gabe the barman approached their table with two plates, each containing a cheese and ham toastie, and Madeline caught the wink he gave to Rebecca, a wink she had the nerve to return.

"So Gabe is still on, I'm guessing, but Todd's still off?"

"Yes, Gabe is still very much on," she said, her eyes twinkling, "though I do miss Todd."

Madeline leapt at the chance to change the subject to something a little less serious. "So tell me more," she said. "Take my mind off my bad news. I want all the gossip – when and where, times and dates."

Rebecca was happy to oblige. As she tucked into her meal, she gave Madeline all the gory details of trips to her shed, the spare room, the patio table in the sunshine and of course the lap pool. It seemed there was no surface left untouched. Clearly going to her place for dinner would be a different experience from now on, Madeline thought. How can you ever un-see what you've seen, even if it is only in your mind's eye? She was only half listening, which seemed a bit mean, since she'd asked for the details in the first place, but she had rather more pressing problems to deal with, and Gabe and Todd weren't a part of them.

At length she became aware that Rebecca had finished speaking and was sitting eating her toastie, watching her. Madeline picked her knife and fork up and began to eat, but found she had little appetite. Tales of Todd and Gabe hadn't done the trick.

"I think I'll finish this, then I might go straight home. Sod Sainsbury's today. I wonder when his funeral will be?" An event she needed to avoid like the plague, but how could she?

"I think that's a wise idea. We'll cut this short. You go home and put your feet up in the garden and chill out a bit. Bad news can do terrible damage to your health, so you need to take it easy while you adjust. We can catch up again next week when you're feeling more in the mood and less sad."

Madeline tried to smile, and failed.

No need to be so melodramatic. James wasn't one of the family, you know.

Rebecca's advice sounded good, though, and she nodded in agreement as they ate.

"Better not have any more alcohol," said Rebecca. "Do you want a coffee instead, and maybe a slice of something?"

Madeline shook her head 'no,' her mouth full of cheese and ham. She was having enough trouble forcing the toastie down without adding anything else. She hoped she wasn't going to be sick.

They finished their meal and drinks, paid up, and headed back out to the stifling car park and two very hot cars. Just before Rebecca got into hers, she said, "I saw that man you talk about that goes into Sally's for lunch. He was in the newspaper. You know, the really miserable one? The report said he'd been really ill with food poisoning. Edward knows of him, apparently. He's the one who pointed the story out to me. I think he's in finance or something, same as Edward. Did you see it too?"

"No, and I've not seen him for a few days, now you that mention it. Did the report say much about it, about what caused it?" She felt her heart start to beat faster, sweat rising to the surface on the back of her neck. Again. Guilty conscience, maybe?

"No, it didn't say, but it looks like a one-off case, so the Health Authority aren't involved. I suppose that's a good thing."

"Yes, I suppose you're right. I wonder why it made the papers?"

Why the hell had it made the papers?

"Oh, I expect because he was taken to hospital. Must have been bad. Urgh. Imagine that – yuck. And in this heat. And I bet he's on his own. How miserable."

They said their goodbyes, and Madeline got in her car. She immediately wound the window down. The heat was nearly unbearable.

"My god, it would be, and in this heat too," she said to Rebecca through the window. She did her best to look sympathetic. "Anyway, have a lovely weekend and I'll speak to you soon." She waved and smiled as she turned the engine on. She drove off thinking of the damage she'd done to Big Sod, Grey Man, and two now very Dead Men.

Chapter Forty

Josh typed into the status box:

Sad news. James Peterson, book club leader and local business owner, has passed away this morning due to a suspected heart condition. He will be greatly missed by our group. He was a man passionate about books and someone who kept us glued together for the fun of it. I'm sure we will all miss him terribly. I'll let you know of the funeral details when I have them. #RIPJames. #bookclub

He clicked Post and off went the message into the ether. It was only a moment before a response came back.

@Josh_man. That's sad news. Sorry to hear that. He was quite a character. #RIPJames

@Jaybaby. That he was, and so shocking. We only had book club last night. He didn't seem too well when we all left. Perhaps we should have noticed something then, but he just said he was hot and needed an early night."

@Josh_man. It's no one's fault. Just nature taking its course. #lifeisshort

@Jaybaby. Won't be the same without him, though. I told the police when they came over to the campus he didn't seem well, but I don't think they're treating it as a suspicious death. Case opened and closed. I guess his family will take care of his affairs.

@Josh_man. I guess. Keep us posted when you hear.

@jaybaby. Will do.

Josh closed the browser and lay back on his bed to think. What a shocker. What would happen to book club now?

Chapter Forty-One

"So you're telling me he had angina, took a Viagra, and that's what killed him?" Jack wanted to double-check what Mitchell had just told him.

"Pretty much. Angina is a condition that needs a higher blood pressure to supply the heart with blood. Lowering the blood pressure decreases the flow of blood to the heart and can cause a heart attack. In this case, it was fatal. And it's not an uncommon problem."

"Go on."

"Well, many men use Viagra recreationally. That is to say, on occasion, like when they need a little extra help, rather than because they have impotence. And it's quite popular in the party scene now, with young men mixing it with ecstasy or even cocaine to get that euphoric high. Sextasy, it's called. Stupid and dangerous, but then people taking street pills are hard to educate. Could be fatal for them, but we never think it will happen to us. And it's incredibly easy to come by."

"So you think old James just fancied a bit of extra help and bought himself one, and it proved fatal?"

"That would explain it, but that's your job, not mine. I'm just telling you what killed him. The mix of chemicals he took simply lowered his blood pressure way too far for his heart to cope. Stopped his heart. End of story."

"Thanks, Doc. So that's it, then?"

"Unless you find any evidence that it was forced on him, I'd say so. Let me know if you find anything, but a pretty open and closed case in this instance. I'm off home now if you want me. Speak soon." She hung up, and that was the end of that.

Jack sat back in his chair, a few bristly hairs of his moustache between his thumb and forefinger. He twirled the coarse hair, contemplating what Mitchell had just told him. It all fitted nicely with seeing Vivian later that evening. An evening that should have been fun had simply gone bad. He dialled Amanda to tell her the news.

"Sextasy, eh? What will they dream up next?" Amanda wasn't particularly surprised to hear the results.

"What a way to go." Trust Jack to voice the glaringly obvious. "So that's that then – misadventure. Easy one to put to bed for a change." Jack was trying to be funny.

"Ha ha. Yeah, yeah, I get it. You can be so crass sometimes. The guy is barely cold and you're making jokes at his expense. Poor old Mrs. Stewart was beside herself, all of a muddle and on her own. Poor thing. I hope her neighbour is looking in on her."

"You can't look after everyone, Lacey. You'd have a house full, and they're not your responsibility. She'll be fine. Give her a call tomorrow and let her know he didn't suffer or something." He couldn't help but smile as he said 'didn't suffer,' and Amanda felt herself smile at the notion too.

"Now stop it!" she chided. "It's not funny!" But it was, really.

"I'm headed home now," she said. "I'll see you in the morning." She picked her bag up off the desk, slinging it over her shoulder as she headed to the back staff entrance.

"Yeah. Goodnight, Lacey." The line clicked dead.

Chapter Forty-Two

MADELINE FELT TRULY EXHAUSTED. THE DRIVE HOME WAS ONE OF those where you were at the wheel, but you faded out to someplace else. Somehow you got to your destination and wondered how the hell you did because you don't remember one bit of driving it. They say only one in three drivers is actually fully paying attention, and the rest, well, they're not. One in three is not many when you think about some of the roads you drive on, but Madeline had managed to get home and park the car away without causing a casualty. That she knew of. For a change.

She slipped inside to the relative coolness, grateful she'd got home in one piece. The hard, flat surface of the door was a comfort as she leaned back against it like a supportive crutch. Picking up the mail from the floor, she noticed a familiar envelope from the telephone company and tore it open. It wasn't red. Finally: the credit note she'd been waiting for.

Better bloody late than never, I suppose.

Dexter trotted up and greeted her.

"You'd never believe my day if I told you and you could understand," she said to the cat, screwing the credit note into a tight ball and tossing it over her shoulder.

He cocked his head as if to say "Try me."

Her bag and keys hit the hall table and shoes flew through the air as she flicked each one off in turn. Dexter was not impressed.

"Let's just say I've had a bit of a shock, and I'm feeling a little panicky."

He didn't say a word but looked like he wanted her to fill him in.

"I need a cold drink and then I'm going to sit in the shade outside, so if you want to know more, come find me in a minute."

He looked like he might just do that, and watched as she headed to the kitchen cupboard in search of the favourite blue bottle. There was tonic in the fridge and ice in the tray and it clunked in the tall glass as the cubes hit, the sound of tonic fizzing making her drool. She topped it off with a healthy pour of gin, then headed outside to the shade, cat in tow.

Even though the sun was baking in the early afternoon sky, it was lovely sitting watching the garden without getting too hot, taking in the full blooms, the vegetable patch and the fields beyond. Dexter pulled up alongside and jumped into her lap for a bit of motherly love. He started buzzing immediately and she rubbed him under his chin. He turned it up as far as it would go to get her to rub even more. If he could have said "Right, I'm ready when you are," he probably would have done.

Madeline gave a big sigh as she caught sight of the Giant Orange Machine, reminding her of where this had all started

"I've been a bad woman," she began.

He watched her, still purring loudly.

"I've done some dumb things recently and now I'm a bit worried I might get found out. It started with a woman and her iced buns, but now I might be in trouble for something a bit more serious than sticking my finger where it wasn't wanted."

A blackbird flew in and sat on a low branch of the magnolia tree at the edge of the patio. Dexter noticed it and sat up more alertly, wondering if he could be bothered going for it, if he could get to it in time before it flew off and made a mockery of him. The blackbird didn't move and neither did Dexter.

She sipped her cold drink. "And now I'm wondering what will

happen, and how it might happen, so if anyone wants me, I'm not in. That way, they might just give up and go look at another clue." She had another thought. "Maybe I could even get Gordon to go away with me this weekend, go to Brighton maybe, or Bournemouth?" She knew, though, he'd hate that idea straight away. Having just come back from London on a hot train, he wouldn't be up for a hot evening's drive down there. The traffic would be hellish, for one, and he didn't appreciate short notice, for another. An impromptu weekend away wasn't going to happen. Or save her.

"I'll just have to stay busy and keep out of everyone's way, head out to the garden centre again…" The thought of the garden centre reminded her of another episode. "Oh hell. And there lies another tale."

Dexter looked up at her, confused, but stayed on her lap, busying himself with washing his front paw like it was a sudden emergency and then nestling his head down for a snooze. An ample sigh made his whole body rise and fall heavily just the once.

"I feel just the same, Dexter. Perhaps I should have a nap too." And so she laid her head back on the lounger, breathed deeply for a couple of beats, closed her eyes for a moment and let the light breeze waft over her in an almost caressing way. Not five minutes later, Madeline was sound asleep.

Chapter Forty-Three

MADELINE AWOKE TO HEARING HER NAME BEING CALLED. HER eyelids felt like someone had put little dumbbell weights on them; she had to battle them open. It reminded her of the heaviness after anaesthetic.

"Madeline. Maddy? Are you okay?" Recognising Gordon's soft voice, she tried to sit upright, having slithered down the lounger somewhat. Her hands immediately went to her head and mussed-up hair,. She had a terrible case of bedhead. Finally, waking a bit more, she replied, "Yes, I'm fine. I must have dozed off. What time is it?"

"It's just coming up to five pm. Are you sure you're all right? I don't think I've ever known you to fall asleep in the afternoon." He was smiling down at her, looking like the caring husband he was. They had their moments.

"What are you doing home so early? Is everything alright with you?" Madeline was fully awake and sat upright now. No, this definitely wasn't the norm for a Friday afternoon. Gordon smiled warmly again.

"Yes, quite. Everything is fine. I just thought I'd make my way home early and take my wife out for dinner, if she fancied it. It's such great weather, I thought we'd go off and find a pub somewhere by a river and sit and enjoy it. What do you think?"

Well, it would make up for me not going Sainsbury's shopping, and as I had no clue what was for dinner anyway, it's a good idea.

"What a lovely thought. Thank you." Her plan to lie low came flooding back to her. "Yes, let's do that. In fact, why don't we freshen up now and head straight out. We could take a stroll after dinner." She beamed her best smile up at him and thought about how lucky they were not to have a crappy marriage like Rebecca and Edward. Gordon might be a bit humdrum sometimes but who was she to talk? Her waistline was not as small as it had once been, and the extra chin had developed nicely over the last couple of years, but still, she knew she loved him, and he loved her and they were faithful. They were as solid as any couple that had been together for most of their adult lives.

Standing, she gently shooed Dexter to the ground and brushed his hairs off her skirt, then followed Gordon inside. After a quick shower and a change of clothes each, and a bit of extra make-up for Madeline, they were on their way, headed south down the quiet back roads and on to Oxted. 'The George' wasn't exactly by the river, nowhere near a river at all actually, but it was a nice pub with somewhere to take a walk afterwards when you were feeling a bit overfull. It had been refurbished just the year before, and the new fitout came with new cuisine too, a Spanish influence that she and Gordon both found quite nice.

They pulled into the car park and she thought about the text she'd got at lunchtime with Rebecca, about James's death. She was reluctant to bring the subject up at all, but she knew she needed to tell Gordon. She hooked her arm through his and they both went inside. It was quite a nice light and airy place – they'd done a good job on their refurbishment – and Madeline propped the bar up while deciding what to drink. Having already had two G&Ts today, she suspected she'd be safer to stick to a sparkling water and was just about to open her mouth and order but Gordon beat her to it.

"Two gin and tonics, please," he said to the barman.

So much for only having water, then, but there is a quiet comfort in him knowing my tipple of choice.

She didn't mind, and he knew she rarely drank anything else apart from a glass of wine at Sunday lunch. Picking up the menu, she began to scan it, taking in the sharing boards and the steaks, all of which she could quite happily devour. The afternoon nap had made her hungry.

"I don't need to look," he said. "Steak for me, and you choose a sharing board." He was such a creature of habit, but then they both were. She made her selection and placed their order with the barman, and then they went to sit outside in the garden. The evening sun felt lovely and warm on their skin.

"Let's sit over there," Gordon said, pointing to a quiet corner, though there were only a handful of people in the garden at the moment. Give it another hour and it would be packed. They sat down together, sipped their G&Ts, and fell into a comfortable silence.

After a few minutes, she took a deep breath, screwed up her nerve, and told him about the text, about James's death. Obviously, she wasn't going to mention what she'd actually done to cause it, but if the police did come knocking again, which they likely would since she was a book club member, she figured it was best that Gordon be forewarned.

"Oh dear, darling. No wonder you were asleep. That must have been the shock. Why didn't you say something earlier?" He genuinely looked sorry, and her heart melted a bit at the concern in his voice. He reached for her hand and petted it. "There, there," he said soothingly.

"Well, you didn't know him, so I didn't think it would be of interest to you. He was the dominant one at book club and could be a pain in the arse sometimes, but now? Well, he's gone. Heart condition, apparently. I'm not sure if I'll go to the funeral yet. I don't know when it is at this point." She watched another couple enter the garden. They were holding hands and looked very much in love. They took seats in the farthest corner from Gordon and Madeline.

"Oh, but you must go," said Gordon. "Pay your respects and all. The other members will be going, I'm sure, so you'll want to show your support for each other. A nasty time for you all." As always, he was the voice of reason, and he was quite right: she really should go. But it didn't sit well in her stomach at all, knowing that she'd killed him. Though it wasn't intentionally, she was still guilty. And would the police be there?

"Would you like me to come with you? I'm sure I could if you wanted me to," he suggested gently. "It might be nice to meet the other members of the club. I don't know anything about them."

"It's not really the right place to go to meet folk, is it?"

"Not generally, that's not what I meant, but there's always a spread on somewhere after when the service is over and people gather for tea and sherry. I could say hello to them then."

She knew he was right; it looked like she was going to go to James's funeral after all. "All right. I'll find out when it is, and if you can come, then lovely." She smiled over the top of her glass. It was then she noticed the colour of his eyes again, for the first time in a long time. Whether it was the events of the day, the afternoon nap or her third G&T, she was seeing Gordon like it was twenty years ago again. He really was quite handsome. She leant forward, took his hands in hers and pecked him slowly on the lips.

"What was that for?"

"Does there need to be a reason? Just thanks for being so supportive, that's all."

"It's what friends do. And lovers, as a matter of fact." He smiled so nicely, like she really was the love of his life. Maybe she still was. Their sharing platter arrived and the waiter set it down between them, the beautiful cured cut meats, dips and breads all arranged perfectly. Madeline picked up a small piece of bread, dipped it in olive oil and tucked it into Gordon's half-open and surprised mouth. She watched him chew. He really was a handsome man. Could she still be the love of his life? She hoped so.

Chapter Forty-Four

AMANDA DROVE TOWARDS HOME THAT EVENING WITH MRS. STEWART on her mind. She decided to drop in on her on the way, just to make sure the old woman had someone looking out for her. Her Google Maps app voice informed her the destination was on her left. Amanda pulled up outside and sat thinking for a minute – did James have a next of kin? Mrs. Stewart would know, and probably the other legal things like where his will was, if there was one, who to contact and all the other things that need sorting when someone dies. Since they'd known one another for some time, Amanda would be surprised if she didn't.

She grabbed her bag, headed to the front door and rapped with the old-fashioned brass knocker. The sound seemed to echo down the whole street. It was a quiet part of town, and glancing at the nicely manicured front gardens filled with copious amounts of random colour, she guessed rightly that the street was home to mainly elderly folks. The younger generation tended to go for a more uniform colour scheme and more low-maintenance plants these days than annuals from a garden centre. Leafy greens and whites were more common in those neighbourhoods. She heard light footsteps on the other side of the door, and a frail voice asked nervously, "Who is it?"

"It's Detective Amanda Lacey, Mrs. Stewart. We spoke this morning." There was a click of the lock and the door opened inwards. Mrs. Stewart stood looking quite small on the other side of it.

"Hello again. Please, come in." She started walking back down the hallway, to the kitchen, no doubt: they were always down the back.

"Thank you." Amanda followed her footsteps and added, "I just wanted to pop my head in and see how you are. How are you doing?"

"Tea?" Mrs. Stewart enquired without answering the question.

"No, thank you. I won't keep you long. Are you feeling a little better? Is someone looking out for you?"

"Yes, I told Bridget next door what has happened. She's been extremely thoughtful. I'm to go round for morning coffee in the morning, when I'm feeling a little better, you know. But I will call her if I need anything in the meantime." She seemed satisfied with that arrangement and Amanda nodded her approval.

"I have to ask about Mr. Peterson's next of kin. Do you know who we should contact, or are you in touch with them?"

"Yes, I've let his son know. He's not local. He lives in Australia, so he's on his way over. I rang him when I got back here this morning. Do you know what happened yet?"

"It seems he had a heart attack. You knew he had a heart condition, I expect?"

"Oh yes, for a couple of years now. I guess we all have to go eventually. Still, I will miss him deeply. We've been good friends and I won't pretend the bit of money hasn't come in useful. I guess there's a funeral to arrange now." She stared off, lost in thought, and Amanda took the opportunity to finish their conversation there.

"Yes, there will be." She paused, then added, "I'll leave you in peace then, Mrs. Stewart, and say good night to you. I simply wanted to make sure you were okay."

"Yes. Good night to you too. And thank you for dropping by."

Amanda made her way back to the front door and out into the riotous colours of the street. The evening air was still warm and a light breeze blew, making it feel like a warm hair dryer blowing on a low speed round the back of her neck. She unlocked her car then drove over to Ruth's place. She didn't want to go home to an empty house. Not tonight.

Chapter Forty-Five

AMANDA SAT IN HER CAR OUTSIDE RUTH'S PLACE FOR A FEW moments. The windows on the front of the house were all wide open in an effort to encourage a breeze through, and she could see the curtains billowing a little inside. Amanda hated seeing death; it was never pleasant for anyone, and that was one of the reasons she'd decided to drop in on the old woman. Friendships that have developed over many years tended to be strong ones, she knew, and death was much harder to bear when the end finally came for one of them.

It had made her think about her own situation, her and Ruth. They'd been together for some months now but Ruth still hadn't introduced her to her family. Amanda herself hadn't got much family left, having lost her parents years before to a drunk driver. She had been an only child, so the subject of meeting Amanda's family had never come up between her and Ruth. But seeing Mrs. Stewart looking so frail and lost made her realise that if anything were to happen to Ruth, she'd be just as alone and it saddened her. She wanted to be a part of a family, with Ruth. Maybe one day they would even adopt a child or find someone willing to help out creating a baby of their own making. Other gay couples did; maybe they would too. Seeing Mrs. Stewart all alone had made her realise she definitely wanted more. She would broach the subject with Ruth soon, just not tonight. At this moment, all she really wanted was a hug, a glass of wine and to curl up with the woman she loved. But this weekend, she would bring the subject up when the right moment arose.

She made her way down the side alley and in through the back gate towards the back door, which was wide open.

"Hello!" she called.

"I'm back here," came the reply from somewhere behind her in the garden. Amanda turned and saw Ruth coming out of the shed, gardening gloves protecting her lovely fingernails while she did whatever she did in there with potting compost and the like. Amanda was not one for gardening, though she appreciated other people's efforts. Smiling, she made her way down the paving stone path, trying not to step on the grassy joins: at school that had always been bad luck. For some reason she still kept the tradition up: no stepping on grassy joins or cracks if she could help it. She wasted no time taking Ruth in her arms and hugging her tightly.

Ruth was unsure where to put her gloved hands without making a mess, so she held them in the air behind Amanda's back and squashed her warmly with her elbows.

"You okay? I don't want to get you all dirty. Here, let me take my gloves off and let's try that again so I can join in." Amanda let her pull away for a moment and take the offending gloves off before re-engaging in an even tighter hug. Ruth rubbed her back as she did so; Amanda often saw some rough stuff with her job and generally needed a little comfort after work. Being in the police really did give a person cause to moan about a bad day at 'the office,' she knew. Ruth waited for her to pull away then gave her a quick peck on the cheek.

"Let me get you a cold glass of wine, then you can fill me in if you want to – or don't if you'd rather not. Come and sit on the patio while I get it." They walked hand in hand back up to the house, and Ruth parked Amanda in a comfortable chair, pecked her on the cheek once more and let go of her hand. "I'll be right back." She hurried into the kitchen, poured two glasses of Sauvignon Blanc from the bottle in the fridge, and returned to Amanda with them in hand.

They clinked their glasses and sipped companionably for a moment before Ruth asked gently, "What's up? You look wrung out."

"We were called to a death this morning. An older man with heart problems. But it was the poor old housekeeper who found his body that I keep thinking about. She's pretty much all alone and he was too, though they had been friends for many years. Just got me thinking about not having much by way of family myself, and who would take care of my affairs, that kind of thing. My funeral, my cat."

"You don't have a cat."

"I might have to get one, if I don't have any family around," Amanda said, smiling weakly, trying to make a point without getting too maudlin.

"Now you're being dumb. You have me, silly. I know we don't have the most conventional relationship, but it works for us, doesn't it? It will be me taking care of your affairs when it happens, but not yet, eh?"

"And I know that, and yes it does work for us. It's just sometimes..." Amanda's voice trailed off without finishing the sentence. She'd told herself she wasn't going to go there tonight. She changed the tone to something a little more positive and added, "Anyway, I'm here now, and I'm going to drink this glass of wine then walk down and get us some fish and chips – unless you've already eaten?"

"I just had a sandwich earlier on, so I'm sure I have room for a fish and chip supper. I'll walk down with you if you'd like?"

"I'd very much like." Amanda felt better already. But she was going to bring the subject up again over the weekend. It was something she very much needed to sort out.

Chapter Forty-Six

SATURDAY

RUTH LOVED THE WEEKENDS – WHO DIDN'T? SHE WORKED HARD during the week, keeping unsociable hours sometimes, but that was because she enjoyed it, and when Amanda was busy with her own work, she figured she might as well take the opportunity to catch up. But Saturday and Sunday? They were for play. Even if Amanda was working, Ruth would catch up on some of her chores or grocery shopping. It seemed only fair and part of what they did for each other, even though they still lived separately. But today they had the whole day together. She turned over to face her. Amanda was still asleep, her blond hair sticking up all over the place like a wild woman's. Ruth smiled; she could be pretty wild sometimes, and last night she'd stayed over after they'd shared a cold bottle on the patio and feasted on fish and chips in the park. Boy, was she wild.

But Ruth knew Amanda was bothered about something more than simply a hard day at work. She had alluded to it out in the garden – their relationship together and meeting her family. The problem, if you could call it that, was that Ruth's family didn't know she was gay. In fact, no one other than Amanda and a few casual hook-ups knew she was gay. It had never come up, and she'd never spelled it out. Not her work colleagues, no one. They all thought she was a busy, driven businesswoman who didn't have time for a male friend, but the truth was she preferred female friends, and her favourite and the love of her life was Amanda.

The bedside clock said it was just coming up to 7 am, which was much later than her usual get-out-of-bed time, so she gently pushed the covers back and slid out, trying not to wake her lover. Amanda whimpered slightly at the movement but didn't open her eyes; she pulled the covers back up to her chin. Ruth dressed in her running gear, grabbed some cash, which she stuffed into the hidden pocket in her shorts, and set off with Sam Smith crooning in her ears. Not exactly upbeat running material, but then she didn't feel the need this morning. Today, she wanted to think.

The sun was up and the day promised to be another beauty. It felt good warming her face and shoulders as she got into her stride, headed out towards the park and a few laps round. The monotony of laps gave her the space to churn things over in her head without worrying about traffic turning at junctions, cars reversing out of driveways, kids on tricycles and wheelie bins on pavements, things that turned a straightforward run into an obstacle course. The park was fairly empty; 7 am was too early for the weekday commuters who took the opportunity for a slower start to their days when they could. Apart from a couple of other runners and the odd dog walker, she was on her own, just as she liked it. She picked up the pace and sweat started to bead across her forehead and on her chest, something she always found motivating when it came to working out, and egged her on even more. The more she sweated, the harder she pushed. Sam was reaching the end of the first track of Ruth's 'thinking running' playlist, and as she had it on shuffle, she had no idea what was coming up next. Life was an adventure sometimes, and Adele filled the gap with her haunting rendition of 'Hello.' She thought of the music video, in which Adele stood by the river, her gorgeous hair billowing around her in the wind, looking serious and sounding incredibly emotional. It reminded her of Amanda last night. But she'd come out running to think, not re-live music videos, and she swept the images of Adele away and replaced them with Amanda.

How could she tell her that she'd still not come out yet, that her family didn't know, that no one knew? Amanda would assume it was because she was ashamed or something, and that simply wasn't the case: Ruth had just hadn't felt the need. And, more to the point, what if they didn't approve? Ruth wasn't sure she could bear that. But she knew that Amanda wanted to meet her family, and she wouldn't be able to put it off for much longer without it becoming an issue. Although maybe it already was. Deep down, she knew what she had to do. But how should she do it?

After ten laps she'd worked up a fair sweat, rivulets running down her chest and back, soaking her shirt through and making it stick to her skin. She'd had enough of running and thinking, but still wasn't sure she had the answer. As a cooldown, she jogged lightly back towards Richmond Road and to the little coffee shop just past it, where she ordered two lattes to go. Amanda would be awake by now.

"I'VE GOT A QUICK ERRAND TO RUN FOR WORK FIRST OFF." AMANDA was up now and ready for the day. "Won't take me longer than an hour, and then let's go out for the whole day. It's not often we get a day together."

Ruth had her head in her morning crossword; the record time to beat was long past and 11 across was giving her grief. "I hate it when I can't do it straight off," she said crossly, and pushed the folded newspaper to the side in a huff. Sulking wasn't what she did usually, but 11 across was irking her. She'd go back to it later. She turned her attention to Amanda now. "Sounds like a good idea. Anywhere in mind?" She was up for a day out with Amanda; it might give her a chance to say something if the time was right. After Amanda's hint last night, the topic of meeting her family was sure to come up again soon, and a weekend day was probably the best time to do it. She knew Amanda too well.

"Let's get some brunch in town, sip some coffee, flex the credit card for some new gear, and if we really want to push the boat out, we could catch an early show with a late supper. Go the whole hog. Be edgy." Amanda was grinning from ear to ear.

Ruth grinned right back. "That sounds like a nice plan. I'm up for that. How long do you need to get back and ready?" Ruth looked down at her own faded jeans and thought she'd better change, even though she'd dressed not long ago.

"Just got to pay someone a visit, so give me an hour? Then I'll be back and I'm all yours." Amanda's eyes glinted as she said 'all yours,' and Ruth stood to peck her on the cheek as she passed her on the way upstairs to change.

"Perfect," she called over her shoulder. "Don't be any longer now I've got the idea of brunch in my mind. Not had bacon for ages."

Chapter Forty-Seven

Madeline stood in the hallway, thinking quickly, as Detective Amanda Lacey knocked on the door, more loudly this time. Madeline had seen her arrive and was ready for her. She'd wondered how long it would be before they'd figured she'd been at James's place on the night he'd died. She knew the police had got in touch with all of the others, one by one, and it seemed she was the last, probably because she'd been actively avoiding them for obvious reasons. She'd never meant for it to turn out so badly for James; she'd just wanted to teach him a lesson, but it had all gone wrong. How the hell was she to know about his damned heart problem? And now Amanda had finally caught up and had come knocking on this otherwise lovely Saturday morning.

Taking a deep breath, Madeline pasted a smile on her face and opened the door wide.

"So we meet again," Detective Lacey opened, a smirk on her face.

Act surprised, Madeline, and be pleasant.

"Detective Lacey, how nice to see you again. Come on in." She hoped she wasn't overdoing it with her enthusiasm. Her plan was the same one she'd used with the landscaper's 'disappearance,' – tell the truth, and don't go into too much detail. The guilty can often do that, she knew – overcompensate, add too much detail – and detectives tend to notice these things. Madeline wasn't about to be caught out.

"I assume this is about poor old James's death?" She shook her head solemnly. "How sad, and what a shock." Leading Detective Lacey back into the lounge, a place she was now becoming quite used to, unfortunately, she asked, "Can I get you some tea?"

"Yes, please. That would be nice, thanks."

Huh. Not the answer Madeline had been looking for. She left the detective in the lounge while she went out back to the kitchen. She gathered cups and a plate of biscuits, something she figured a murderer wouldn't do, and waited for the kettle to boil. It was raining now; the clear morning had turned wet and the view out of the kitchen window looked sad and dismal. The Great Orange Machine was still standing in the corner of the garden, with Dexter in the cab, dry, looking over towards the house. Madeline felt Amanda before she heard her.

"Miserable day, isn't it? Though we do need some rain." Amanda was going with the idle chit-chat opening before leading to the real questions. Loosen her up a little, get her talking. Madeline knew the moves: too much CSI.

"Yes, but you're quite right, we do need it, though I believe it will be bright again later."

Dexter, at the sight of them both in the kitchen window, took it as a sign he was needed, and they watched him jump down from the digger and trot across to the back door of the house. The cat flap clicked as he entered, a single meow informing them he had indeed arrived. He took no time in introducing himself to Amanda's legs. She bent down to scratch him. Ginger hairs gathered on her trousers and fingers, transferred from his damp coat.

"This is Dexter," Madeline said by way of introduction. "Sorry about his hairs. He always seems to be shedding, and brushing him doesn't seem to keep them at bay. But you didn't come here to talk about Dexter this time, I know, so how can I help you?" Madeline hoped that, with the sight of the Great Orange Machine, Amanda wasn't going to bring that particular subject up again.

"You were at the book club on the night of his death along with the others. We don't have all the results from the tests back as yet, but can you tell me what happened from your experience?"

"Of course, though there isn't much to tell, really. We all turned up as normal, had wine and crackers, and he said he needed to finish earlier than usual, though he didn't really say why. It was such a hot night, had been all week, and I just put it down to needing an early night. I don't think many of us had slept well with the heat, and he must have been feeling it more – being a bit older, I mean. We left a little earlier than usual, probably more like eight thirty rather than our usual nine pm. That's it. The first I heard about it was a text from Derek the following day. Shocking."

"Did James say anything before you all left, other than about finishing early?"

"No. He said he was hot, though, and that he would sit out the back and try and cool off. He got himself some water. Do you think it was the heat that upset him? I've heard of heat stroke before."

"We don't know as yet. Just checking with you all what happened."

Madeline poured tea into two cups and offered Amanda one along with a chocolate biscuit.

"Thanks," she said. "Did you know James well?"

"Only through book club. He was our self-appointed leader, if you like, and we went to his place every fortnight, shared a bottle of wine or two and talked books. He ran a business in town and was a widower. That's about it."

"How long have you been going to book club?"

"Gosh, quite some time. Must be a good couple of years." Thinking for a moment, she continued, "Yes, must be about two years. I think we've all been going at least that long. Derek, Pam and Annabel were some of the originals, and I joined through Lorna. She introduced me."

"And how would you say your relationship with James was? I believe he could be a bit difficult at times."

"Well, he was our leader, so yes, he got a bit annoyed if we hadn't managed to read what we were supposed to be reading, but that was just part of his way. I got on fine with him, to answer your question.

We all did, otherwise we wouldn't have gone. A small group like ours, you've got to like each other to make it work." And that was the truth: you did. Amanda seemed to be letting this sink in and Madeline didn't offer anymore.

Don't fill the gaps with unnecessary details or lies.

"Did he have a regular partner in his life that you know of? I know he was a widower, but was he seeing someone? Did he ever mention anyone?"

"Not that I knew of, and I've never heard the others mention anything so I'm guessing no. He liked his own company; he'd been on his own for so many years. Maybe he'd become used to that way of life, didn't need anyone. I'm guessing, of course." She fell silent for a moment, thinking of her next move. "He was a popular man, well known in the area and very generous. Such a shame he's now gone."

Shut up, Madeline.

Madeline was staring out at the wet garden again, not looking at anything in particular, but knowing what she'd done to two men made her feel a little emotional. It wasn't unexpected, really, given the hormones buzzing about inside her, and so she wasn't surprised to feel a tear trickling down her cheek. It was perfect timing, so she turned to Amanda to let her see it. "Yes, such a shame." She bowed her head a little. Hopefully that was the end of her questions, for now.

It worked like a charm. Detective Lacey thanked her and got to her feet. There wasn't much else she could have asked anyway, because nothing suspicious had taken place: it was just a man with a dodgy heart found dead in his home, with no evidence of anyone else involved.

"Like I said, we'll get the rest of the test results back soon enough and will know more then," the detective said. "If you think of anything in the meantime, you have my card. Just let us know. I'll see myself out."

"Of course." But there was no way Madeline was going to let her show herself out, so she followed her back to the front door at a distance, just to make sure she didn't divert into another room or something.

Too much CSI making me nervous.

When Detective Lacey had finally gone through the door and was safely ensconced in her car, Madeline once again let out the breath she'd been holding. Her shoulders sagged back to their normal position and she mentally patted herself on the back for holding it together. Fingers crossed that was the end of it. But would it be?

Chapter Forty-Eight

"So how the hell can I tie the two ends together?" Amanda asked herself as she drove away from Madeline's house. She knew there just had to be a connection between the two incidents. Either that or Madeline Simpson was bloody unlucky and it was a coincidence – and she had to admit that stranger things had happened. Some years ago, she'd been involved in an investigation into the sudden death of the husband of a wealthy woman. He had died in the same circumstances as her first husband had – in another county. She and Jack had followed the evidence trail and looked into the old case, but everything had stacked up nicely. In the end, it had pointed squarely to bad luck, and neither the wife nor anyone else was ever charged with any wrongdoing. Gut instinct is not hard evidence, of course, and certainly doesn't stack up in a court of law. Back in the eighteenth century the courts would convict a person if they merely had a 'look' about them; there had been no need for solid evidence. Amanda thought this could have come in handy on some more recent cases she could mention. Maybe this one even. But those days were gone, and she knew she needed to come up with some solid evidence, somehow. She asked Siri to dial Jack on his mobile, and the ringing of his phone boomed out of her car's speakers.

"Yeah? What's up?"

"Jack, I've just left questioning Mrs. Simpson, again." She knew what he'd be thinking so she let him.

"I thought we'd agreed to stay clear – the 'nothing to see, move along' scenario."

"Yes, but that was before I realised she was also at James Peterson's place the night before he died. She's a book club member."

"What? Tell me more." That got him listening.

"Well, that's just it again. Nothing to tell. That night, she went as usual, like she had for the past couple of years. Said he wanted to close early, and they all left together and went home. Shortly after... well, you know the rest." She paused. "I know there has to be a connection, but what?" She could almost hear him twiddling his moustache as the car filled with silence. She let it carry on a while, waiting for him to say something.

"So what's next?" he said finally. "What are you thinking? Because as it stands, I can't see a link apart from one woman."

"Well I'll be damned if it's a coincidence," she said. "So I'm going to go through it all again, take another look at what we have, see if anything shakes a clue free. That missing landscaper has never surfaced, and he's never been seen since, but if she had something to do with that, god only knows how she got rid of his body, because apart from a few cat hairs, there was no other evidence to look at." She glanced down at her own trouser legs, which were still covered with ginger hair; that more or less explained how Dexter's hairs had ended up in Des's van – they stuck to anything and everything. That tidied up the only 'lead' they had, just as Jack had said earlier. "But one missing and one dead and one person who knew them both needs another look, in my view."

"Let's look again on Monday, then," agreed Jack. "No rush now, and I've got a golf game in thirty so I'll give it some thought. Remember, we still don't know if there is even a crime with the landscaper, and the book club man just seems to be a good night gone wrong, as the doc confirmed. I'll give it some thought, but now I'm off to enjoy some weekend. Why don't you do the same?" Without waiting for her reply, Jack disconnected.

Amanda drove back to Ruth's searching the back of her brain for any possible reason why Madeline Simpson would be involved in both cases. What was her possible motive? And how could she physically do it? A missing person and an explained death that was down to a heart condition? She had virtually nothing to go on. Was there even a case, or cases, to be solved?

Chapter Forty-Nine

LATER THAT SATURDAY MORNING, RUTH AND AMANDA CLIMBED into the car together and headed off into Croydon for something to eat before heading into the far richer shopping experience of the west end of London. Amanda found parking easily, and they walked arm in arm to 'their' coffee shop. Opening the door for Ruth, Amanda stood aside to let her enter and they headed to a side table, 'their' table, just a little way down from the front window. No mean feat on a Saturday morning.

Ruth picked up the menu, though she knew exactly what she was having. Like father, like daughter. "I'm having scrambled eggs with a side of bacon, and then I might have some of that lemon drizzle cake. And coffee."

"I say ditto to that. I'll go and order." Amanda left Ruth sitting at the little wooden table, soaking up the artisan ambience she loved so much. They'd been going there since forever ago and, even on a busy day, found it a place to relax. Amanda placed their order, then returned and sat opposite her, placing her hand on top of Ruth's and leaving it there for the world to see. Or those who might look their way, anyway. She was testing the waters and Ruth knew it, so she left her hand where it was.

"You look like you've got something you want to say." Ruth knew what was coming but didn't want to steal Amanda's thunder by pre-empting it.

"You always have been the observant one. You should have been a detective too." She smiled. "And yes, I do want to say something." She took a deep breath and ploughed on with it. "I want to meet your family. I think it's time they knew about us. We've been together for almost a year now, and, well, I think it's long overdue." Amanda sat and waited, hoping she hadn't ruined what was going to be a nice day together.

Ruth just looked at her, but she wasn't upset. "I know. And you're right."

Amanda relaxed at her words.

"They don't know, though," Ruth went on. "About me being gay. I've never told them. I'm not ashamed of what I am, or of you. It's just that it's never come up and I've just let them assume what they assume."

"I figured as much."

"Are you disappointed, Amanda, that I've never come out and told anyone?"

"No, I'm not disappointed. Probably a bit surprised, though. I mean, you've known you're gay for years. I'm just surprised it's never come up and been talked about." Ruth looked at the table; Amanda knew she had made her point. She carried on. "So how do we tell them, then? As a couple, and spring it on them? Or you tell them on your own? Because I think it's time they knew." Amanda was trying not to push, but at the same time she wanted to plough on. After nearly a year it seemed stupid to her to still have never been introduced to Ruth's family and for Ruth still to not have told them.

Ruth looked back up at her. "Look, I know it needs to be done, and I need to do it, but let me think about the best way, eh? I'm worried, how they'll react, that's all. Remember what it was like when you told your parents? How they reacted?"

Of course Amanda remembered: they hadn't spoken to her for nearly two weeks before they decided to try and understand her choices. They'd never been really close – Amanda had always been the black sheep of the family – and her revelation had just given them more ammunition for their argument that they'd gone wrong somewhere. Amanda hoped Ruth's experience would be a whole lot better.

The waitress hovered with two plates of bacon and scrambled eggs and Ruth was grateful for the distraction, but she also knew that wouldn't be the end of it. The waitress put their plates down and left them to their brunch.

Ruth carried on. "I hear you, I really do. And I will tell them. I know I have to do it. But let's enjoy our day together, and talk more about it tomorrow." She gave Amanda's hand a squeeze and left it for a long moment, her loving smile confirming her promise. Anyone interested enough to notice them together would guess rightly they were indeed a couple. And a very close couple at that.

OUTSIDE THE CAFÉ, A WOMAN WAS TUCKED AWAY BEHIND A TREE, watching their table. She had been there since they had first gone inside: both the women were familiar to her. In the back of her mind she'd always known about Ruth, but had never seen any outward signs to confirm her suspicions. It didn't bother her – why should it? But obviously it bothered Ruth. The thing that bothered Madeline the most about what she'd witnessed was not that Ruth was dating another woman, but *who* that woman was – Detective Amanda Lacey.

Chapter Fifty

MADELINE SLIPPED OUT FROM BEHIND THE TREE AND INTO THE BUSY flow of Saturday shoppers, blending in easily. Had Rebecca been with her, she'd have stood out, or rather Rebecca would have, but she was on her own. She was glad she didn't have to worry, because she didn't want Ruth to think she'd been spying on her, even though she had been, at least for a little while. The fact that Ruth was still hiding her secret made Madeline wonder why, at her age and in her situation. She no longer lived at home, so she was free to do whatever she wanted with whomever she wanted. Her concern, though, was most definitely Amanda, and purely in a selfish way. Why had Ruth never introduced her friend to her and Gordon, and did Amanda know Madeline Simpson was Ruth's stepmother? After all, she'd been to the house, sat in her lounge and interviewed her over a missing person *and* a dead person; surely she'd put two and two together?

No, she doesn't know I'm Ruth's stepmother – we have different surnames.

But the other question was more pressing: who else suspected Madeline was involved in the two incidents? After all, everyone knew that Madeline had been there at book club. Did Ruth suspect? Or Gordon? Or Rebecca? Would they put the two events together and think she was involved? Was it that simple?

Panic started somewhere inside of her, and that familiar feeling of heat building around her waist and racing up her back and chest took her over like something from *Alien*. Beads of sweat made themselves known across her forehead and cleavage, making her hair stick to her clammy skin like greasy tendrils. She had to stop walking and hold on to an empty bench while it passed. She was truly hotter and stickier than she had been all week; the worry over being found out was accelerating the temperature tantrum. Unable to push it away, she dealt with it as best she could: she bent over slightly to catch her breath and let the heat pass over her. A cold glass of water would have been useful, but no such luck out in the busy street, so she struggled on slowly until she reached M&S and the welcome blast of cold air that hit her when she entered the store. As usual, there was a chair just inside so she sat and took a moment to calm herself properly and dab her sticky face with a tissue.

A security guard who was hovering nearby had seen her struggling and made his way over to ask if she was okay.

"Yes," she lied, fanning herself with the tissue. She thanked him for his concern and he smiled and went back to his post. He had caring eyes and a pierced ear with a single diamond stud.

Funny the things you notice.

From the chair, as she focused on calming herself, she could see the busy shoppers – the children with their parents, the elderly with their children now grown, and those who were shopping alone, like her – and wondered if they lived alone, or if they had someone to look after them when they needed it. She felt a pang of sadness and her eyes filled with tears.

Steady on, Madeline. Don't lose it here in the lobby of M&S, for God's sake.

When the temperature tantrum had fully passed some ten minutes later and she didn't resemble a sweating beetroot anymore, Madeline stood up slowly and headed for the food hall and a cold carton of juice. If she was going to get something nice for Gordon's birthday next week, which was the purpose of this shopping trip, she couldn't sit there all day. He'd gone to watch Crystal Palace play Spurs at home. He'd be most of the day, stopping for a pint afterwards with some of the other season ticket holders that he'd met up with. They'd been doing it for as long as she could remember. A bit of 'bonding time' was a good thing for him and the other men; it was not just a girly pastime. She was all for Gordon's days out, and he looked forward to the games too, especially if The Eagles, their nickname, were picked to win. A win always meant he'd pick up a celebratory bar of chocolate on his way home – all for Madeline.

Leaving M&S and the glorious coolness of the store, she headed back out into the sunshine, hoping she didn't bump into anyone she knew.

Chapter Fifty-One

Aside from the temperature tantrum, seeing Ruth and Amanda together, and the subsequent panic attack, Madeline had had a nice morning shopping and had picked out a lovely shirt out as a birthday present for Gordon – well, Madeline thought it was lovely anyway. Hopefully he'd wear it – what do you get the man who doesn't ever want anything, doesn't collect anything and, apart from football at Crystal Palace, doesn't really do anything? Every gift-gifting occasion was fraught with danger and dread for her, and this one had been no different. Still, he could change it if he wanted to.

Mission accomplished, she headed to a café for lunch on her own. She was knackered, and she thought a nice meal and some tea would soothe her mangled nerves. And she wanted some time on her own to think about the possibility of Amanda being in her life a bit more – a lot more – than she could cope with right now. Would she forever be looking over her shoulder if she was?

"I'll have the quiche with salad, please, a scone, and a pot of Earl Grey tea." The pretty young waitress, whose name badge read 'Anna,' took her order and gave her a number stuck on a table-sized pitchfork that looked like it could wound someone quite badly given the chance. With weapons of mass destruction on every table, Madeline bet no one upset the staff intentionally. Taking pitchfork number 14, she found a table for two in the corner. Tables for one didn't really exist, and the odd one that did generally faced the wall. And who wants to face the wall?

An hour later, and with a full-to-bursting stomach topped up with tea, Madeline turned into Sainsbury's, her last job before returning home. After yesterday's news and then going out for dinner, the weekly shop had been missed, meaning it still had to be done and not just forgotten. There was no getting away from it. The car park was jammed, and she felt her hackles rising again. If she hated Sainsbury's on a Friday, she hated it even more on a Saturday. She didn't even try to find a space near the door but instead drove straight to the back of the car park and grabbed one of the last spaces well away from the rest of civilisation.

"Let's make this quick and uneventful," she mumbled to herself, and set off with a smile plastered on her face. The only positive was it would be cool inside. She found an abandoned trolley and pushed it towards the main entrance. All clear so far. After finding the list that was floating around inside her bag, she headed towards the first aisle. It looked like Christmas Eve inside: people jostling, trolleys piled high with food like it was the Apocalypse tomorrow and no one had told her, but she kept calm, head down, determined to get out again in one piece – both physically and mentally.

Twenty minutes later, she ticked the last items off her list as she popped them into her trolley. She had quite a pile of groceries, so there was no point going through the self-serve checkout. Plastering her smile onto her face once more, she made her way to the shortest queue with a human cashier to play a game of 'how-long-will-it-take-her-to-ask-for-my-Nectar-card.' The answer to that question, when she started on her purchases, was precisely fifteen seconds – hardly time for the woman to say the obligatory "Hello, had a nice day?" It all sort of rolled into one long sentence, like she'd followed her training to the letter and was getting everything she needed to say out in one fell swoop so she could then fall silent for the rest of the transaction. To her credit, thought Madeline, she did it effortlessly and deserved a gold star for her name badge.

Transaction completed, Madeline steered her trolley back into the hot sun and the waiting hot car, hoping the ice cream she'd bought would make it home as a solid, not a liquid. But as she came in sight of her car, she realised with a sinking heart that it wasn't going to be as straightforward as she'd hoped.

"Ah, hell!" she exclaimed, exasperated. In the distance she could see her car, and could also see that the car on the driver's side had parked so close to the door that even Rebecca would have had difficulty getting in. She'd been left with about nine inches of space to try and shimmy into the car.

"You inconsiderate git!" she yelled, and quickly closed the remaining distance to her car. Her blood boiling, she stood behind it, now, and could see that he (because it had to be a "he") had parked well over the white line, encroaching in her space. She stumped round to the other side of the car. It wasn't much better there: that car had parked right on the line, so Madeline had a tiny bit more than nine inches on the right. Probably ten at best.

"For heaven's sake!" she yelled up to the sky. A couple of youths sniggered at her as they passed her on their way back to their own car; they had enough beer in their trolley to sink – or hopefully crash – the old banger they were about to drive off in. Madeline flicked them the bird, all class, and they returned the gesture with a collective "Oooh!" followed by another collective laugh. She felt stupid, and bloody angry, so she turned away and considered what to do. Even if she could put the groceries in the boot, how was she supposed to get in? Climb over the back seats and shimmy into the driver's seat, arse in the air as she went? It wasn't looking hopeful.

Hands on her hips, she took in the worst offending car, the one closest to her driver's-side door. It was completely covered in stickers, like they were holding the whole knackered vehicle together. An old coat hanger was wedged in for an aerial where a proper aerial had once been, and from what she could see, the old jalopy had four dangerously worn-down tyres. It wasn't a car you'd feel safe taking a ride in, and you wouldn't want to come across it on the road either.

Don't people realise how irresponsible it is to drive on bald tyres, whatever the weather?

She made a note of the vehicle's registration plate to report it to the police, anonymously of course, feeling it was her duty as a good citizen. Death traps like that shouldn't be on the road, she harrumphed inwardly. If it hurt anyone, she'd never forgive herself for not acting.

Turning back to the problem at hand, she decided there was nothing else for it. She had to climb in through the boot 'à la arse-in-the-air' – or risk losing the ice cream forever. Madeline took a quick survey around, hitched her skirt up around her waist, exposing her ample hosiery-clad thighs, and began to struggle into her car, hoping a bored security guard watching the CCTV monitors somewhere wasn't having a good old laugh at her expense as her big lilac undies filled his screen.

Chapter Fifty-Two

WEEK 7
Monday

EVERY SIX OR SEVEN WEEKS MADELINE'S OFFICE-EQUIPMENT workplace was graced by the presence of Jordan, a sales rep. He would call in to see Stanley, Madeline's boss, and she couldn't stand him. He was a lot of a creep, not a bit of one, and even though she'd shown her distaste at his leering, he persisted. Deidre got her share of it too. While it was nice to get appreciative looks from the opposite sex once in a while, they didn't count from Jordan. Stanley, being an older man and from a time when 'male bonding' involved some good old-fashioned sexist comments and bottom pinching, thought good old Jordan was a bit of a hoot, and didn't see that his behaviour was offensive to the women, never mind against sexual-harassment legislation. There was really no point in bothering with a grievance, Madeline knew. Either you stayed and worked with it or you took another job elsewhere. As Madeline quite liked the job and the hours, she got on with it and just kept her head down when Jordan was due to visit.

The click of the kettle switch said the water had boiled, so Madeline poured it onto a Lady Grey tea bag in the pot and waited for it to steep a little. The light, fragrant aroma of bergamot drifted up to her nostrils as she stood gazing out of the little back office window. The view was nothing more than the silvery-grey tiled roofs of other offices and industrial buildings, and the tracks of the railway line that sped folks into Victoria Station or back the other way and to the south. It wasn't dreary, exactly; it just wasn't particularly nice, but it was typical of life on the outskirts of South London. The saving grace of the view today was the deep blue sky that once again stretched as far as the eye could see, making everything look ten times better than it did on a rainy day, even though it was the same view. Even the worst places on earth looked better when the sun shone.

She poured the tea and added a dash of milk then grabbed three chocolate digestives from the packet before putting it back in the little fridge. She stuffed a whole one straight into her mouth and hurriedly tried to eat it all before she got back to her desk, making it seem as though she'd only had two biscuits. Deidre and Stanley both knew her trick, however, so the only person she was fooling was herself. And her waistline wasn't particularly happy with it either.

At 9.55, the familiar sound of car tyres on the gravel car park could be heard through the small open office window, and both Deidre and Madeline knew what it signalled: the slimy git would be making his way through the front door at any second. He didn't disappoint. They could smell the tsunami of cologne before the door was even shut behind him. Noses wrinkled; Deidre and Madeline exchanged knowing glances but said nothing. A loud over-the-top voice broke the peace with its exuberance.

"Morning all. Cracker of a day, isn't it?" Jordan's fixed, cheesy smile stretched across his face like it had been painted on, clown fashion. He always wore his dark hair slicked back like Gordon Gekko in *Wall Street*, as though he fancied himself Gekko mark 11, but he never wore a tie, meaning his top shirt button was always open, with dark wisps of hair spilling out like a burst pre-war cushion. He was, however, always full of the joys of spring and positive minded, and extremely popular with kids when it came to the local astronomy event he'd started and now organised every summer. He could be a very generous individual with his time and money, but he was also generous with his leering – something most women didn't much care for. Jordan was single.

He needed a greeting so Madeline obliged. "Morning, Jordan. Can I get you a cup of tea or coffee?"

It was always left to Madeline to sort guests' drinks out, so she just got on with it.

"Tea's fine, thanks. Anything else on offer, gorgeous? You're looking as edible as usual." His suggestive wink and the slimy clicking of his always moist-looking mouth turned her stomach.

God, does he ever have any luck getting a woman with those chat-up lines? Surely no one falls for them?

Walking away before her stomach rolled again, she flipped over her shoulder, "I'll bring you a couple of digestives if you're that hungry." She went to put the kettle back on, mumbling, "Pity there wasn't some rat poison under the sink. That might put the brakes on his innuendos and sexist comments." But really, she had had her fill of poisoning people. It was causing her too much stress.

While the kettle boiled, she grabbed the packet of biscuits back out of the fridge, hurriedly crammed another one into her own mouth and placed two more on a small plate for His Highness. Stanley never ate biscuits or drank tea or coffee, only water, so this little 'breaking of bread' was all for Jordan.

"My chocolate-demanding hormones must be particularly active today," she muttered with a half-full mouth, dropping crumbs all over the floor. When the tea was ready, she put it all on a tray with a fresh glass of water for Stanley and took it downstairs to his office.

Jordan was already sitting in front of Stanley's desk, deep in conversation, so she put the tray down and handed the water to Stanley. As she leant over, her leg accidentally brushed Jordan's knee. He slammed the brakes on his conversation immediately, changing his face from businessman back to the painted clown smile. Madeline nearly puked as their eyes met for a second.

"Sorry!" she stammered, but it was too late. His hand rubbed up her calf and towards her knee in quick-smart time. To her chagrin, she found herself screaming in surprise and bolting for the door like a frightened schoolgirl. The sound of the men's high-pitched laughter followed her out, laughter at her expense, and she closed the door behind her with a thud. Heart racing, and suppressing a shiver of revulsion, she took a moment to calm herself before she fled back to the safe sanctuary of her desk.

"What has he done now?" Deidre said in alarm. "I heard you scream and you look like you've had a fright."

"Slimy git stroked my sodding leg!" Madeline sputtered, now well and truly pissed off. "He's gone too far this time and Stanley doesn't sodding care – thinks it's so funny. I'm getting sick of it," she shouted, raising her voice loud enough for everyone to hear. Her pulse was racing hard as she sat back in her chair, trying to calm herself down again. Sweat beads were forming on her upper lip, yet again.

"You know, Madeline, he really is a dirty pervert, that guy," Deidre grumbled. "I don't know why Stanley rates him, and I don't know why we have to put up with him." Deidre had also had her fair share of his lecherous advances.

"One day he'll get his comeuppance – you mark my words," Madeline said, and meant it. "I know he does some good stuff with the kids, but for the sake of all womankind, he needs to stop being such a sodding letchy pervert. I can see why he's never got a steady girlfriend. Who'd want to get close enough? Nice car and nice house or not."

Madeline gazed out of the office window towards the car park and wondered what that comeuppance would be. How could she teach him a lesson and piss him off – but without killing him? She'd had enough of killing people. The sky was still an incredible blue outside, but in the distance a few clouds were just visible. She saw them –and the start of another plan.

Feeling a little calmer, she asked casually, "Any idea what the weather forecast is going to be over the next day or two, Deidre? We could do with some rain."

"My roses are desperate for a good drink. The watering can is never as good as the real stuff from the clouds. I do believe they have forecast rain the day after tomorrow for most of the afternoon. It's the kids' cricket tournament, so I suppose it could be called off. A shame, really. And it's also the day of that astronomy fair thing that slimy git gets involved in."

Bugger, and my day off as well. What a shame indeed.

But she now had an idea of how to give Gekko II a spot of inconvenience, and get his stupid slicked-back hair wet at the same time. His car was parked at the far end of the little car park under one of the shady trees. She knew it couldn't be seen from Stanley's office so, leaving her desk, she went outside and walked over. His car really was beautiful, she thought as she approached – a navy-blue F-Type Jaguar, a two-seater sports car no less, that fitted exactly with his greased-back hair and expensive cologne. The beautiful leather interior with the familiar feline jumping cat logo on the centre of the steering wheel reminded you of the luxury brand you were driving, in case you happened to forget. It really was beautiful and something she didn't want to damage, but *she* didn't actually need to. But *he* could. And would.

Moving around to the front of the car, which was mostly shaded by the tree's branches, she leant across the windscreen and lifted the wiper arm away from the glass. She slid the rubber blade off the arm and then did the same with the other side. They came off easily in her hands and she gently replaced the now-naked arms back on the windscreen. To look at them, you would never know anything was missing. But when the rain came and Slimy Git turned the wipers on, well, that would be a different story. She sniggered at the thought of what would happen. His windscreen would need replacing from the damage, sure, but the inconvenience of having no wiper blades when it rained would be far worse. And he'd have no clue where or when the rubbers had been lost. Or taken, in this case. That should wipe his cheesy clown smile off his face, and it would be Madeline smiling come Wednesday afternoon when it poured down.

She wondered exactly where he would be when her latest little plan took effect.

Chapter Fifty-Three

ON HER WAY HOME FROM WORK THAT EVENING, MADELINE WAS driving back down Purley Way towards home when a car pulled out of a junction up ahead. There was nothing to note about the style of driving – it wasn't erratic or anything like that – but what did pique her attention was what the car looked like. It was the same sticker-covered old blue car with the coat-hanger aerial that had jammed her in at Sainsbury's on Saturday afternoon.

She grunted to herself in disgust, remembering how she'd been forced to enter her car via the boot, and the youths who had watched in delight, pointing and hooting, as she'd hitched her skirt up and displayed her ample thighs and her Bridget Jones–style M&S lavender-coloured undies for all the world, or at least all of the car park, to see. Those lavender undies were now in the wheelie bin by the garage, never to be worn again. If only she could throw that part of her brain in the wheelie bin too.

The Blue Stickered Car indicated left now, and Madeline, freshly enraged, decided to follow, keeping a little distance, but interested to see if the owner lived locally. A short detour wouldn't be a problem. It was Monday, and Sunday leftovers for dinner would be an easy meal to prepare. The blue car turned right and she followed. In fact, she followed it all the way home, which as it happened was only three or four miles away. It turned into Sanderson Road and pulled up outside a mid-terraced house. Madeline pulled up a bit further on, not wanting to be seen. With the motor still running, Madeline watched to see who was driving the car and where they lived. She wasn't surprised to see a middle-aged man, quite unkempt-looking, get out and head up an equally unkempt garden path. Would he knock or did he live there, she wondered? He pulled his keys from his pocket and opened the front door.

"So, I've gotcha," she said to herself triumphantly. "There's no escaping me, you ignorant sod. You caused me too much embarrassment to let this slip. I've just got to decide on your penance: should it be harsher than your original crime, or just something to teach you a bloody lesson?"

Thinking about James, she decided she needed to err on the side of caution. "But you're certainly not getting away scot-free," she spluttered into the rear-view mirror as he closed his front door.

There was nothing to be gained by staying parked outside, and she was melting in the still very warm sun anyway, so she made her way back home, thinking about how best to get back at him and get that heap of junk with its four bald tyres off the road at the same time. It was later on, while she was doing the dishes and cleaning the kitchen down and Gordon was watching the soccer game he'd recorded, that the answer came to her. Quickly, she Googled it on her phone to double-check it would work then closed the page and deleted the browser history just in case. Now she had to put the plan into action.

Chapter Fifty-Four

Tuesday

From @Stargazer, So the guy who rolled his van last week on the Wickham road has died. Complications from an infection, I believe. #droppinglikeflies

@Stargazer, That's not good news, and a reminder to wear a seatbelt, I guess.

@Jaybaby, Yes, and something should be done about that bend. It's a known blackspot. #needsattention

@Stargazer, Any idea what the complications were that killed him?

@Jaybaby, Yeh, my mum is a nurse on his ward, and said it was infection in the shoulder wound after getting it set. Didn't respond to antibiotics. #superbug

@Stargazer, Seems a little extreme?

@Jaybaby, Had undiagnosed diabetes too, to help complicate things. Boils the size of saucers apparently. And he was massively overweight too. Puts strain on your body.

@Stagazer, Shit! #betterdiet

From @Inwonder to @Stagazer, Wow! Sad news. Didn't know him, but he had a broken collarbone and some bruises, I'd read.

Hi @Inwonder, You well? Not seen you on here for a few days.

@Stargazer, Snowed under with work. #busybusy

@Inwonder, Yep, another one bites the dust. Who'd have thought it would end like that for him? #Lifeisshort

From @Jaybaby, Buckle up all. Changing the subject. Any news on catching the groper? #groperman

From @Inwonder, Not heard of him being caught, but I heard about another attack last night. Someone every week. Playing fields this time. Too close to home!

@Inwonder, Holy shit! Female I assume? She okay?

@Jaybaby, Believe so to both. Scared her shitless. #Mustbehorrid

@Inwonder and @Stagazer, You ladies take care out there until this fucker is caught. #Getthefucker

From @Benj to @Jaybaby, Watch your language, buddy. Public forum and all.

@Benj, Sorry mate. It worries me, that's all.

@Jaybaby, I hear you. They'll nab him soon. He's bound to make a mistake.

@Benj, Fingers crossed. I hear someone's swiping washing, mainly ladies' underwear. Connected? #Pervert

From @Inwonder to @Jaybaby, I reckon that's pranksters. Wouldn't want mine. #Neednewundies

@Inwonder, Thanks for sharing that with the world!

@Jaybaby, You are so welcome. If you're offering to buy...

@Inwonder, Nah, strapped for cash as always. Keep dreamin'.

@Jaybaby, Off to read now. Goodnight.

@Inwonder, Stay safe and sweet dreams.

BENJAMIN, THE MODERATOR, SMILED AT THE BANTER THE TWO OF them had developed over the recent weeks. Jason and Alice – Jaybaby and Inwonder – were two opinionated and active voices on The Daisy Chain, and he often sat back to watch and listen, though he'd take what Jason said with a pinch of salt. His over-exuberance was well known – and better than TV any day. Benjamin hated having to wade in and remind Jason to watch his language, even though he agreed with the sentiment, but bad language was not tolerated and, as moderator, he had to keep control. He sat, thoughtful. So the van driver had died and there had been another groper attack last night. What a sad state of affairs. The attacks were getting more regular, and the frightening thing was that no one ever saw anything, and no one could ever give much of a description. Apart from 'male, fifties and balding,' which meant he could be one of hundreds of thousands of men. The clock on the top right corner of his Mac said 10.30 pm. Time to log out and get some sleep.

Chapter Fifty-Five

"So, are we all complete? Everything organised?" Jordan asked his friend Brian.

"All set, Jordan, all set. We just need the weather to be kind to us for the outdoor stuff, so fingers crossed." Brian was the main organiser of the event. It was an annual thing: the kids would work hard on an astronomy project all through the summer holidays, and then, before they all went back to school after their long summer break, they would hold an exhibition and festival in the school hall and the surrounding grounds. There were stalls and raffles and bouncy castles and food vans. Over the last few years it had become quite a big part of the local social calendar. Other schools now took part, which had converted it into more of a local derby challenge, with public schools trying to beat the private ones. It had started off as a bit of fun, and something to help occupy the kids during their holiday time off, but the beast had grown – in a good way. And Jordan, who was the founder, was now the judge of the competition. He'd been fascinated for years with the moon and stars and everything that floated up there, and had been running this program, his brainchild, for the last ten years. This year was to be a celebration of that milestone. He had wanted young idle holiday minds to learn and create rather than wander the streets and get into bother. It was a shame he wasn't as thoughtful about women as he was about the children he encouraged.

"Right, then. I'll lock up. It looks great in there, doesn't it? A job well done, Brian. Thanks for all your help with it. Tremendous achievement." And he slapped Brian squarely and good-naturedly on his back. Brian lunged forward a little at the force but smiled anyway.

"Steady on, Jordan,. You don't know your own strength. Does look great, though, eh? I wonder who'll win it this year. There are some top-notch entries in there. You have a favourite?"

"Ah, can't catch me out like that," Jordan said, touching the side of his nose in a 'not telling, don't be nosey' manner. "My lips are sealed."

If only they'd stay that way. Jordan had a way with folks that they either loved or loathed, mostly depending on their gender. He was harmless enough, but most women gave him a wide berth; his humour was a bit off for most women's liking. Men, on the other hand, thought he was a 'Jack-the-lad,' a fun bloke to be around. He told jokes to make your hair curl, and dressed like he'd walked straight out of Wall Street rather than South Croydon. As long as you kept him away from your wife or girlfriend, there was never any harm done.

"Fancy a quick pint before you go on? We might catch the end of a match of something if we get going. What do you say?" Brian asked.

"I say yes. Why the hell not, old boy. That was thirsty work in anyone's book – don't mind if I do!" Jordan twanged the braces of his trousers like Charlie Chaplin, and spoke in a voice far older than his years. To others he often sounded a bit upper-class, and many wondered if he had been born into his money or had indeed earned it – on Wall Street. Few knew much about the smaller details of his life except that he was single, lived in a nice secluded house that was run by his housekeeper, and drove a great-looking Jaguar. Some suspected he was lonely; some never gave him a second thought. Jordan, being Jordan, didn't notice either way.

"I'll drive us, Brian, and then I'll drop you back at home if you like. Get in." As they approached the beautiful sleek navy-blue F-Type Jaguar two-seater sports car, Brian admired it openly.

"What a thing of beauty."

"She is, isn't she? And never a cross word out of her," Jordan said, chuckling. "Not much fun to pinch her bottom, though. A bit too firm for my liking." He roared at his own joke, throwing his head back and laughing up to the sky. Brian, well aware of what Jordan was like, smiled and shook his head at his friend and slipped into the passenger side. The soft leather interior of the sports seat wrapped around him like a blanket.

"It fits me perfectly, Jordan. It's like it was made for me."

"It fits everyone perfectly, Brian, but you're welcome to be its owner until I get you home if it pleases you. Choose something from the playlist, buddy, and we'll let our hair down on the way. It's such a great day."

Brian queued Moby, and 'Extreme Ways' pulsed from the top-of-the-range sound system; the sound was crystal clear. Jordan slipped the roof down as they pulled out of the car park, and his greased-back hair started to blow a little around the slick edges. Jordan hadn't been lying when he'd said they'd let their hair down, though Brian's comb-over blowing wildly wasn't what he'd had in mind. Still, the guy was happy just to be sitting in his car, and when they pulled up in the pub car park a couple of minutes later, heads turned to see who was arriving. Brian scrambled to mend his tangled, wispy hair as they headed inside for a pint – a few steps behind Mr. Confident.

Chapter Fifty-Six

THE ONLY WAY MADELINE COULD MAKE SURE GORDON STAYED asleep while she slipped out was to give him one of her sleeping tablets. He'd taken the odd one before when stress from work had kept him awake at nights, so she knew he was okay taking one. It was just that usually he *knew* when he'd taken one. This time, however, with a whole pill crushed up and mixed with the filling of blackberry pie and covered with whipped cream, he'd never noticed it. But he was certainly feeling it.

Funny that.

He was sleeping it off in his chair in the lounge. The recorded football game had ended long ago without being seen, apart from the first ten minutes. Liverpool had beat Arsenal at home 4–3. Pity he'd missed it; it would have been an exciting game.

For her latest plan to work, she needed to be quick so as not to be seen and raise questions, which was why she had waited until dusk and was wearing one of Gordon's old football caps with her hair tucked up. Stashed in her car was the necessary equipment to do the job, as well as the materials for plan B should she need them. She set off back to Sanderson Road and retribution. With not much traffic on the road, it was only a few minutes away. She parked a few yards away to watch the house from a distance for a while to gauge things, like whether anybody was home. The Blue Stickered Car was still parked out front, just where it had been earlier, and the front room light was on inside the mid-terraced house; the curtains were still open. That didn't trouble her: with the lights on inside the house, its occupants would have difficulty seeing what was going on outside. Obviously closed curtains would have been ideal, but beggars couldn't be choosers. It was now or never.

"Come on, girl. Get it done and get back home. Gordon might need the bloody loo and wake up." Madeline found comfort in talking to herself; she always knew to listen but rarely answered back. Pulling her cap a bit further down for good measure, she slipped out of the car, grabbed the diesel canister from behind the driver's seat and walked casually across the road, watching for movement and prying eyes. Nothing. The Blue Stickered Car loomed, all the crappy stickers giving it an odd glow, and close up in the dusk it looked even worse than she remembered. Luckily the petrol cap was on the road side, meaning she could pour and monitor the houses at the same time. As the car was old, the petrol cap didn't lock, so Madeline didn't need to force it. In seconds, she was tipping the diesel canister up and letting the fuel rush down the nozzle and down into the tank. For her plan to work, she needed the tank to be nearly empty, or at least only half full, and judging by the amount of diesel going in, her wish had come true.

When her canister was empty, she quickly fixed the Blue Stickered Car's fuel cap back into place and walked back to her own car, checking her surroundings as she went. Her heart was beating hard in her chest and she was sweating like a race horse; the cap covering her head was not helping. She placed the empty diesel canister back in the boot. She hadn't needed plan B, a bottle of bleach, which, had the Blue Stickered Car's petrol tank been full, she'd have added instead for maximum damage. From her research, she knew that diesel fuel in a petrol engine would do a great job of screwing up the filters and engine. Bleach would have done a more corrosive and longer-lasting job, but Madeline didn't want him to suspect sabotage. She just wanted to teach him a lesson, and set him wondering how he'd managed to put diesel fuel in his tank...

Back in the driver's seat, she scanned again for twitching curtains and nosey neighbours but all was quiet. She'd just started the engine and was all set to go when she saw a man leave his house a couple of doors along and walk down the front path. Not only had the movement caught her eye, but the way he was dressed was all wrong for a warm evening. The hat and coat he wore looked like a disguise, like he was trying to hide something, a bit like Madeline had been doing only moments earlier. But where was this man going? From her vantage point she watched as he turned towards the park, his outline looking creepy in the orange glow from the streetlights. There was something familiar about him. Madeline put her car in gear and cruised slowly past him, and did a double-take as she recognised him.

It was Grey Man, and she now knew where he lived.

Chapter Fifty-Seven

Wednesday

"Morning, gorgeous." Amanda leaned in and dropped a quick peck on the top of Ruth's damp head. Ruth had been out for her run and was already back and showered, deeply engrossed in the crossword puzzle, her scrunched-up brows telling Amanda she was struggling with another clue. "You stuck?"

"Morning, and yes, I am. Nothing seems to makes sense this morning, and I'm stuck with three of them, can you believe. I've not been so stuck for a long time. It's not usually this hard."

Amanda put a capsule in the coffee machine and the fresh pungent smell permeated the kitchen. "You want another coffee or some toast put in the toaster?

"Yes please to both. Might clear my foggy brain. It's either me, or the puzzle setters at the paper have done the dirty and printed one for much more intellectual people than me." Ruth knew she was sounding a bit whiney and petulant, but she hated being beaten at anything.

Amanda could hear it in her voice and smiled knowingly. Ruth just needed to forget it; it was only a silly crossword.

"What do you want to do this evening?" Ruth asked her. "Fancy the movies in town, some pizza beforehand? We've not been to the movies since the last 007 film, and that's some time ago. And I fancy pizza too. What do you say?"

"Sounds good," Amanda said, buttering toast and handing a piece to Ruth. "Let's not even look what's on and go and sit through something random just for fun. Sort of a little adventure. What do you reckon?"

"I'd rather know beforehand, but if that's what you want to do, we can do that. In fact, if you want a night of adventure, then I suggest we order a pizza that we've never eaten before – a whole evening of new tastes. And we should add drinks to that too: we can't order what we normally have. It has to be something different. Agreed?"

Ruth was smiling at the idea and Amanda smiled back, giving her a buttery grin as she chewed her toast. "Deal. You're on. That should be fun. Let's hook up later and confirm the time a bit closer when we know what we've both got going on. But right now, I need to get showered and out of here pronto." She headed off upstairs, the last piece of toast between her fingers.

Ruth turned back to her newspaper and quickly scanned the rest of it. All quiet on the news front: nothing of any note to report. She stood up and put it with the recycling under the sink.

It occurred to her as she took the used pod out of the coffee machine that they weren't a particularly environmentally friendly product – how many millions of plastic coffee pods were there in landfills across the globe? "Perhaps we should find an alternative," she muttered to herself, and headed upstairs to blow-dry her hair into something a little more presentable. She had a big meeting that afternoon with Liberty and every detail counted.

Chapter Fifty-Eight

THE CARNIVAL ATMOSPHERE ALWAYS EXCITED HIM. AS OLD AND grown up as he was, Jordan was still a big kid at heart, and that was one reason he enjoyed the astronomy event. To watch the eyes of the kids light up when their work won a prize or when they saw the mechanics and technology they'd worked on transform into a robot or a game was priceless, and he wondered if some of the creations would ever get to market in some form. How cool that would be for a youngster? Indeed, Jordan had himself tried to make a couple of the games he'd seen fly, but he wasn't a developer and didn't have the right contacts – yet.

He checked his watch and adjusted its strap nervously. Even in casual clothes he looked like someone straight out of *GQ* magazine. There wasn't a hair out of place on his slicked-back head, and he had just the right amount of cologne on, he thought. Suede loafers, starched chinos and a Ralph Lauren polo shirt completed the 'I've got money' look. A casual onlooker would say he just needed a cravat to finish it off with, something Jordan had indeed contemplated but had decided against. It was a kids' event, after all, albeit a serious one.

He jogged lightly down the stairs, grabbed his keys and wallet and headed out to the garage and his beloved Jag. As he waited for the garage door to fully open, he could see the dark grey clouds gathering in the sky in the distance. While it was still hot and sunny at the moment, rain was definitely in the forecast. He desperately hoped it held off until after the event. The ignition fired, the deep rumble of his V6 engine sounding like a big cat raring to go, and he let it throb for a moment. Jordan loved his car and was just in the mood to open her engine up a bit, let some of that 340 horsepower out and crank the speed. Smiling to himself, he checked his watch again.

"Sod it, I've got a few spare. Let's take a spin, baby!"

Grinning in anticipation, he turned left out of his driveway instead of right, away from the school. The only place where he could give the Jag some throttle was the bypass, and that was where he headed, hoping there'd be no police cars or cameras around. The sound system was a clear as always, Guns N' Roses bouncing out of his perfectly tuned speakers as he headed in the wrong direction for a quick burst of pleasure. He pressed the accelerator gently and the engine took the hint, clicking past 80 then 90 mph. He pressed her to 100 and sang along with Axl Rose. For ten whole minutes he enjoyed the uninterrupted speed until the clock on his dashboard told him playtime was nearly over. But it was the first splashes of rain and the arrival of the dark clouds that dampened his spirits.

"Ah, bollocks," he exclaimed, slowing the car down, making a turn to head over to the school at a more leisurely pace. The drops came heavier and faster, and it was only when he turned his wipers on that he realised he had a problem. As rain started to pelt the windscreen, the wipers, for some reason, weren't clearing the water away as they usually did. What *was* happening, though, was the empty metal arms were dragging over the windscreen, and screws that should have been holding rubber blades in place were gouging into the glass, making one hell of a noise. And deep scratches.

"What the hell?!" The rain was a monsoon now, and Jordan no choice but to pull over. He came to a standstill on the shoulder and sat thinking for a moment. If he got out now he'd most certainly get drenched to the skin, but he was running out of time. If he didn't fix the problem soon, he wouldn't be judging anything, so he had no choice: he'd have to get out and take a closer look. Remembering the umbrella behind his seat, he grabbed it and opened the door to investigate the problem in the bouncing rain. He pulled the closest wiper arm away from the windscreen to take a closer look and with a sickening feeling he realised the rubber blade was gone. He reached for the other wiper arm; same deal there. The scratches on the glass glared back at him through the deluge.

"What?" Water poured relentlessly down his scalp as he stood, stunned, beside his wounded baby.

The only explanation he could think of was that someone had stolen the rubber blades, probably for a joke. But who would do such a thing? And why?

"What a damn mean-spirited thing to do!" he shouted into the rain. Traffic swished by, not paying him any attention. His pressed chinos and fancy loafers were now saturated. Getting back into his car, he took out his phone and called the Automobile Association to rescue him. They'd be there in an hour. He wasn't going anywhere soon. He thumped the steering wheel with all his might and screamed, "No, damn you!" at the top of his voice. No one heard him.

Chapter Fifty-Nine

Thursday

From @Stargazer, Who went to the astronomy competition? Shame about the rain.

@Stargazer from @McRuth, I did. Some very cool stuff, and yes, pity about the rain. You see anything really interesting?

@McRuth, Definitely. Some of the students are way out there with their tech knowledge – out of this world, literally. #wishiwas

@Stargazer, Puts us older gen to shame, eh?

@McRuth, Ah, but we have life experience. Can't complain. Judging was very late this year? You know why?

@Stargazer, Yes, @Belfort had car trouble. Some lowlife swiped his wiper blades. #nogoodintherain

@McRuth, I bet those car vandals are having a laugh. #toerags

@Stargazer and @McRuth from @Belfort, Evening all. Just saw the ping and the thread. I was hacked off. Tremendous damage. #newwindscreen If I catch them...

@Belfort, Don't blame you. Gorgeous car too.

@Stargazer, Yes, and thanks. Take you for a spin one of these days, eh?

@Belfort, Oh, how exciting! Yes please!

Ruth watched the conversation carry on for a few more minutes without taking part any further. She was well aware of Jordan's, aka @Belfort's reputation and his great-looking Jag, though @Stargazer, Lorna, appeared not to have heard about him – though she was married anyway. Although that definitely wouldn't stop @Belfort from perving on her. And she knew from her time moderating the site who the dominant characters were and who were the followers – Lorna, a regular nice woman, fell into the latter category. She hoped Lorna never experienced Jordan in the flesh, so to speak. Jordan, being Jordan, had chosen @Belfort as his online handle after Jordan Belfort, the main character in *The Wolf of Wall Street*. It fitted him perfectly. Lorna's handle, @Stargazer, fitted her perfectly too.

Ruth sat looking at her screen, thrumming the table in thought. She was sure Madeline had mentioned Jordan a couple of weeks back but couldn't quite remember what she'd said. No matter. Probably nothing.

Chapter Sixty

Friday

The funeral was today, Friday, at 2 pm, at the crematorium following a service at Purley Baptist Church, then on for refreshments. Madeline was still undecided whether to go or not. It wasn't that she didn't *want* to go and pay her respects; she just didn't want to meet up with the damn police if they were there, particularly Detective Lacey, or as Madeline now knew her secretly, Amanda, Ruth's partner. Did Amanda know that she was Ruth's stepmother? As far as Madeline was aware she hadn't made any connection, but how could she know for sure? Not wishing to risk it, and unwilling to hide in the bushes and watch the service from a distance, she had voted to stay home. Gordon had gone off to work. He'd offered to attend with her, which was sweet of him, but if she wasn't even sure about going, there was little point him taking time out for it.

I did kill him, after all.

Stirring a sugar into her coffee, she gazed out of the kitchen window. The light rain made the garden gloomy; the grey sky was thick with drizzle. Drizzle was so pointless and depressing.

"Just get on and rain, then sod off again, would you?" she demanded at the window and beyond. The Great Orange Machine was still in the garden, just where it had been left, and it taunted Madeline every time she looked out, like some sort of penance for the bad deed and the secret that lay beneath it. Water dripped off its bucket and its caterpillar wheels and coursed down its metallic orange carcass, and it seemed even more vibrant in colour, like a fresh navel orange. Dexter often sat on it and she knew he knew her secret; he'd been there that day, watching. And she suspected just what he was saying to himself when he looked her way. *Murdering bitch.* But that was over and done with. She hadn't really set out to kill Des, of course, though who knew what she thought she was doing when she raised the spade and whacked him? It was just that some days her anger and frustration went through the roof at the flick of a switch, and that day the switch had been the telephone bill. And then the cheeky bugger had tried to put his price up, so she'd whacked him. And buried him. Seemed the right thing to do at the time.

Sid's Transport couldn't get there soon enough for Madeline's liking. She'd rung them straight after Amanda had left last week, but the Great Orange Machine was still standing in place, annoying the hell out of her. They promised to pick it up as soon as they could, but wanted to know who was going to pay for its removal.

How the hell should I know? It's not my sodding machine.

Eating the last two chocolate biscuits, she sipped her coffee, still dwelling on whether to go to the funeral or not. The kitchen clock said it was 10.30 am, so there was still plenty of time to decide.

"I'll go if it stops raining by twelve pm," she said to her coffee mug. "If it's still raining then, I'm not going. That seems like a fair decider." The rain wouldn't make one ounce of difference to whether the police were there or not, but Madeline had to decide somehow.

Chapter Sixty-One

SHE WAS STILL IN THE KITCHEN AN HOUR LATER. PONDERING. Madeline watched the rain drip off the gutters and droplets run down the windows. It made her start to think a bit, about herself, and about how sad the whole sorry mess was – a mess she'd created. It was all down to her. There she was drinking coffee, looking out over the grave of the first man she'd killed and wondering whether to go and pay her respects to her second victim. Plying him with Viagra had been meant as a bit of fun at the time, but quite clearly it hadn't turned out that way.

Her other indiscretions drifted into her head and she put them all in order, gazing out to the drizzle-soaked garden. The incidents spun like a vinyl record on a deck, the words on the label whizzing round, virtually unreadable. But she knew what they said, those words, because she'd written them, created them, with her actions.

Madeline had been wrangling outbursts of anger and suffering from temperature tantrums for months, but hadn't done anything about them. She had allowed them to spin out of control, spin like the record on the deck, playing a song that no one was interested in listening to but herself. Her road rage had been dangerous at times: she had driven perilously close to other people's bumpers and intimidated innocent strangers. She had stuck her nose – and in one infamous case, her finger – where it wasn't wanted. She had taken actions that had ultimately been murderous on two occasions – and if she included the poisoning of Grey Man, there could very easily have been a third. This was not the Madeline she knew. She was ashamed.

Her thoughts drifted uneasily back to Grey Man. What was it with that guy? Why did he stick in her thoughts so much, more than any of the others? The record in her head carried on spinning, and suddenly it came to her why Grey Man crept into her thoughts so often.

Because she kept seeing him, that's why.

The vinyl continued to spin round on the deck as the pieces fell into place. It had been niggling at her for some days, since she'd tipped diesel into the Blue Stickered Car's petrol tank and realised that Grey Man lived a couple of doors down. She'd seen him head out, looking similar to yet not entirely like the man she'd poisoned, and according to news reports there had been another attack that night.

And there was also that night she'd taken Lorna home – who had she seen heading to the park? Grey Man. And who had she seen walking briskly along the platform in the tube station in London after another attack? Grey Man. Suddenly it had become clear exactly who the police were looking for. The little description they had of him fit perfectly, and the times and dates she knew about all fit too.

"Hell. It's got to be him!" she said out loud, much to the alarm of Dexter, who was quietly napping in the corner on the big comfy chair. He raised his head, glared at her, and went back to his own world.

Madeline stood and began to pace. What on earth was she going to do about this? She could arrange an accident for him, add him to her current body count, but she didn't want to bring the police to her door a third time. And she certainly wasn't keen to go anywhere near a police station, especially with no real evidence against Grey Man. And besides, how would she explain how she'd come to see him each time? Would making a formal complaint against Grey Man just give them even more reason to dig into *her* life? No, she couldn't think of risking it – not yet. Maybe when things had died down further... *Not the best choice of words, Madeline*, she thought wryly, but still, they made sense.

In the meantime, she'd just have to hope and pray no one else was attacked.

Getting up from the table, she flicked the switch on the kettle again, made herself another coffee, then sat back and watched the rain start to fall properly. It was quite cathartic.

Chapter Sixty-Two

AT 12 PM IT WAS STILL RAINING, SO THAT MEANT SHE WASN'T GOING. At 1 pm it was still raining but Madeline's conscience was telling her to grow up and put her big-girl knickers on – though not the lilac ones, which she'd thrown out anyway – and go and pay her respects properly. The other book club members would be there, and it would look bad, odd even, if she didn't show. And if the police *were* there, wouldn't they think it was suspicious if she wasn't? Her inner dilemma had been sorted. The kitchen clock told her she'd better get a move on. If she was going, she needed to get changed.

Dashing up the stairs to the bedroom, she grabbed a black skirt, a blouse and her black heels, then went to the bathroom to add some make-up and fluff her hair up a little. The finishing touch to her funeral ensemble was to change earrings and find her wristwatch. The woman looking back in the mirror didn't look half bad – not quite up to Rebecca's standards, but still, not bad.

Perhaps I should make a little more effort every day, and not just for funerals.

"What do you reckon – do I look like a murderer?" Dexter, who had jumped up onto the bed, was washing himself, his hind leg pulled up behind his ears, like it was the most important thing in the world.

He stopped at Madeline's question and just looked at her, then resumed what he was doing as if to say, "Do you really want me to answer that? Credit me with some intelligence."

She transferred some essentials into a smaller black handbag and was ready to go.

"Shit! Look at the bloody time. I'm going to be late." She ran down the stairs, leaving Dexter thinking it was his birthday being left behind on the bed. She bolted out through the front door and into her Audi, then drove out down Godstone Road towards the church at Purley. The rain was falling quite fast now, big droplets splashing on the windscreen, making visibility much poorer than it would have been in the drizzle. She hoped the big umbrella was still in the boot, though it wasn't the best place to keep it, in hindsight – if it was hurling down when she got there, she'd be soaked just getting the damn thing out.

"Better check the time of arrival," she said, and rummaged in her bag for her smartphone. With one eye on the windscreen and the other on Google Maps, she typed in the address. Sixty-five minutes via the A22 bypass route. And a big, long line of solid red blobs – backed-up traffic at a standstill.

"Damn. Must have been an accident. Shit! Shit! Shit! Now I'm almost certainly going to be sneaking in at the back during the service. And I bet there's nowhere left to sodding park either. Damn it." She thumped the steering wheel in frustration. Realising she'd have to go the back way, following the smaller local roads, she made the necessary turns to get on to Coulsdon Road and headed north. While it wasn't as stuck as the bypass, it was busy with dawdling locals. She hadn't the time to stick to the 30 mph speed limit, so she pushed her speed as far as she dared. She passed the Coulsdon Manor and golf club, and approaching the intersection in record time. Looking at her watch again, she knew the timing was going to be tight and she hoped there wasn't going to be too much traffic at the junction ahead.

As she got nearer she realised she was out of luck. A shopping trolley of a car was sitting at the front, trying to turn right. It was making no effort at all to nudge its way out; there was probably an old person or a learner at the wheel. Thumping the steering wheel again in frustration, Madeline scrutinised the four cars ahead, trying to determine if they were going to be as nervous getting out as the one at the front. The 'click-click' of her indicator was winding her up, so she turned it off and watched the flashing amber on the car in front instead. On. Off. On. Off. On. Off. It was equally annoying, and she took another deep breath, trying to calm her inner tension.

The rain was falling heavily, great blobs hitting the windscreen, the wipers doing their damnedest to keep up but struggling. A thin mist started to cover the inside of the windscreen, fogging everything up and making visibility even worse. She reached forward and wiped the glass with the back of her hand, making smeary marks instead of clearing it.

Finally the driver of the shopping trolley up front plucked up their courage, found the pedal on the right and pushed it down, and the trolley cruised round the corner with the second car close on its bumper. The next two weren't as bad, but still, they took their time. When it was finally Madeline's turn, she took a cursory look both ways and decided she could make it before the oncoming truck reached her. She pushed the pedal to the floor and gunned it. She'd had enough holdups already. But the tarmac was drenched, and instead of grabbing the road, her tyres spun wildly, searching for traction in the water, before finally propelling the car forward. But it was too late. Madeline's car clipped the front bumper of the truck and it spun her around, sending her hurtling sideways into a lamppost on the other side of the road. The airbag exploded in her face with a wallop.

It all happened so fast. At a standstill, powder sifting over her face, she very slowly pulled her head up to check what state she was in. Her shoulder hurt, her face hurt – everything hurt, it seemed, including her mood. And there was a stranger shouting through the passenger side window, a man, who then opened the door and shouted again, this time right in her face. Who the hell was he? Rainwater was dripping off his hair and that's all she could think about.

"Are you okay? Heavens. Are you hurt?" he shouted, over and over again, but Madeline had gone dumb. Her brain reeled.

"Are you okay?" He tried again, a little calmer, and she managed a nod.

Looking over at the other side of the road, she saw the truck she'd hit was in someone's front garden. Its rear end had opened up and brown stuff was spilled all over the road. It smelled like shit.

"What's that smell?" she asked the dripping face in front of her.

Why does it matter, Madeline? You've just had an accident.

"You hit a truck carrying manure. Look, don't worry about that now. Can you move your arms and legs okay?"

She moved each of her legs in turn and both appeared to function just fine, but when she went to unclip her seatbelt, a sharp jolt of pain shot through her right shoulder.

"Aarghh! Shit, that hurts!" The impact of hitting the lamppost must have broken something around her shoulder or collarbone, because the wave of pain and nausea almost made her pass out. She put her head back and closed her eyes a while, willing it to fade away quickly. All she could hear was the downpour hitting the windscreen hard outside, and Madeline knew she was about to lose control and fade off someplace.

And then it all went dark.

Chapter Sixty-Three

SHE CAME TO IN THE BACK OF AN AMBULANCE. SHE CHANCED A glance as best she could at the temporary strapping on her shoulder. It throbbed like all hell. The rain had dulled the daylight, from what she could see through the back window of the ambulance, and it felt almost dusk, even though it was probably only about two o'clock in the afternoon.

"Ah, you're back with us. How do you feel?" A friendly-looking man in a dark green uniform was taking her vitals as they sped towards hospital, lights and siren blazing. She could see the reflections of red and blue bouncing off houses and other vehicles through the side windows as they passed through heavy traffic, and she imagined vehicles moving over to let them through, like the parting of the Red Sea. This time it would be a sea of red tail-lights.

Not the time to be getting biblical, Madeline. Or perhaps it is?

"Like I've been in a car accident, funnily enough." She knew she sounded sarcastic and he was only doing his job. He looked a little taken aback.

"Sorry. I don't mean to be rude. I'm supposed to be at a funeral, and it was very nearly my own." Taking a deep breath to calm down, she answered his question. "Sore head, desperately sore shoulder and a bruised ego. Other than that, I guess I'm okay."

Be nice, Madeline. He's just trying to help and do his job.

"Well, you're lucky you're not hurt any worse. Your shoulder can be fixed, and as soon as we get you to the hospital, they will give you some stronger pain relief than what we have on board. You may have to have surgery on that shoulder, but we'll know more when they've examined you properly. Hang on in there." He did have kind eyes, and she managed a slight smile in reply before turning back to watch the blue and red reflections again.

What the hell have I gone and done now? Madeline the Maverick?

It was only a short journey to Croydon's University Hospital, and she was soon being trolleyed out the back of the ambulance and wheeled inside. The sound of the pelting rain was replaced by the voices of doctors and nurses as they went about their business with other patients. An orderly wheeled her into a cubicle, where she was told a doctor would be there shortly to assess her injuries in more detail. She closed her eyes to wait; the stress of the day so far was catching up and making her feel incredibly drowsy. Or it could have been the meds the ambulance crew had administered. She zonked out again.

"MRS. SIMPSON. CAN YOU HEAR ME? MRS. SIMPSON?" WHOEVER IT was had a bright singsong voice, and Madeline managed to peel her eyes open. "There you are." He was all smiles.

"Hello."

"Welcome back, Mrs. Simpson. I'm Dr. Graham, and I'll be taking care of you until we get you up onto a ward. From what we know so far, it looks like you've more than likely broken your collarbone and have some other cuts and bruises. You've had a nasty bang on the head too, so some concussion. I've organised x-rays so I can see what we are dealing with, but we'll probably keep you in at least overnight, maybe two depending on how bad that break is. Concussion can be a funny thing, and we don't take chances with it. Better here where we can monitor what's going on."

Bloody marvellous.

"Okay. Thanks. I don't suppose I can do much about it, really. Would you know how the driver of the truck is? Did he come in here too?"

"Not heard, I'm afraid, but I will check for you. The police will probably want to speak with you, but not until we've fixed you up a bit first." His singsong voice made everything sound so cheery, as though a chat with the police and an x-ray were something to look forward to, like jelly and ice cream.

"I need to tell my husband where I am. He'll be worried. Gordon – his name is Gordon, and he works at Calder and Rushmore. He's an architect, you know. A partner, actually." She knew she was rambling, but the nurse wrote it all down anyway. She guessed he'd give the information to a young police officer or admin person to do the necessary.

"I'll make sure he's notified; don't you worry. Now let's get you off for that x-ray." He signalled to a hospital porter to take her on the next part of the journey to getting fixed up.

A G&T is what I need, and a damn good sleep.

Chapter Sixty-Four

IT HAD BEEN A ROUGH SHIFT FOR BOTH DETECTIVES. FRIDAY NIGHT was never the best time to be in law enforcement, and even though Jack and Amanda didn't walk the beat and patrol the nightclubs and bars like uniforms did, they still had to clean up the mess if something went wrong. Tonight, a young woman had been attacked by her husband, who had a history of drunken behaviour and had taken it out on her with his fists. This time he'd gone way too far and she was lying in intensive care. She'd be lucky if she made it through the night. He, however, was in the wind, and Jack and Amanda had gone in to the station to check up on a few things and were sitting drinking mugs of tea, talking through the case in the staff canteen. Other officers were on their breaks and the room was filled with the smell of fried food and strong coffee. In the far corner of the room, a group of officers were sharing a joke, all sitting round one big table. It must have been something highly amusing, but the laughter was getting on Amanda's nerves.

"I wish they'd quiet down a bit. I can't hear myself think."

"Ah, leave them alone. This job is tough enough without having to watch your volume in here. If you can't do it the break room, where can you do it? The only other place is the pub. Not always practical."

"Yeah, I know. I'm just a bit on edge. That poor woman might not even make it through the night, and it doesn't seem right that folks are laughing. And before you say anything," she put her hands in the air as though in defeat, "I know, I know – it's not their fault." As if on cue, another loud roar of laughter bellowed out from the group. Amanda winced. "What's so sodding funny anyway? What are they laughing at?"

Jack shrugged his shoulders in reply and said, "I'll get us another mug each before we get back to it. Want anything to eat?"

"No, just tea. Thanks." She watched Jack head over to the cashier to order two more mugs.

While he waited, he wandered over to the group of officers in the corner and stood listening as one man spoke. The whole group, including Jack, erupted once again. Jack shook his head as he walked away, still laughing along with them. He picked the two mugs up, still smiling, and carried them over. He set one down in front of her.

"So what's so funny over there? Dirty jokes?"

"No, actually. Dumb chicken jokes, like the ones you used to tell at school, only far worse. Listen to this." He cleared his throat as though he was talking to a large audience and was on stage somewhere. "A little kid was standing behind an old man at the garden centre. The old man had five giant bags of chicken manure in his trolley. The kid asked the guy why he was buying bags of poop. The old man replied that he was going to put it on his strawberries. The kid screwed up his face and said 'I dunno where you grew up, but at our house we put sugar and cream on our strawberries.'"

She laughed despite herself. "Hell, that really is bad. Why on earth are they telling crappy jokes?"

"Because a couple of them were called out to that accident at the top of Coulsdon Road earlier today, when that manure truck hit a car coming out of the junction and ended up in someone's garden. Spilt its load everywhere, apparently – a right mess."

Amanda looked blank. "So?"

"So it was chicken shit. That's why they're telling 'shit' chicken jokes."

"Oh, I see," she said slowly, finally getting it. "Was anyone injured?"

"Truck driver's okay, but the woman driving the car that tried to cut in was taken to hospital. Definitely her fault. It was PC Daniels over there that went to interview her when she'd come round. The irony is she was on her way to a damn funeral. Can you believe it? Needs to watch where she's going a little better if you ask me, or it'll be her own funeral."

Amanda set down her tea and went over to the group. Everyone quieted down at the look on her face. She spoke directly to PC Daniels.

"What was the name of the woman in the chicken shit accident, the one on her way to a funeral?"

PC Daniels got his notebook out and flipped back a couple of pages. "Here it is. A Madeline Simpson. Why?"

Chapter Sixty-Five

SATURDAY

"How are you feeling today?" asked Ruth, sitting down on the edge of Madeline's hospital bed.

"I'll be better when I can get out of here. Three days, they say. I thought they kicked you out at their earliest convenience." Madeline wasn't happy; in fact she was bloody grumpy. Again. The broken collarbone needed an operation to fix it and she'd got concussion and some nasty bruises. The operation was scheduled for later that day, so she was set for a few days' stay in hospital. Her arm was going to be in a sling for six weeks, and she wasn't looking forward to the inconvenience of it all.

"Did you know, you're seventeen percent more likely to die after an operation at the weekend?" she blustered. "Just been reading about it online. Mine's today. Saturday. Seventeen! Who'd have thought it?"

"Don't be so maudlin, Madeline. You have to get that shoulder fixed, and your stay in here will go quick enough. Just enjoy the rest while you can. I wouldn't mind having a lie-down for a few." Ruth smiled warmly; she was just trying to lift Madeline's spirits. "Do you need anything from home, a book or a fresh nightdress maybe?"

"Gordon is on his way in later with them. Thanks. But I could do with something to chew on. The tablets I'm on are making my mouth taste foul. Some fruit pastilles, perhaps. Or wine gums would be nice."

Ruth's lip quirked up at one corner.

"What did I say?"

"Your mouth tastes *foul*. As in chicken – fowl. As in the fertiliser truck that you hit." Madeline's mind wasn't computing so Ruth filled in the gaps for her. "You hit a chicken shit truck." Ruth was laughing now and Madeline began to laugh along with her.

"Oh I see – fowl." She giggled, despite herself. The meds must be making her loopy. "Yes, very funny. I saw a short report in the paper. I guess I made a mess, eh?"

"Oh, that you did, that you did. You should see some of the jokes on the site – every chicken shit joke you could think of. Some of them have been quite funny actually."

"Great. I'm glad I'm able to brighten someone's day," Madeline said, sarcastically, her good mood evaporating as quickly as it had come. She was fed up already at being in a hospital bed and desperately wanted to go home. But on the upside, at least she'd had some time to do some thinking, with all the hanging around, and she'd thought a lot about Ruth. Perhaps her own near-death experience had brought it to the surface. Madeline took the pause in conversation to change to another subject, one a long way away from herself.

"Ruth," she said tentatively.

"Oh-oh. This sounds ominous."

"I've been thinking while I've been in here, and thinking about you." Ruth looked a little concerned now and Madeline did her best to lighten what was about to be quite a serious moment, one that could backfire or go well. With a slightly embarrassed smile she carried on. "I just wanted to say, I know about your girlfriend, Ruth, and your dad and I are fine with it."

There: she'd said it directly. There could be no mistake about what she was referring to. She watched as Ruth's face drained of all colour.

Madeline ploughed on, rephrasing it slightly just to be sure as she got the message on the second try.

"What I'm trying to say, Ruth, is I know about your blonde *female* friend. And you. And your dad and I are absolutely fine with it. I think I've known for some time, actually, but I'd always hoped you'd finally say something yourself one day." Madeline paused for a moment then carried on a little more. "I've seen you two together, actually. Amanda, I believe her name is."

That caught Ruth's attention. "How do you know her name?"

It wasn't really the first question Madeline had expected Ruth to ask, but she answered, "She's a detective, right? She came round to ask me some questions when that landscaper first went missing. Remember his digger at the house?"

Ruth nodded, but didn't say anything further.

"So what I'm saying, what your father and I are saying, actually, is we are fine with it all. Really we are. It's your life – you do what makes you happy. It's for no one to interfere with. Not us, not anybody. I just wanted to let you know in case you'd been worrying about ever telling us."

The air around Madeline's bed was heavy with silence as Madeline waited for Ruth to say something more.

"You surprise me, Madeline. I thought you would be the old-fashioned type, the type to disown me for bringing the family name into disrepute. Not that we actually have the same family name, but you know what I mean. Disown me perhaps. I know others have had that experience."

"Well, I'm not others, and give me some credit. Old-fashioned, eh? Cheeky sod," she smiled, her eyes catching Ruth's as she smiled too.

"Well, some would say it's not what 'the family' would approve of," Ruth continued, "and plenty of people would be pissed that there might not be grandchildren in quite the same way. You know, be totally selfish and make it their problem when it really needn't be a problem at all." She'd obviously been thinking about what they might have said had she told them herself.

Madeline carried it on. "Grandchildren aren't the be all and end all, and anyway, there are ways to do that should you choose to. I'm sure you're aware of that already. And you're forgetting we have two grown sons as well, so I'm sure there will be little feet running round to spoil one day." She paused, then added, "Unless they are both gay too, of course." Ruth burst out laughing, raising the eyebrows of the nurse nearby, and they both got the message to quiet down.

Then she did something neither of them quite expected: she leant over and gave Madeline a hug. Probably one of only a handful in the time they'd known one another, but it was a hug nonetheless, and it felt good. And a long time overdue. Madeline couldn't have felt happier.

"So what does Dad say? About knowing, I mean."

"He was a little shocked when I first mentioned it, but you know your dad – Mr. Laidback. Unless it concerns Crystal Palace, *then* it's something to get upset about," she said, smiling again. But no, he's absolutely fine. I think he just thought you were too busy for men, but now we know. We're both glad you have someone in your life. *Are* you happy?"

"I am, yes. And yes, she's with the police and we live near each other. She's a lovely woman, actually, though I don't expect you saw that side of her if she was working. She's very focused."

Agree with you there.

"I don't remember too much about the interview, to tell you the truth. I don't suppose I was much help to her. The guy just left suddenly." *Well, that was the truth.* "Did they ever find him, do you know?"

"Not that I've heard, but Amanda would know, I expect. Why don't you ask her?"

"I will, yes." Ruth looked thoughtful for a moment, then added, "You go out to the garden centre, the one on the Wickham road, don't you?"

"Yes, all the time. Why?" Odd question to ask.

"Remember that crash a couple of weeks ago, where the guy turned his van over?" She had Madeline's full attention. "I saw on The Daisy Chain that he'd died, complications with his injuries and undiagnosed diabetes apparently."

Madeline could feel the colour drain from her own face as she zoned out. That meant another one added to her ever-growing list: it was now three.

"Madeline? Madeline? Are you okay?"

Madeline could hear her but she had gone into dumb mode once more, her brain whirring but nothing coming out of her mouth. It took a few moments for the news to sink in and for her to respond.

"Oh dear, that's so sad," she finally managed. "Perhaps if he'd been wearing his seatbelt... though I was, and look at me lying here." She wafted her good arm over the hospital bed. Was she sounding convincing? "You just never know what will happen next."

Her thoughts drifted back to that hot day in the car wash, and she felt ashamed at what she'd done to his tyre. It was supposed to be for a bit of a laugh and a lot of inconvenience. It was never meant to kill him. And it had been the same with James – just a bit of fun, and that had gone wrong too. She wondered about all the other 'bits of fun' she'd organised and wondered if any of those had also backfired – that she didn't know of yet.

But why had Ruth mentioned it? Did she suspect something, and if so, what exactly? Glancing at Ruth, who was looking directly at her, she couldn't quite read what was on her face, but there was something. Doubt, maybe? Was she putting events together and connecting them all to Madeline? Had she noticed there were too many connections? But why would she think of Madeline? Was she being silly? Paranoid? There were too many questions she couldn't answer. It was time to change the subject to something completely different and put an end to the doubt – for the time being.

"So when are you off to France to see your other mother?" Madeline said cheerily.

Chapter Sixty-Six

WEEK 8
Sunday

"Just feel that sunshine on your face, Madeline. Isn't it wonderful?" Ruth was sitting on the patio with her face tilted up towards the sunshine on another beautiful summer day. They'd had a lovely lunch. Gordon had cooked steak on the barbecue to go with the coleslaw and potato salad he'd made earlier in the day under Madeline's supervision. Ruth had brought a bottle of rosé and a baked lemon cheesecake from M&S, and they were all stuffed. Gordon had retired inside to watch the match he'd recorded but was probably asleep in his chair; football for him was really just an excuse to doze off in peace. Madeline's own head was laid back, also tilted to the sunshine, which was warm without being too hot, and it felt great.

"Mmmm, lovely. I'm just glad to be out of that hospital and back home with some real food, and I'm absolutely stuffed full. I shouldn't have forced that last bit of cheesecake in. Or was it the last mouthful of wine that did it?" She giggled like a teenager, and she could hear Ruth giggling too,. Obviously they'd both had enough to drink.

Since that day about a week ago by Madeline's hospital bed, when she had told Ruth that she already knew about her and Amanda, there had been a definite shift in their relationship. Gordon and Madeline still hadn't invited Amanda to their home. On Madeline's part it was due mainly to the fact that there was a dead body in the garden, and had nothing whatsoever to do with Ruth and Amanda's sexual orientation. Madeline just wasn't ready to let Detective Amanda Lacey get too close when she might still be a suspect in several deaths. But Ruth and Madeline were now both more relaxed with each other, and that unexpected hug she'd given Madeline in hospital was still vivid in her memory, a memory she hoped would become a reality again sometime soon. She'd have to wait for Ruth on that one.

Opening one eye against the bright sunshine, Madeline turned to look at Ruth, knowing she would have her eyes closed in the sun. She was a female version of Gordon in her looks: she had the same oval face and the same hazel-brown eyes, and her short wavy hair was the same light brown as his had been when they'd first met, before the salt and pepper had taken over. The sunshine picked out the lighter highlights Ruth occasionally added in. With a light summer tan, she really was a striking woman.

That was where the similarities ended, though. Where Gordon was placid, Ruth was fiery; where Gordon was average height and soft around the middle, Ruth was tall and athletic and firm, spending her free time running rather than watching footy. But each to their own ways. Ruth cleared her throat now like she was about to say something, so Madeline resumed her position and enjoyed the sunshine for a moment longer. She wasn't quite prepared for what Ruth said next and was glad she was already sitting down with her eyes closed.

"You know, Madeline? I think I've worked something out."

Oh shit. What does she think she's worked out? The Great Orange Machine? James? What?

Madeline acted dumb. "Hmm?" Sleepily. "What have you worked out?" Her heart rate started to pick up speed and push blood around her veins a little faster. Could Ruth really know something about her antics or was she still being paranoid? Hearing her move, she assumed with her eyes still closed that Ruth was sitting up properly, giving her strength and more authority. This didn't bode well, but she ignored the feeling as best she could. Her pulse, on the other hand, couldn't. Ruth dived straight in.

"All the recent goings-on – I think they're all linked."

Madeline's mind was working overtime but she didn't move a muscle.

Act cool, Madeline.

"What do you mean? Which events are you talking about?" Her voice was even and casual, she hoped.

"The missing landscaper guy, that poor chap with food poisoning, the book club man, even the crash victim on the Wickham road." She had moved in her chair again, and Madeline could feel her direct stare even though her eyes were still firmly closed. If she'd turned towards her, Ruth would probably be able to read the 'Yes, I know' message that was written across her forehead. What to do? There was an empty space where neither spoke, and it needed filling.

Stay cool.

"What about them?" Madeline said at length.

"I think they are all connected. There is a common theme running through them."

She was still staring at her; Madeline was sure of it.

"What makes you think that? And what is the theme?"

Ever the damn puzzle solver, what had she deduced?

"Because they all tie back to one person, that's what they have in common. One person came into contact with all four of them at some point. There's just one of them that I'm not entirely sure about yet, but I will figure it out."

She was right, there: was she on to her?

Madeline was starting to sweat and couldn't blame it on a temperature tantrum this time, or the sunshine.

"You always have been good at puzzles, so what bit can't you figure out?"

"How on earth that crash happened, how the person did it, or why – but then I'm asking 'why' about all of the incidents." Ruth paused to let that sink in, and Madeline stayed exactly where she was, eyes still closed and melting under Ruth's gaze, which was far hotter than the sun shining down on them both.

Then Ruth dropped her bombshell. "So why don't you fill me in, Madeline."

Oh shit.

Madeline had to sit up and talk to her now. She'd obviously pieced things together and seen the common thread – Madeline Simpson. She sat up fully, waited till her eyes adjusted to the brightness, and turned towards Ruth. Ruth was indeed staring right at her, her eyes razor sharp, a mixture of disbelief and concern on her face. Madeline's face must have said it all: there was no point in denying what she'd done. Ruth's face lost some of its colour.

"I knew I was right. Shit, Madeline! What have you been up to?" Her voice had risen a couple of decibels, but if they were going to have this conversation right then, Madeline didn't want Gordon in on it.

"Shhhh! Keep your voice down, will you. Why do you think it's me?" she asked, thinking she might as well see just what it was Ruth had put together.

"Because you were the last to see the landscaper alive. The food poisoning guy ate at Sally's. The crash victim died on the road that you travel along to go to your favourite garden centre, and you were on your way there that day. And the book club man was *your* book club leader. Easy, really. Have I missed anyone out?"

Like I'm going to tell you if you have. Blue Car Man comes to mind, as do Skinny Suit and Jordan. Oh, and the red BMW, and Pink Fluffy Woman.

Ruth went on, "I just haven't figured out the why, and what you've done with the landscaper guy. And for the record, I haven't told anyone. Yet."

Well, that's good to know, though I don't like the 'yet' bit.

"And I'm guessing that's why you've not been in a hurry to invite Amanda round for lunch, her being a detective and all. In fact, she's already been here, hasn't she, to interview you over the landscaper, and the book club guy? You've already met her, and yet she has no idea who you are to me."

Should I come clean or carry on my charade?

"So you think it's me? I'm responsible for them all? Just because I seem an obvious link? Do you have any proof for these wild accusations?"

"No, of course I don't have any proof. But I am right, aren't I? It is you, isn't it?"

Madeline avoided that question and asked one of her own. "What are you planning on doing with this notion, with no proof?"

Ruth looked away and took a moment to answer. Sweat was beading on Madeline's forehead and cleavage, and she wiped it away with a leftover serviette from lunch. Neither one spoke, and she wasn't going to fill the gap this time. She held her breath until Ruth spoke again.

"Nothing. For the moment."

She released her breath with a soft whoosh.

"I'm not going to do anything. But on one condition. You tell me why, you get some help and you put a stop to anything else you have planned right here and now." Her eyes were fiery as she spoke, as if Madeline were a naughty schoolgirl and she was the headmistress.

What choice did she have? She'd been caught. There was no point in denying any of it if she wanted a relationship with Ruth, and for Gordon's sake: it would break his heart if the two of them split when they were just starting to get closer. He'd want to know why. And she didn't want Amanda to find out.

Madeline nodded, her eyes never leaving Ruth's as she accepted her demand. "Okay, that's more than fair. And thank you, but I'm curious to know why you're not going to report me."

Ruth sighed in apparent resignation, that she'd been right all along and now Madeline had basically admitted it. She looked disappointed and relieved at the same time, but Madeline felt almost ill with remorse. She'd always felt that each of her actions had been justified, but now, sitting there with Ruth, she wasn't so sure. Tears welled up in her eyes and she struggled to blink them away.

"I would have thought that was obvious, isn't it?" Ruth said.

Madeline shook her head that it wasn't.

"You're my bloody stepmother, Madeline. And think of Dad, for heaven's sake. What it would do to him with you banged up inside? Jesus Christ! You can be thick sometimes."

Shame washed over her at the thought of Gordon again. During all the things she'd done, she'd never once given any consideration to him, about what would happen if it all came unravelled and she was caught, just how distraught he would be. She'd been totally selfish and in it for her own pleasure, just to teach a bunch of stupid annoying strangers a lesson and for her to feel like she'd won. The car park incident, the diesel in the petrol tank, all of it, even fingers in buns. She'd never set out to kill James, even though he did annoy her sometimes, or the big sod who'd made her wait at the car wash. Every single thing she had done had been in the name of spitefulness and anger. And now she'd been caught.

As the realisation sank in, tears started to well in her eyes, and she let them roll down her cheeks. Ruth passed her a tissue from her pocket and Madeline dabbed her eyes with it. She smeared her mascara a little but didn't really care. Ruth stood and walked over to her stepmother and wrapped her arms around her shoulders, pulling her in tight. Madeline returned the embrace, just glad in a way that someone knew, and that it was someone she could talk to.

The tension she'd been feeling ever since the landscaper, Des, had first dug the hole in the garden had been hard to bear. She'd taken that tension out on him in the worst way possible. He certainly hadn't deserved to die – even though she'd tried to justify it at the time. But what about her feelings of rage and spitefulness *before* she'd killed him? What was that all about? She had no answer there but the obvious: it had all been part of the change, the menopause. Perhaps she should have got help with chemicals from the doctor, just like Rebecca had urged. Millions of women went through menopause without killing every idiot who crossed them, didn't they?

The tears kept coming, rolling away off her jaw, and she let them flow until she'd cried enough. Ruth wiped Madeline's sticky brow and wet cheeks with a tissue of her own. Madeline knew her face would be all red and blotchy.

"I'll go and get you a cold glass of water. Be right back." Ruth disappeared inside the kitchen. Through the open window, Madeline heard the cupboard door bang shut and a glass fill from the tap. A moment later Ruth was back.

"I popped my head into the lounge. Dad's sound asleep." She sat back down. "This is between you and me, Madeline, okay? Don't go and be tempted to come clean with him. He doesn't need to know. You'll only hurt and worry him, and he doesn't need either. If you want to discuss it with anyone, you discuss it with me and only me, you understand?"

Madeline nodded, grateful, and took several large gulps of the water. She really wanted to tip the whole glass down the back of her hot neck to cool off.

"I should have known you'd figure it out. You've always been so clever. Thank you, Ruth, for not reporting me. You won't tell Amanda, though, will you? You'll have to keep it a secret, our secret."

Ruth shook her head. "I won't tell her."

In an odd sort of way Madeline felt relieved, like the proverbial weight had been lifted off her shoulders, one she hadn't even realised was there.

"Why don't you start from the beginning, and tell me what's happened and why," said Ruth gently, and sat back in her chair.

And so Madeline did. She told her all about trying her best to deal with the anger, the sudden tears, the temperature tantrums and the spitefulness. About the need to win and the fact that it gave her satisfaction, but that at the same time she was concerned about getting caught. James's death had not been the plan, nor Big Sod's, nor the landscaper's. The silly episodes like the diesel in the Blue Stickered Car's petrol tank, Jordan's windscreen wiper blades, and the holes in Pink Fluffy Woman's sticky buns were pure and simply spite, though she wasn't that person normally. Hell, she'd never been that person until her hormones had started to screw her over.

At the end of Madeline's confession, which had felt quite cathartic, Ruth was speechless. Madeline wondered if she'd changed her mind, or was even recording the whole conversation. Ruth stared at her blankly, disbelieving, though she had heard it all from the horse's mouth. Madeline suddenly felt very worried.

"You've changed your mind now, haven't you? Oh hell, no, please Ruth!"

"No, I've not changed my mind. Relax, Madeline. I just didn't realise the enormity of what you've been up to and how many people you've hurt. This is serious stuff, and we've got to get you through this unscathed and keep you out of prison."

"On that we agree," Madeline said. Thinking, she added, "There is one good thing to come out of it though."

Ruth looked at her more closely. "And what's that?"

"I'm pretty sure I know who the groper is and where he lives."

"What? How do you know that?"

"Because, a bit like you, I can do puzzles too, and I've been putting two and two together. Where I've seen him and where the attacks have taken place – they all marry up. He lives next door to the guy with the blue car, the one whose petrol tank I poured diesel into. But I couldn't say anything." Madeline looked thoughtful.

"Until now. And like me, you've no evidence, and even if you had, you wouldn't be going to the police with it. So who is it, then?"

"Ironically, it's the same guy I tried to poison. That's why the attacks stopped for a while – he was sick and in hospital. Probably put him off his stride for a bit. Who knows – I may have even stopped another attack happening."

Ruth looked at Madeline as if to say, "You've got to be kidding. That justification isn't going to wash with me." She looked off, thoughtful, wondering how she could intervene without implicating Madeline or herself. After a time, she nodded over at the Great Orange Machine, which was still sitting on its pile of dirt.

"So what did you do with him then? Where is he?"

"I'm not going to tell you anything about that. Not because I don't trust you, but because I don't want you implicated either. The less you know, the less you can get into trouble for. So no. I'm keeping quiet. All you need to know is he won't be coming back and he'll never be found. End of story."

There was nothing to be gained from her telling Ruth any details, and they both knew it. They sat in silence for a while. Finally, Ruth spoke up again.

"And why did you do it?"

"Because the phone company pissed me off with another incorrect bill."

Ruth looked at her like she'd gone mad – and maybe she had, a little. It did sound a bit extreme when you thought about it.

"You knocked him off because of a phone bill? Have you gone nuts?! What had that got to do with him?" Ruth's voice rose to a squeak, and her eyes were as wide as saucers.

"Well, that and he tried to put his price up for the pond hole because the ground was so hard and I wasn't having any of it, cheeky bugger." Even to Madeline's ears it sounded a bit over the top now.

Ruth rubbed her hands over her face as if deep in thought, or just disbelief. "Hell, remind me to never piss you off."

Madeline smiled weakly. "Now you're being silly. I'd never hurt a hair on your head and you know it. And before you get all worried, I wouldn't hurt Gordon either."

Ruth stood up and paced on the small patio area, occasionally looking out to the digger and then back to Madeline again. Dexter was lying on the bucket sunning himself, and despite herself Madeline smiled at the secret only the two of them knew.

"And what's so funny?" Ruth was definitely not smiling.

"Nothing, actually. I was just smiling at Dexter sunning himself over there, not a care in the world. He kills something, it's not an issue. I kill something and it is. I'm coming back as a cat when I leave this earth."

Ruth rolled her eyes again in disbelief. "I'm going to get myself a stiff drink. Want one?"

Hell yes.

Chapter Sixty-Seven

THURSDAY

Since James's death two weeks before, the little group hadn't met up as a book club. One reason was that they met fortnightly anyway, but the other was that no one was really sure if they should, and how they should carry on. Added to that, Madeline had been laid up in hospital and then at home after her run-in with a chicken poop truck. Finally, Josh had taken the initiative and sent everyone a text suggesting they all met up at the pub for an informal discussion on where to go next. It was an excellent idea and they'd all agreed.

They met at the Baskerville, the pub Madeline and Rebecca had their lunch get-togethers, and also where James's funeral tea had been held. It seemed appropriate somehow, as if he with them in a way, though Madeline thought it more likely he was looking down on them – literally and figuratively. And frowning at her.

At any rate, while it was a bit further out than his old house for her, it meant she could have a G&T and a bag of salt and vinegar crisps while they all chatted. Madeline was looking forward to getting out again, which was putting it mildly. There was no way she was staying indoors until her shoulder was healed; she was going stir crazy. Dexter hadn't been much good on the conversation front, and she was bored to death with reading and television. She was also looking forward to seeing the rest of the group. Lorna had been to see her in hospital, and the others had sent their love via text messages when they'd heard about the crash.

How ironic was that? The woman who killed him almost killed herself on the way to his funeral. It sounds like a plot for a good book.

Madeline was the first to arrive. She wasn't really supposed to be driving with her arm in a sling, so she had allowed plenty of time to get there, taking things steady. For a change.

"Thank god I've got an automatic," she'd said to Gordon, who had voiced his concern about her driving herself anywhere. "No need to change gears or anything like that, though going around roundabouts is a bit tricky."

"Gin and tonic please, and a bag of salt and vinegar," Madeline said to the barman. It was Gabe, the same one who served her and Rebecca each Friday lunchtime, and he recognised Madeline straight away.

"Hello, love. Your friend not with you tonight?" Bloody typical. Rebecca had pulled and she wasn't even in the same damn room. At least he'd remembered Madeline, though, and for that she was grateful. Apparently she wasn't completely invisible in Rebecca's presence.

"No. Gabe, isn't it?" He looked a little taken aback at the mention of his name, but she knew quite a bit more about him, quite intimate details in fact, from Rebecca's stories, though she didn't say so. "She'll be in with me tomorrow lunchtime if you're working, so you can carry on flirting and whatnot with her then," she said with a wink, smiling to show she wasn't being mean. She just thought it would be fun to see him blush. He didn't disappoint, going crimson and giving her a nervous smile in return before turning away to fix her drink. A moment later, he handed it across the bar to her.

"That's four-fifty, please," he said. She paid him, thanked him and gathered her crisps, putting the little bag inside her sling and leaving her free hand to carry her drink. She chose to sit in the same spot as she did every Friday lunchtime, even though it wasn't Friday. If those chairs had ears, they'd have been privy to a lot of juicy details over the time she and Rebecca had been meeting.

As she sat waiting, her thoughts drifted off to when Todd had found her with Gabe and how upset she'd been, though it could have been a whole lot worse if it had been Edward who'd found her. She and Edward needed to get their marriage sorted out before much longer, or they'd both find themselves single at an awkward age. Who would want to start dating all over again, hooking up on Tinder in their fifties or sixties? It all sounded too hard and she was glad she had Gordon – comfy, reliable old Gordon. She loved him.

Thinking she should order some sandwiches to share with the others when they arrived, a sort of cheese and cracker replacement, she headed back to the bar to order a mixed platter. No sooner had she put her purse away than the others all arrived en masse.

"Madeline!" exclaimed Lorna. "You made it!"

"Yes. I didn't crash the car on the way here. I managed it all the way this time," she said, laughing. "I'm quite a capable driver generally, really I am."

"I know you are. I'm sorry – I just meant it's great to see you, that's all."

"And I appreciate it." Madeline gave her a one-armed hug, trying not to crush her damaged shoulder in the process. The others each embraced her individually, though gingerly, and she felt her heart swell with happiness.

"It's really good to see you all. I've really missed human contact this last week or so, and bloody hated it in hospital." She beamed at them all and they stood, beaming back. "I've ordered some sandwiches too."

"Bravo, Madeline. Great idea," said Derek in his best schoolteacher voice. Madeline secretly reckoned he would be keen to take over the book club leader role and she wondered when he might get round to suggesting it. Before the night was over, she suspected.

"Let's go and sit down, shall we?" Annabel steered the group to where Madeline had been sitting, noticing her drink and crisps alone on the table. She pulled up some extra chairs and it was Pam who took the floor first.

"Let's get started then. If I might, I'd suggest we go round the table and see who is keen to continue and what their thoughts are with regard to venue, day etcetera, and if they have any interest in becoming the chair, I guess, for want of a better word. Would that be okay for everyone?" The group gave a collective nod, not wanting to say anything while Pam had the floor.

"Why don't you start then, Josh, and we'll work our way back round to me." She smiled at Josh, who took the reins with a bit of a splutter at being first cab off the rank. He took a moment before he spoke.

"Yes to carrying on. I don't see why we shouldn't, though it's sad James has gone. Happy for it to stay on the current day fortnightly, and no, I don't think I want to be considered as chairperson. Not my thing. Wouldn't mind it being held here, actually, then we can all have a drink and maybe share some sandwiches together."

As if on cue, a platter of cheese and pickle, ham and mustard, and beef with horseradish arrived. Everyone leant forward and took a soft filled triangle.

"Great idea, actually, Madeline." Josh nodded his approval and she nodded back.

"I can be useful at times."

It was Lorna's turn to speak, and she agreed with Josh's points, adding that she herself would not want to be chair either. Around the table they went, with both Pam and Derek expressing they would like to be considered for the role. No surprises there, really. Madeline certainly had no interest; she had enough trouble trying to read the books in the first place and it wouldn't do for the chair to be so slack.

The business concluded, the group turned their attention to the sandwiches, their beverages, and each other. Madeline felt a rush of pleasure at being out in the company of friends again, out of hospital and out of the house. She sipped her drink and thought back to that fateful afternoon with Ruth. Madeline had been hugely relieved to unburden herself to her stepdaughter, and more than relieved that Ruth was going to keep her dreadful secrets. They'd chatted a little more about why she'd done the things she had, her feelings, and how Ruth could help her in the near future. Madeline had agreed to go back to the doctor in the hope she could suggest something a bit more natural than the chemical option she was so keen to hand out, but maybe she'd have no choice in the matter. One thing was for sure, though: it had to stop. She couldn't carry on being Mad Madeline and doing the things she had been. Spending the rest of her menopause in prison was not an option.

The last beef and horseradish was looking at her longingly, begging her to eat it, so she picked the triangle up and bit into it with gusto. Yes, book club in the pub was going to be a great idea.

Chapter Sixty-Eight

THE BOOK CLUB MEETING HAD BEEN MOST ENJOYABLE. THEY'D toasted James, and elected Derek to be the new chair for the rest of the year up until they broke for Christmas, Pam would take over in the New Year, which seemed fair. They'd all said "Aye, aye" in agreement, and that was set. At 9 pm they were all done – drinks drunk, sandwiches eaten. The only things remaining on the table were a few ice cubes sat in the bottom of otherwise empty glasses.

"Can I give you a lift back, Lorna, or have you driven over?"

"Thanks, Madeline, but I drove over even though it's not far. I've been taking your advice until this pervert guy is caught. I can't believe he's not been found yet. Must be a master of disguise or something."

"And he keeps attacking by all accounts," Derek added. "I hope he doesn't escalate things and really hurt someone. Weird people can sometimes change their MO and escalate their crime to something even nastier. Shocking state of affairs, it really is."

Another one watching too much CSI, though it's probably true.

Everyone mumbled in agreement as they gathered their things and headed out to the car park. Feet crunched on gravel, car doors slammed and last-minute goodbyes could be heard as engines started and the small group dispersed in both directions. Slipping inside her own car, Madeline sat for a moment before starting the engine. There was no doubt in Madeline's mind who was behind the attacks on women, but again, where was the proof?

She pressed the ignition button and the engine fired into life; the air-conditioner was still on full throttle from her arrival earlier. She turned it off before the blast blew her head off. At 9 pm only a little cool air was all she needed, and she much preferred the natural air from outside, so she wound her window down fully. Her head was full of 'what-to-do' scenarios: tell the police what she suspected, against Ruth's advice, and put her name back on their radar but possibly help save some other poor woman from being attacked? Or be totally selfish and stay quiet in the hope they caught him without her help soon? There had to be another way. Madeline just didn't know what it was yet.

"Maybe an anonymous tip-off would work?" Another conversation with herself and the windscreen. "Or I could confront him myself?"

She pondered both options for a moment, but decided neither would work: it all came back to the fact that she still had no evidence. What was she going to do – call the police and say, "It's a man that lives on Sanderson Road," or actually knock on Grey Man's door and say, "I know it's you but I have no proof"? Nope: he would just laugh in her face or, worse, assault her. She decided to leave it for her unconscious computer again; she put the car in gear and headed out, knowing her head would eventually tell her what to do. She gave it until she reached the end of her road to come up with the answer. Until then, she tried to think about something else, although that was easier said than done.

The answer came a lot sooner than she thought it would, long before she got back to Oakwood Rise. Madeline smiled with satisfaction, indicated, and turned the car back in the direction she needed to go. She stopped at a petrol station along the way for a bottle of water and a bar of chocolate. Then she called Gordon and told him she was staying out with the others just a while longer, and not to wait up. One more white lie wouldn't hurt. She carried on with her journey – back to Grey Man's road.

Madeline was going on a stakeout.

Fifteen minutes later she was parked down Sanderson Road and watching what she remembered to be Grey Man's house. Funnily enough, the old blue car was still sitting in exactly in the same spot, and she sniggered because she'd won that one too. She'd managed to keep that death trap off the road – her little "fuel injection" had probably clogged his engine very nicely. Madeline high-fived herself mentally, though she knew she shouldn't be doing so – Ruth would certainly be disappointed if she saw her celebrating. She took a swig from the water bottle and settled down to wait. Who knew if she'd even see anything. Maybe she'd just fall asleep with boredom.

Chapter Sixty-Nine

BILL WINTERS LOOKED LIKE A DIRTY OLD PERVERT. BUT THEN HE was one.

With his long grey coat and unstylish hat, he knew he'd blend in. His natural appearance was so perfectly nondescript: no one would give him a second look. There was nothing remarkable about him, literally, and that's just the way he wanted it to be. He was invisible to everyone.

With his coat sleeves covering the cigarette burn scars on both his arms, he'd got used to being hot, the sickly-sweet onion smell of stale body odour repelling people and keeping anyone from getting too close to him. He knew he repulsed the locals he came into contact with: he'd seen it on their faces, seen their wrinkled noses, though they'd stopped noticing him at all now. And that's the way he wanted it to stay. To blend in. To hardly exist.

But he had certain needs, needs that couldn't be fulfilled conventionally, and he'd found another way to satisfy his cravings. That's what made him a pervert. He took what he wanted, whenever he got the urge. No matter what.

Ready to go, he opened the front door and went out into the warm evening dusk – in search of some relief. A dog barked in the distance. It must have known he was coming.

Chapter Seventy

Biting into her chocolate bar, Madeline wondered if she'd have felt more in stakeout mode with doughnuts instead. *CSI* style. As it happened, only thirty minutes later she saw movement from his house: the front door opened and a figure walked down the path. He wore the long coat she'd seen him wear before, and a hat – totally the wrong clothing for a warm summer evening, even at 10 pm.

After letting him walk a little way down the road, she quietly opened her car door, grabbed her mobile and set off in pursuit on foot, though keeping well back. All she planned on doing was to follow him from a distance, see where he went and what he was up to. It was possible she had it all wrong, though she was pretty sure she didn't.

It must have been twenty minutes later when they both turned into a park area. The night was fully dark now apart from the moonlight and the orange glow from a few street lamps. The darkness and the trees gave her some cover. He wasn't far ahead of her, and she kept him in her sights while she scanned the rest of the park as best she could in the light available. This late, Madeline assumed they would be on their own, but just in the distance and over to the right she saw a small white poodle taking a walk before bedtime with its owner, who appeared to have the gait of a woman.

"Who the hell is that out here at this hour? Silly woman," she whispered to herself. "Is she stupid or what?"

Shush, Madeline!

Grey Man, in front of her, had stopped walking, and Madeline was thankful for a nearby bush to dart behind. Through the branches she could see him looking in the direction of the poodle and its owner. Her heart raced as she realised what might be about to happen. Suddenly this all felt a bit too real. With her heart pounding in her ears, she quickly pulled out her phone and texted Ruth, saying where she was and what she was seeing. Surely Ruth would know what to do. Madeline was sure she could distract him should she need to, and she wouldn't get the police involved until she was absolutely sure there was a problem.

The 'woosh' of the text being sent reminded her to turn her phone to silent. She thumbed the button down and stayed still behind the bush. Nothing was happening. She and Grey Man both stood stock still in their respective places, one hidden, one not.

A moment later, Ruth's text landed.

Don't be stupid. Keep clear! Amanda and I are on our way!

"Shit," she thought miserably. "What did you tell her for? Now I've got some bloody explaining to do. *Shit. Shit. Shit!*"

Then suddenly there was movement up ahead: Grey Man was on the move. No time to text back a response to Ruth. Madeline jammed the phone back in her pocket, crept out from behind the leafy camouflage and tailed him from a distance again. They were both in a wide-open space now, and Madeline had nothing for cover. But Grey Man was not looking at anything or anyone except the poodle woman, who was headed for the old toilet block.

"At this hour?" thought Madeline incredulously. "In the dark? Really? She must be desperate or stupid, or both."

Hanging back as far as she dared, she watched as the woman crouched and tied her dog just outside, under a single light fixed to the corner of the building. As she stood again and passed under the full light to go inside, Madeline recognised who it was. Her eyes widened in horror.

"Oh dear Lord. Holy hell."

She watched as the woman went into the toilets, followed a few moments later by Grey Man. No, there was no time to wait for Ruth and Amanda: she needed to do something now. Madeline covered the distance as fast as she could; her injured arm in its sling made running awkward.

She flung open the main door and yelled the woman's name.

Grey Man whirled around, startled, and at the same time the middle cubicle door opened. Lorna looked right at Madeline, her face a mask of fear and confusion.

And then she spotted Grey Man.

Chapter Seventy-One

RUTH SHRIEKED. "WHAT THE HELL?"

Amanda looked at Ruth and stopped her biscuit halfway to her mouth. "What's the matter?"

"Come on – we've got to go. I'll tell you on the way."

Perplexed, Amanda set her mug of tea on the little table and started to get up.

"Hurry!" Ruth shouted. She grabbed her car keys and ran out of the front door. Amanda followed her at a trot, wondering what the hell was going on and where they were going at almost 10.15 at night. She pulled the front door shut behind her and jumped into Ruth's car, not quite closing the car door before Ruth took off like a maniac down Richmond Road.

"Are you going to fill me in on what's going on or do I have to guess?"

"I'll tell you the whole story later but right now, my stepmum is in trouble and I think we might need police backup. Can you get backup out to Wandle Park? I think she's gone after the groper guy."

Amanda's eyes nearly bugged out of her head. "She's what? How do you know that – and how does she know? And who is she?"

There were too many questions to choose from, so Ruth took the easiest.

"She just texted me to say she was following him. Being a stupid hero or something, but either way she's out there with him and she's on her own. She needs help, Amanda – can you organise something?"

Amanda yanked out her mobile to phone the situation through, and then she phoned Jack, who said he'd meet them there. She relayed the message to Ruth, who felt only a little easier that help was on its way; she just hoped she could get there in time.

"Hang on, Madeline. Hang on," she said to herself.

Chapter Seventy-Two

"Hey, what are you doing in here?" Lorna demanded. "This is the ladies." The grey-clad man standing by the basins like a deer in the headlights said nothing. She turned to her friend.

"Madeline? What's going on? Was that you shouting at me just now?"

Madeline was out of breath but managed to nod yes, it was.

"But I don't understand. What are you doing here, and who is this?" She flung a hand towards Grey Man, who still hadn't moved. Madeline was between him and the door, and he – quite rightly – assumed she'd tear his legs off if he budged.

"This," Madeline said, pointing to Grey Man, "is the pervert attacker, and he had his sights set on you." Her breathing was starting to slow but she was full of adrenalin. She went on, "He lives just on Sanderson Road and I followed him tonight to see if my suspicions were correct." Madeline looked at him and narrowed her eyes. "And I guess they were. I would have poisoned you far worse had I known back then, you filthy sodding pervert!"

He just looked at her as though she'd gone mad, but then the penny dropped and he registered where he knew her from – and what she'd done to him.

"That was you?" He sounded incredulous. She could see his mind working hard to process what she'd just said.

"Yes, that was me, you miserable excuse for a man, and now we've got you trapped. The police are on their way." Madeline really hoped they were because how could two women, one with her arm in a sling, hold on to one pissed-off man? Alas, there was no sound of any police cars coming to the rescue.

Why exactly did I text Ruth instead of phoning the police? To save my own ample arse, that's why. Idiot!

For a moment the three of them stood still, a peculiar little tableau lit by the single ceiling bulb. Grey Man was the first to react. He made a go of pushing past Madeline, but the adrenalin pumping round her veins gave her a strength she didn't know she had. Even with one arm in a sling her legs worked fine, and she stuck one out to trip him up. He stumbled but didn't go all the way down, grabbing at the toilet door handle behind him to steady himself. Like a trapped animal, he turned and lunged at her unexpectedly, snarling like a rabid dog, and she stepped backwards, away from his grasp. Her feet lost their traction on the damp tiled floor and, with only one good arm to save herself, she went down like a sack of flour.

She heard a high-pitched scream from Lorna, saw the light from the bulb overhead, and then saw a shocking constellation of stars as her head caught the edge of the porcelain hand basin with a sickening crack. Down she went, hard, stopping absolutely still on the dirty cold tiled floor. Darkness enveloped her. Madeline could do no more.

Chapter Seventy-Three

THE ATMOSPHERE IN THE CAR WAS AS THICK AS FOG AS RUTH SPED along the empty road. She knew there'd be plenty of questions later, but right now Madeline needed her help and there was no time for discussion. They were only a couple of minutes away when, somewhere in the near distance, she heard the first siren as a police car made its way to the park to meet them.

"Which part of the park? Any idea?" asked Amanda.

"She didn't say."

"Well, I'm hazarding a guess that, if it's him, he'll be headed to the toilet blocks, so let's start there. Though you'll be sitting in the car and letting the police do their job. It's too dangerous for you."

"Like hell I'm staying in the car," squawked Ruth. "That's my stepmum out there!" She roared into the car park, sending gravel flying in all directions.

"Keep driving – go over the damn grass! It's over there," instructed Amanda, pointing. "No point trying to run."

Ruth didn't need to be told twice. She jammed her foot to the floor, speeding across the hard ground and towards the light of the toilet block. The only thing she could see in the distance as they approached was a little white poodle tied up outside. Over the other side of the park, she could see red and blue flashing lights through the trees.

She braked to a standstill outside the toilets and jumped from the car with Amanda close on her heels and calling at her to stop. She ignored her. She could hear crying sounds coming from inside the small building, and as she flew round the open doorway, she stopped short and gasped. Madeline was lying on the floor, thick dark blood pooling around her head. A woman was kneeling over her, crying hard and willing her to wake up. Ruth stood frozen and in shock, and it was Amanda who pushed past her and took over to assess the situation.

She knelt beside Madeline and felt her neck for a pulse, calling out her name softly as she did so. She could hear Jack behind her now, calling for an ambulance, but Amanda knew it was too late. Madeline's body was still and silent. She was gone.

She turned to Ruth and gently shook her head, acknowledging that Madeline, her stepmum, was dead. Ruth sank to her knees on the hard, tiled floor and took Madeline's lifeless hand in her own. Amanda stroked her head as a wail, more animal than human, came from Ruth's throat.

JACK FINISHED HIS CALL AND TOOK CHARGE. THIS WAS NOW A CRIME scene. He left Ruth with Amanda, and steered Lorna away and outside as best he could. The poor woman was almost hysterical. Once they were outside, Lorna untied her poodle and clutched it to her chest. Gently, Jack asked her just what had happened.

"I was out walking Bubbles before bedtime as usual," she sobbed, "and I needed to use the ladies and then I heard someone call my name, and then a commotion outside the toilet door." Fat tears ran down her cheeks, and she stroked the dog's head.

Jack looked up from writing in his notebook and tried to soothe and coax her on at the same time.

"Go on," he encouraged. "What happened next?"

"I opened the toilet door and there was Madeline, and then I noticed a man in there too and then it all got so confusing." She wiped her face with the back of her hand, smearing her mascara. Jack handed her his handkerchief, and she dabbed her cheeks and blew her nose into it loudly.

"Can you tell me what this man looked like? Did you see where he went?"

"I didn't see where he went," she said, snuffling, "but he was about my height, had a hat on and wore a long coat, almost like a disguise." She looked into the distance as though searching for the answer on a nearby bush, then turned back to Jack. A little more calmy, she added, "Madeline said he was that groper guy and he had his sights set on me. He must have been following me." She shuddered, so Jack took his jacket off and wrapped it around her shoulders. Another siren could be heard getting closer. The ambulance, though far too late, would be arriving soon.

"And what happened next?"

"She said something about how she'd poisoned him, and he got very angry and lunged at her but she slipped. There was such a thud; I remember that bit very clearly. When she fell he just ran off. I didn't know what to do!"

Her tears started up again and she cried quietly into the handkerchief, wiping her eyes occasionally. The cloth was now smeary grey in places.

"I wanted to help Madeline," she continued, "so I stayed here, and then I heard you arrive. I didn't want to leave her. I hoped she'd come round but she didn't."

A moment or two passed and Jack waited for her to gather herself again. When she finally did, she asked, "Do you think you'll catch him?"

"I hope so, and now we are looking at homicide rather than just sexual assault charges, so it's suddenly got a whole lot more serious for him, and for us. We have officers circulating his description now. He can't have got too far on foot from here."

Lorna remembered something else Madeline had said and brightened. "I think I know where he lives!" She was almost jubilant. "Madeline said he lived on Sanderson Road, though I don't know what number. She'd followed him here, and then saw him following me, I think."

Jack scribbled down the street name then gave it to another officer to do the necessary and find the house number. Quickly. He doubted the man was there now, not if he had any sense, but you never knew.

He thanked Lorna and asked if there was anything else she could remember and she shook her head no. She was shivering with a vengeance now. The shock of what had just happened, how close she'd come to being attacked, and having witnessed Madeline's death were simply too much for her.

Jack looked up to see Amanda coming out of the building, her arms around Ruth, who was silent and also obviously in shock. Behind him, Jack heard the ambulance pull up and its doors open. He walked over to the crew and quietly informed them of the gravity of the situation. While they could help both Lorna and Ruth somewhat, for Madeline, sadly, it was too late.

They were once again dealing with a crime scene, a death, but this time it was Madeline Simpson herself.

Chapter Seventy-Four

Ruth sat in the back of the ambulance alongside Lorna; each was wrapped in a blanket. It was a summer night, but the shock they had both experienced had chilled them to the marrow. Lorna's teeth occasionally rattled as she shivered uncontrollably, and Ruth sat totally mute. Madeline was gone, and as she lay there on the cold tiled floor, the crime technicians went about their work, the painstaking job of gathering evidence of what exactly had happened that evening.

"I wish I could cover her up or something," Ruth said quietly. "It's not a place I want her to be. I wish they would hurry up and lift her somewhere more comfortable." She knew her words were futile, but she wanted more for her stepmum.

"I know what you mean. I feel the same," said Lorna. "I expect they will bring her out soon. I can't believe it. I just can't believe what's happened." Her voice trailed off with the light breeze, but Ruth was barely listening anyway. Her thoughts had drifted to how she was going to tell her dad. Gordon was going to be devastated; he and Madeline were rarely apart as a couple for any length of time. She wasn't looking forward to telling him but she'd have to find the strength somehow. He had to know soon; he'd be wondering where she was.

Amanda, having completed her report, approached the ambulance where Ruth and Lorna sat. "How are you both feeling now?" Her eyes were filled with concern.

Lorna nodded her head. "Okay." Ruth started to cry gently again, tears running down her cheeks like raindrops.

"I've got to tell Dad." It was a half wail, half sob, and Amanda put her arm around her tightly.

"I know, hun. I'll come with you and we can tell him together if that helps." Ruth's head bobbed a yes, but the tears kept flowing steadily.

"Jack can finish up here with the rest of the team so we'll just be a minute, okay?" Amanda rubbed her shoulder soothingly before leaving her and going back to talk to Jack.

"I'm going to take Ruth to tell her stepdad the bad news. Between you and me Jack, I can't believe Madeline Simpson is, I mean was, Ruth's stepmother. I'd no idea. I've never met her family, not socially anyway."

"Ah, don't fret. It is what it is. You go and do what you need to do with her and I'll finish up here with the lab rats. The mortuary van should be here shortly so it's probably best if you take Ruth away now before it gets here. What about the other woman, Lorna? She okay to go home, do you know?"

"Yes, I called her husband a moment ago. He's en route – only lives around the corner. Any news on finding the perp? I'm guessing he wasn't stupid enough to go back home and wait for us to knock on his door."

"You're right there – no sign – but they're doing a thorough search of the place now, see what they can dig up. Forensics will be having a field day, I'm sure. Handy the vic said the street name before she went down. Won't be long before we get the sicko now. I bloody hate perverts and sexual attackers. Should be castrated if you ask me."

Amanda nodded in agreement and jingled her car keys in her pocket. "Right. I'll be off, then. Call me when you know something. I'll go and get this over with. I might be a while – we'll see."

"Take your time," said Jack, and turned back to speak to another officer who was waiting to talk to him.

Amanda walked back to Ruth and helped her from the ambulance and back into the passenger seat of her car. She looked numb still. The tears had stopped for the time being, but Amanda could tell they were lying close to the surface, ready to spring out again at a moment's notice. What a way to meet your sort of father-in-law for the first time.

The engine turned over and Amanda slowly pulled away from the chaotic scene and the flashing red and blues, driving across the grass and back out of the park. She headed towards the A22 and an address she'd been to a couple of times before without knowing the relevance of it.

Oakwood Rise would once again be the focus of her attention, though tonight for quite a different reason.

Chapter Seventy-Five

JACK WATCHED AS RUTH'S CAR DROVE OFF WITH AMANDA AT THE wheel. He'd had his suspicions about her, the reason she never dated men, and having seen her here tonight with her 'friend,' as she'd referred to her, he knew they were much more than that. Even under these circumstances it was obvious how deep their relationship was, and how much Amanda cared for her. What a tragic night it had been, and now Amanda not only had to tell the victim's husband she'd been killed, she had to deal with the trauma and upset of her lover too. He knew she was in for a rough few days. His phone buzzed and he answered it.

"He's not here. He's gone, Jack." It was Hancock, one of the other detectives. "You'd better come on over, though. There's something you're going to want to see."

"Can't you tell me over the phone?" He was tired and in no mood for show and tell.

"No, best not." Hancock gave him the house number.

"I'm on my way."

Jack could see which house it was without needing the number. Flashing blue and reds lit Grey Man's street like a Christmas pageant. He could see Hancock in the doorway of the mid-terraced house. He turned and went inside as Jack approached, and he followed him inside.

"Down in the basement."

As they descended the old wooden steps, the air was thick with the smell of damp. The old lime-painted walls flaked like bad dandruff and stray cobwebs drifted lightly around his shoulders. A single bare bulb hung from ceiling wire, illuminating the dank room in an eerie low light.

Hancock shone his torch to show him what he wanted him to see.

"What the hell?"

There on the wall was a *CSI*-style collage of all the news reports on the attacks that Grey Man, or Bill Winters as they now knew him, had collected, going back two decades. There were curled old yellow clippings dating from the '90s, reports from various towns across the south of England, along with a few mementos he must have snatched from his victims during the attacks. The little wooden box on the old table contained a handful of cheap necklaces and a silky scarf, no doubt snatched while committing his dirty crimes.

"Looks like she was right with her suspicions, Hancock. Just a shame she had to die trying to stop him. Any sightings of him yet?"

"None so far, but he's on foot, so it shouldn't be too hard. Now we know exactly who we're looking for, we should have him soon enough. He can't get far. Seems he doesn't drive either, so that goes in our favour. We'll have him before dawn – mark my words, Jack."

Epilogue

GORDON STOOD LOOKING OUT AT THE GARDEN THROUGH THE SAME window Madeline had spent so much time looking through herself. The Great Orange Machine had finally been picked up and Ruth had asked the driver if he wouldn't mind just moving some of the piled-up soil back into the hole before he took it, which he'd obligingly done.

"Sad news," Sid had said when Ruth had told him Madeline had passed away, and he'd been happy to help.

But the area looked a bit of a mess now, with loose soil and bits of grass strewn all over. It needed Madeline's love and attention. But she wasn't around any longer to give it.

Dressed smartly in his black suit, Gordon was thankful it was a clear day and not raining. Standing by a graveside would be bad enough without the added discomfort of rain, though he couldn't help his own tears from falling that morning. He wiped one away as Ruth entered the kitchen.

"I was just thinking about whether to build the damn pond myself for her, fill it with fish like she'd wanted. I think she'd have liked that. What do you think?" He sniffed loudly and took his handkerchief out of his pocket to blow his nose and dry his face.

Ruth rested her hand on his shoulder in comfort. "She would like that, I'm sure, but let's talk about it more later. The car is here, now, Dad. It's time to go."

"All right. Don't want to keep everyone waiting." He dabbed his damp nose again and gathered the little strength he had left. He walked slowly down the hallway and out through the front door, where the rest of the family were waiting for him.

Ruth turned to glance out at the garden herself, and saw Dexter at the exact same spot they'd just been talking about, digging a hole for himself, changing his mind, then digging another. She watched him crouch down as he relieved himself into the earth, then stood and covered it up, scratching more earth from around the original hole he'd dug until all the evidence of his little visit was gone. Satisfied, he walked away, flicking his rear leg and the dirt from his back paws as he went.

Ruth stood there, stunned. Realisation dawned on her and goosebumps spread over her body. She shivered as everything became crystal clear. It wasn't Dexter's having a pee so much as how he'd covered it up. She couldn't help but laugh out loud in disbelief while she stood there alone in the kitchen. She now knew how Madeline had disposed of the landscaper, and exactly where he was laid.

"Holy hell, Madeline! You clever woman, you! And to think you could drive a damn digger!" She chortled to herself. "Don't worry, Mum. Your secret is safe with me."

Dexter turned and looked at her through the window as he sauntered back to his spot on the patio and curled up to go back to sleep. Ruth could have sworn he winked at her.

WANT TO CONTINUE ON TO THE NEXT BOOK IN THE SERIES? Click here to start reading.

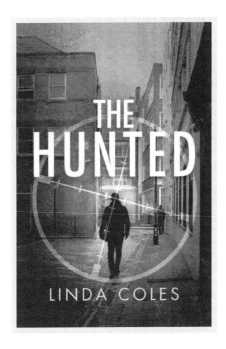

Or you could save money and purchase a book set, here's the next one for you: Book set 2

Also by Linda Coles

If you enjoyed reading one of my stories, here are the others:

The DC Jack Rutherford and DS Amanda Lacey Series:

The Hunted

The hunt is on...

They kill wild animals for sport. She's about to return the favour.

A spate of distressing big-game hunter posts are clogging up her newsfeed. As hunters brag about the exotic animals they've murdered and the followers they've gained along the way, a passionate veterinarian can no longer sit back and do nothing.

To stop the killings, she creates her own endangered list of hunters. By stalking their online profiles and infiltrating their inner circles, she vows to take them out one-by-one.

How far will she go to add the guilty to her own trophy collection?

Dark Service

The dark web can satisfy any perversion, but two detectives might just pull the plug...

Taylor never felt the blade pressed to her scalp. She wakes frightened and alone in an unfamiliar hotel room with a near shaved head and a warning... tell no one.

As detectives Amanda Lacey and Jack Rutherford investigate, they venture deep into the fetish-fueled underbelly of the dark web. The traumatized woman is only the latest victim in a decade-long string of disturbing—and intensely personal—thefts.

To take down a perverted black market, they'll go undercover. But just when justice seems within reach, an unexpected event sends their sting operation spiraling out of control. Their only chance at catching the culprits lies with a local reporter... and a sex scandal that could ruin them all.

One Last Hit

The greatest danger may come from inside his own home.

Detective Duncan Riley has always worked hard to maintain order on the streets of Manchester. But when a series of incidents at home cause him to worry about his wife's behaviour, he finds himself pulled in too many directions at once.

After a colleague Amanda Lacey asks for his help with a local drug epidemic, he never expected the case would infiltrate his own family...And a situation that spirals out of control...

Hey You, Pretty Face

An abandoned infant. Three girls stolen in the night. Can one overworked detective find the connection to save them all?

London, 1999. Short-staffed during a holiday week, Detective Jack Rutherford can't afford to spend time on the couch with his beloved wife. With a skeleton staff, he's forced to handle a deserted infant and a trio of missing girls almost single-handedly. Despite the overload, Jack has a sneaking suspicion that the baby and the abductions are somehow connected...

As he fights to reunite the girls with their families, the clues point to a dark secret that sends chills down his spine. With evidence revealing a detestable crime ring, can Jack catch the criminals before the girls go missing forever?

Scream Blue Murder

Two cold cases are about to turn red hot...

Detective Jack Rutherford's instincts have only sharpened with age. So when a violent road fatality reminds him of a near-identical crime from 15 years earlier, he digs up the past to investigate both. But with one case already closed, he fears the wrong man still festers behind bars while the real killer roams free...

For Detective Amanda Lacey, family always comes first. But when she unearths a skeleton in her father-in-law's garden, she has to balance her heart with her desire for justice. And with darkness lurking just beneath the surface, DS Lacey must push her feelings to one side to discover the chilling truth.

As the sins of the past haunt both detectives, will solving the crimes have consequences that echo for the rest of their lives?

Butcher Baker Banker

A cold Croydon winter's night and pensioner Nelly Raven lies dead and naked on the floor of her living room. The scene bears all the hallmarks of a burglary gone wrong.

It's just the beginning.

Ron Butcher rose to the top of London's gangland by "fixing things". But are his extensive crooked connections of use when death knocks at his own family's door?

Baker Kit Morris will do anything to keep his family business alive. Desperate for cash, he hatches a risky plan that lands him in trouble. As he struggles to stay out of prison, he forges an unlikely friendship with an aging local thug.

And then there's the Banker, Lee Meady, a man with personal problems of his own.

Just how does it all fit together?

As DC Jack Rutherford and DS Amanda Lacey uncover the facts surrounding the case, the harrowing truth of the killer's identity leaves Jack wondering where the human race went so badly wrong.

The Chrissy Livingstone series:

Tin Men

She thought she knew her father. But what she doesn't know could fill a mortuary...

Ex-MI5 agent Chrissy Livingstone grieves over her dad's sudden death. While she cleans out his old things, she discovers something she can't explain: seven photos of schoolboys with the year 1987 stamped on the back. Unable to turn off her desire for the truth, she hunts down the boys in the photos only to find out that three of the seven have committed suicide...

Tracing the clues from Surrey to Santa Monica, Chrissy unearths disturbing ties between her father's work as a financier and the victims. As each new connection raises more sinister questions about her family, she fears she should've left the secrets buried with the dead.

Will Chrissy put the past to rest, or will the sins of the father destroy her?

Walk Like You

When a major railway accident turns into a bizarre case of a missing

body, will this PI's hunt for the truth take her way off track?

London. Private investigator Chrissy Livingstone's dirty work has taken her down a different path to her family. But when her upper-class sister begs her to locate a friend missing after a horrific train crash, she feels duty-bound to assist. Though when the two dig deeper, all the evidence seems to lead to one mysterious conclusion: the woman doesn't want to be found.

Still with no idea why the woman was on the train, and an unidentified body uncannily resembling the missing person lying unclaimed in the mortuary, the sisters follow a trail of cryptic clues through France. The mystery deepens when they learn someone else is searching, and their motive could be murder...

Can Chrissy find the woman before she meets a terrible fate?

The Silent Ones

An abandoned child. A missing couple. A village full of secrets.

When a couple holidaying in the small Irish village of Doolan disappear one night, leaving their child behind, Chrissy Livingstone has no choice but to involve herself in the mystery surrounding their disappearance.

As the toddler is taken into care, it soon becomes apparent that in the close-knit village the couple are not the only ones with secrets to keep.

With the help of her sister, Julie, Chrissy races to uncover what is really happening. Could discovering the truth put more lives at risk?

A suspenseful story that will keep you guessing until the end.

Also by Linda Coles

Jack Rutherford and Amanda Lacey Series:

Hot to Kill

The Hunted

Dark Service

One Last Hit

Hey You, Pretty Face

Scream Blue Murder

Butcher Baker Banker

The Chrissy Livingstone Series:

Tin Men

Walk Like You

The Silent Ones

Coming soon! The Will Peters series.

Where There's A Will

About the Author

Thanks for choosing this book, I really hope you enjoyed it and collect the following ones in the series. Great characters make a great read and I hope I've managed to create that for you.

Originally from the UK, I now live and work in beautiful New Zealand along with my hubby, cat Stella and 6 goats. My office sits by the edge of my vegetable garden, and apart from reading and writing, I get to run by the beach for pleasure.

If you find a moment, please do write an honest online review of my work, they really do make such a difference to those choosing what book to buy next.

Thanks,
Linda

Printed in Great Britain
by Amazon